# CAIN

—————

# CAIN

DIRTY DEVILS MC
BOOK 1

## D. VESSA

# PLAYLIST

"Bloody Creature Poster Girl" – In This Moment
"You Call Me a Bitch Like It's a Bad Thing"- Halestorm
"Heart-Shaped Box" – Nirvana
"Strange Girl" – Halestorm
"Careless Whisper" – Seether
".SALT." – Dead Poet Society
"Cute Girl" – Diggy Graves
"Blank Space" – I Prevail
"Wild Ones (feat. Jelly Roll)" – Jessie Murph, Jelly Roll
"Bloody Mary" – Lyric Noel
"Part of Me" – Disturbed
"High Together" – Shwayze, Cisco Adler

*To anyone who has ever felt like dying their hair a crazy color, do it.*

# 1

Cain

"What did you just say?" I know I didn't just hear this motherfucker right.

"It's gone," Hash, my VP, growled.

"How in the fuck does five hundred pounds of tree just fucking disappear into thin air?" Hash just shakes his head, face hard, letting me know that he's just as pissed off as I am. I'm trying to keep my cool. I really am. But some motherfucker is about to pay with his life for this shit.

"Call church now," I growl at Hash, leaving him behind to round up the brothers as I head inside the compound. Five hundred pounds just gone. How does that even happen?

I take my seat at the head of the table, my fists clenched, resting at my side, face blank as I watch them file in. If we don't find this shipment, we're fucked. Out over half a mil.

We could move some money around from some of the other club businesses, but the Reapers, a rival club from a few towns over, would know the product never made it. We don't need a war on our hands. And I definitely don't need my club looking like a bunch of fucking pussies that can't protect their own shit. I'll be damned if our reputation gets ruined over fucking weed. We never should have agreed to transport this for them.

Rubbing my temples, I ask once all the brothers are seated, "Does someone want to tell me what the fuck happened?"

"No clue. I decided to take a drive up to the Motel Inn, where Ox and Tights were going to stop for the night, just to check shit out since they are still prospects. They never even made it to the motel, Prez. Shot dead on the side of the fucking road. The truck was still there and everything," Scotch said, shaking his head. His face shows that his head is exactly where mine is right now. Fucking fucked.

"Who is on cleanup? I wanna keep this shit under wraps until we figure out what the fuck is going on," I say, dragging my hand down my face.

"The prospects are taking care of it as we speak, Prez." Thank fuck. At least one thing is being taken care of. "Right now, we need to somehow pull 500 pounds of tree out of our fucking asses before anyone catches wind," I say as I look around the table at my brothers' pissed-off faces.

Silence falls over the room. I can see the gears turning, trying to figure out our next move.

"Does anyone have any ideas? I'm fresh out. I can try to hit up the Adduci's, but that isn't really their area, and I don't really want us to be involved with them. We might get some leads, though." I'm just thinking out loud at this point.

Scotch breaks the silence a few minutes later. "I might have something, Prez. If it's okay with you, I can hit up Evan and feel around," Scotch says while looking around the room at the brothers' wary faces.

"I don't know if it's a good idea to bring outsiders into this, brother," I say. Hash and Trick both nod their heads in agreement.

"Look, I know this is club business, but I've known Evan since I was a kid. Evan is basically a pot-smoking hermit. If shit gets out, I know for a fact that's not where it came from."

I look Scotch dead in the eyes, searching for any sort of hesitation, but come up empty. Honestly, at this point, it seems like our only option until I figure something else out. "Alright. Call Evan and set up a meeting. If anything blows back from this, it's your ass on the line."

"Wouldn't have said shit if I was sure of no blowback. Appreciate it, though, Prez," Scotch says as he gets up out of his seat and pulls his phone from his pocket.

Let's hope this doesn't fucking come back to bite me in the ass.

**2**

**Evan**

"Cock sucking motherfucker," I grumble to myself as I flip the light switch that's now not working up and down. Buy an old Victorian house, I said. It will be fun, I said. Jokes on me, right? Victorian homes are so breathtakingly gorgeous, but no one tells you what a fucking money pit they are. My goal in life has always been to have my dream house. And a family. That's one thing I haven't quite locked down yet.

I bought this gorgeous headache last year. It was in foreclosure, and I got it for a freaking steal. And the best part? It sits on ten acres, most of which are woods. Perfect for my little business and to keep people out. I'm also just far enough outside of Ravenna Heights that I don't really hear much of anything. I honestly only ever hear a bunch of bikes come down this way, and they've never bothered me.

This will come as a shock to some, but people aren't exactly my favorite. It's the whole 'they're nice to your face and shady as hell behind your back' thing.

Unfortunately, there is a downside to this place. I seriously underestimated the amount of TLC it would need. I've been running on booze and boxed mac and cheese because I refused to go into town while I was finishing this kitchen. And as a fellow foodie, it's been slowly chipping away at my soul.

Sighing as I feel my phone vibrating in my pocket, I set the bags of groceries down before pulling it out to see that it's Zeke calling. "Hey, what's up?"

"Hey, Ev. Was wondering if you had a minute to help me out today?"

"You know I do, shithead. Just tell me what you need," I say as I roll my eyes.

I remember the exact day I met Zeke. I had just arrived at what was probably my fifth foster home, and let's just say I... wasn't met with the warmest welcome. It probably doesn't help that I'm awkward as fuck when I first meet new people. But Zeke took me under his wing that day and has been the closest thing to a brother that I've ever had. Like recognized like or whatever the fuck they say. Plus, I'm still working on paying him back for that night I'll never forget.

I hear his sigh of relief on the other end. "You're a lifesaver, Ev. Can you meet me at the clubhouse?"

Ah. The infamous clubhouse that I hear so little about. When Zeke first got out of the Army, he caught up with some guy he used to be in with, bought a bike, and the rest was history. I have yet to meet any of them, though. He seems to like keeping that part of his life private, and I haven't wanted to pry.

"Yeah, I can. Text me the address?" I can't help the funny feeling that's building in the pit of my stomach as we both hang up—almost like a huge feeling of dread.

What kind of favor would a motorcycle club need from me?

**3**

Evan

I bring my car to a stop just outside a huge metal gate that has to be at least 20 feet tall. What in the fuck is this place? And how did I not know this existed next door to me?

My stomach is past the point of rolling. It's full-on punching me for being a naive dumbass. Who doesn't ask questions about what they're getting into? "If Zeke fucks me, I swear I will cut his dick off," I mumble under my breath as the gate slowly opens.

"What the fuck..." I mutter as I whip around. How do they even know I'm here?

I slowly drive through the gate and down the concrete drive until a giant warehouse-looking building comes into view. I cut the engine on my Dark Horse Ford Mustang and climb out. Spotting the entrance, I pause just as I'm about to grab the door handle. Do I knock? Or is this like a business, and I just enter? I should have paid more attention when I watched Sons of Anarchy, but Tig was just too hot to not have my undivided attention.

I turn the knob, deciding to just go in.

It takes a minute for my eyes to adjust to the dim lighting, but as they do, I take in the giant living area. Living area? Is that what you would call a room with a stripper pole in the center, a bar up against the wall, and worn leather couches with a few tables and chairs randomly spread throughout? My nose turns up as I hear the stickiness of the floor as I walk further in. Honestly, this place looks more like a frat house.

"Hello?" I call out as I make my way over to the bar and lean against the rail as if I'm waiting for someone to pop up. Based on the floors, it shouldn't shock me that the mirrors on the back wall are dirty. Old stickers from various places cover it. I'd like to say I can see my reflection, but it's more of a half-assed smudgy version of myself.

I jump as a door slams shut behind me, making me whip around to see who has finally decided to acknowledge my presence, only to come face-to-face with a man who can only be described as sex-on-a-stick. He's tall. Has to be at least 6'5, considering I'm 5'7, and he looks like he would swallow me up. I take my time as I scan him from head to toe. The salt and pepper hair lets me know that he's older. Maybe mid-40s? His fitted tee contours to his body in all the right places. He's muscular, but more in the dad-bod sense. The fitted boot-cut jeans are hugging some seriously ripped thighs, though. Damn, the man is fine. If I were asked to build my dream guy physically, this man in front of me would be it.

I sharply inhale at the realization as my eyes shoot up to his face, seeing his eyebrows raised. Fuck. He just watched me check him out. The ground can swallow me up anytime now. I'm nervous as hell and fiddling with the ends of my hair like I'm fucking twelve-years-old. And now he's just staring at me like I'm the biggest idiot. Fuck me. Men don't usually intimidate me, but his stare is almost enough for me to tell Zeke to forget it. Almost.

"Uh.... hi. I'm here for Zeke? He called me and said to meet him." Someone needed to start the conversation since it was clear he wasn't going to.

"Zeke?" The seriously intimidating man grunts out as he studies me. His eyes narrow as they slowly run up and down my body before he turns around and walks right back through the door he came from, slamming it shut behind him without another word.

My jaw drops as the door slams because what in the hell was that? Was I just dismissed? It's been a long time since I've met someone this fucking rude.

And where in the hell is Zeke?

**4**

Cain

Unfuckingbelievable.

When Scotch said he would reach out to someone he thought could help us out, I wasn't expecting that person to be a girl.

Those curves. Jesus fucking christ. They're not in your face. More in a subtle 'I have a little in all of the right places' way. And that rack? I never considered myself to be a tit man, but I wouldn't pass the chance to see how they fit in my hand. And those fucking eyes. Are they different colors? I could have sworn one was blue and the other was green. I had already been staring at her for too long saying nothing, that I couldn't just ask. That would just make me sound like a fucking dipshit, so I did the only thing I could.

I left.

I bang my fist as hard as I can against the door to Scotch's room. "Yo, fucker! Open up!" I don't even let ten seconds pass before pounding on the door again.

My fist is raised, ready to pound again before it flies open. "What?" Scotch glares.

My eyebrows raise at his tone. "Get your ass up. *Evan* is here. You have some fucking explaining to do."

"Fuck." Scotch runs a hand down his face. "Yeah. I'll be right out." He starts to turn back into his room before he stops. "Look... just don't freak out on Evan. She's been through a lot, and I promise she'll keep her mouth shut about all of this, but I really think she can help us out."

I grunt in response. I don't know what the hell he was thinking when he thought it would be a good idea to have her help us out. Scotch knows the rules; nothing with a pussy gets involved in our shit. Unless they're an old lady, but even that doesn't mean they're involved directly. They get the bare minimum side details. It's more of a way to just vent and release some stress.

I just finish pouring a drink as Scotch enters my office. "Sit the fuck down and start explaining this shit."

Scotch lets out a long sigh as he reclines back in the old leather chair in front of my desk. "Evan and I go way back. I met her in one of my foster homes, and we just clicked. She's the closest thing to family I have, and in my eyes, she's my sister. She's the only person I can count on outside of the club."

"Why have you never mentioned her before?" I can't lie and say that I don't feel slightly put off by this. I don't like being blindsided like that. I've known Scotch for over a decade. Even when we were in the Army, I didn't hear shit about someone named Evan.

"Because I didn't think she needed to be brought up. She hasn't had an easy start in life, and Evan just likes to keep to herself. Now if you're done riding my ass, can I explain how I think she can help us out?"

My eyes narrow at his tone. "Watch it."

"No offense, Prez. I'm just protective of her. As I was saying, keeping to herself means Evan hates people, so obviously, she would hate having a job with others." My eyebrow arches for him to continue. "She grows."

Well, I wasn't expecting him to say that. She looked like she would be a tattoo artist or some shit with all of her ink and black and purple hair. Hair I wouldn't mind seeing covering my thighs while she's sucking my cock. "On what scale? Are we talking 'I just want to grow enough to cover what I smoke,' or are we talking a 'moving product' level?"

"She's moving it. I usually go with her when she drops it to her guy," Scotch admits.

Are you fucking kidding me? Not sharing every time you piss, I get. Not sharing every time you fuck a club slut, I get. But if you're part of this club and you're helping out with random drops on the side, I think that's something I should know. "Again, why is this the first time I'm hearing about this?"

Scotch runs his hands roughly down his face as he sighs. "I don't know. I don't want to bullshit an answer because I don't have one. I just didn't think I needed to tell anyone about her."

"You didn't think that you being directly involved in these drops couldn't possibly blow back on the club?"

"I didn't think past just helping my sister out."

My eyes haven't left his as I search for any signs of doubt. Satisfied with not finding any, I say, "Don't let it happen again." I wait for his nod before pushing out of my chair. He knows this is the only chance he gets with me letting something like this slide.

"Let's go have a chat with Ms. Evan."

**5**

Evan

I can't help but stand here *still* with my mouth hanging open like an idiot because he really just walked back out.

I've met a lot of rude and disrespectful people in my life, but he's working his way up to the top of that list. I'm going to rip Zeke a new asshole for making me come here when he damn well could have just come to my house and talked about whatever he claimed he couldn't say over the phone. I'll be damned if I help out if the rest are assholes like that one. Hot as fuck or not.

Taking a seat at the bar, I look around a little more. I bet this place has some wild parties. I was never that girl. I got shit-faced once at a party in high school with a girl named Molly, who I thought was my friend at the time. I was trying to impress some stupid guy on the football team I thought I was in love with at the time. You know, that stupid baby love where you think they're going to make everything all better? Jokes on me though, because halfway into the party, I ended up catching him with this tongue down Molly's throat. I locked myself in the bathroom and called Zeke crying to come and get me. Learned my lesson with that one. Girls will never be your real friends. All it is in the end is one big fucking competition that you don't even realize you're competing in until your heart is ripped out of your chest and stomped on.

The same door that the asshole came through opens again, only this time he has Zeke in tow. My eyes find his, looking for any indication of what is about to happen, but all I see is reassurance. But reassurance for what?

"Hey, Ev," Scotch greets me as he approaches me with open arms.

"Hi, Zeke," I reply, sliding off the barstool I was perched on to wrap my arms around him.

A throat clears behind Zeke as we pull away, and I come face-to-face with the asshole again. "Let's head into my office, Evan, and we can discuss why Scotch asked you down here."

He doesn't even wait for my reply before he's already walking back through that fucking door. I take a few deep breaths to calm myself down before I follow. The dickishness makes me want to stab him in the eye. I sure as fuck don't like being ordered around, unless it's in the bedroom.

"Take a seat." The asshole motions to the chairs in front of his desk that he's already sitting behind. Zeke takes the chair beside mine as I angle myself so I can look at both of them, waiting for someone to explain why I'm even fucking here.

"Scotch has told me you may be able to help us out of the bind our club has found ourselves in," the asshole says as he looks me over, almost like he can't quite believe he's saying this to me.

"Scotch?" I let out a laugh while looking over at Zeke. He isn't laughing. Oh, it's like that? Okay, then. No jokes about his little nickname. "What kind of bind?" I'm one hundred percent not in the business of helping random guys out of binds. Zeke alone? Sure. But a whole fucking MC? No way.

"First, I need to know if what Scotch says about you being trustworthy is true. Our club doesn't hurt women, but if you double-cross us or fuck up in any way, we'll make you fucking pay for it. Got me?"

I jerk back as if he slapped me. "Got you? I don't know you, dude. And I sure as hell never agreed to do you any favors. I think Zeke, or Scotch, or whatever the fuck you guys call him, left a few key details out when he called me asking to help him out. I was under the impression this was just about him alone."

Something moved behind the asshole's eyes. Surprise with a little admiration? It's gone as fast as it came. "Fair enough."

"I wouldn't have called you if it wasn't serious, Ev. We could really use your help."

I have to be the last resort if they're asking me. Do I even want to do this? I love Zeke, but I don't know if I want to be associated with a club. Or, I try it out, and if things become too much, I back out. He would understand, right? Letting out a long sigh as my shoulders slump in defeat, I say, "Alright, tell me what you need, and I'll weigh out my options and see if I can even help."

The asshole nods his head. "A shipment of ours got jacked earlier. We can come up with the cash to cover what was stolen from us, but it's not going to fly with the other...party once they find out it was stolen. We've been trying to keep the peace with everyone, and I'd like it to stay that way."

"So, how exactly do I fall into this?" I inquire. Why would they think I could help at all with something that was stolen?

"I want you to sell us some weed, so it looks like nothing happened to what we were transporting. It will buy us some time to figure out what the fuck is going on."

Well, that definitely wasn't what I was expecting to have been stolen. "Exactly how much are we talking?"

"Five hundred pounds."

And that is when I burst out laughing. Full-on belly-roll

laughing. This dude can't be serious. That's like a million dollar's worth of weed. "That's a good one, dude. Sorry, but I can't help you," I get out as soon as I can breathe.

"I'm not fucking joking," the asshole bites out as he crosses his arms on his desk and leans forward.

"Look, Prez, she doesn't mean it as an insult. Evan isn't from our world, man," Zeke chimes in.

Oh, so he is serious.

"Can you help us out or not? Scotch made it sound like you two are basically family, and where I come from, family helps each other. Not laugh in their fucking face when they come asking."

That had me sitting up straight and glaring. He can't be serious. He has no clue where I came from and what I would do for Zeke. The goddamn nerve on this fucking dude. Zeke rests one hand on my thigh, clearly sensing my need to rip this asshole a new asshole. The asshole's eyes dart to Zeke's hand on my thigh and narrow into tiny slits. Honestly, what is happening? He clearly hates me as much as I hate him, but he almost seems more pissed off that Zeke is touching me.

"First of all, I don't like what you're implying. I would do anything to help Zeke. I'm just not so sure if getting involved with all of this mess is something I need. The last thing I want is a crazy fucking psycho getting wind that I'm helping you guys out, and then I have him making demands at my door." Holding the asshole's eyes, I continue, "Second, I definitely know for a fact I don't have that much ready to rock n' roll right now."

I make sure I keep eye contact with him across his desk. Isn't that what they tell you to do with a rabid dog? If you break eye contact first, it shows you're weak. His muscular, tattooed hand comes up to stroke his neatly trimmed salt and pepper beard, thinking over what I just said.

"I can probably buy us some time. How long are you thinking until you have what we need?"

Oh fuck. I wasn't expecting him to counter. "Um…. I don't really know off the top of my head. I need to go home and look everything over before I can give you a definite answer."

Seeming somewhat satisfied with that, he stands up and holds out his hand, which is covered in a skull tattoo, for me to shake. "You do that, and we'll be in touch very shortly."

As soon as my hand touches his, I feel a little spark. And trust me, I know it sounds fucking stupid. I can't help but think what those large, calloused hands would feel like rubbing over my whole body. My eyes lock with his, watching as they flare with the same heat that I know is in mine.

"Sure," I say before ripping my hand away and bee-lining it for the door with Zeke calling after me.

What the fuck just happened?

**6**

**Cain**

I seriously need to get laid. It's been so long that I swore I felt something when I touched her hand. It's got to be the lack of pussy that's making me lose it.

"You think she's actually going to help us out?" I ask Scotch. The way she just ran out of here has me doubting everything we just agreed on. She's got a set of balls on her. I'll give her that. A lot of patched brothers don't even have the balls to talk back to me the way she just did.

Scotch sighs, "Yeah. She's not one to leave me hangin'. I just don't want any of this blowing back on her."

"It won't. You have my word on that," I assure him. Nothing is going to happen to that sexy little hellcat. She might think she's hiding behind that quiet personality, but I liked what I saw when I pushed just right. I shouldn't be looking forward to pushing more, but I am. She's the first woman that's held my attention for more than five minutes in over a year. Call me fucking intrigued.

"Text me her address." I'm not asking.

Scotch's gaze shoots to me, eyes narrowing slightly. "No offense, Prez, but I would like to be the one that checks up on her with all of this shit going on."

"Not going to happen. Too much on the line, Scotch. You know that. Don't worry your pretty little head. I don't bite." I smirk. Unless it's in the bedroom. "Let's keep this between us until we know it's a done deal. Our brothers run their mouths more than a bunch of fucking 13-year-old girls."

A small part of me isn't ready to introduce her to the club. The brothers will be all over her, and the thought of one of them even laying a hand on her makes me want to cut their fingers off and shove them up their ass. And that's not like me. Fuck. She looks way too young for me, too. Basically, a baby.

"Fuck me," I mumble as I rub my hands down my face.

**7**

Evan

I can feel eyes on me as I fucking floor it, tires screeching as I peel out of their compound. My baby can pack a punch when I need her to. Caressing the dash, I head back to my little fortress of solitude. I'm a little put off that it's right next door. I mean, obviously, there's property between us, but it still doesn't feel like enough space. I know how my brain works. I'm going to constantly wonder what's going on over there now that I know it's there.

I finally let out a sigh of relief when I see my dark beauty come into view. There is just something about this house that chills me the fuck out. I think that's how I knew this would be home. When I first viewed it with the realtor, the state it was left in didn't faze me. I still have a long way to go before she's restored to her original glory. When I first bought the place, I put all of my spare cash into building a large barn in the backyard to hold my plant babies. The same ones Zeke wants me to use to help out his club.

Sometimes, it feels like whenever I take five steps forward; I get knocked back ten. I know he would never let any of the repercussions touch me, but the lingering fear is still there. I learned very early in life that nothing is guaranteed or will ever be as it seems.

And there are obviously other parties involved that they aren't saying, right? I got the vibe that the asshole didn't want me to know who else was involved. He almost slipped up, though. The last thing I need is for one of them to break in and murder me in my sleep. One thing I do know is that all of this shit calls for some comfort food.

Flipping the switch on in my kitchen with Hades on my heels, I decide on queso. Who doesn't love a good cheese dip? My lactose-intolerant ass will be paying for it later, but that's tomorrow's (let's be honest, more like in an hour) problem.

I rescued Hades almost three years ago. I couldn't even tell you what possessed me to wander into the animal shelter at the time, but as soon as I locked eyes with the saddest pair I had ever seen, I knew I had to take him.

Hades was a severely underweight Cane Corso who still seemed too big for the cage they were keeping him in. Fate sealed the deal when the lady working at the shelter told me he was on sale for $125, which was exactly how much cash I had in my pocket.

Settling in on the Ikea couch I got as a placeholder, while I'm figuring out my colors and stuff, legs on top of Hades, and queso resting on my lap, I ponder over everything with each bite.

I know Zeke wouldn't have even involved me if this wasn't necessary. Plus, I've been trying for years to find a way to even slightly pay him back. He's done so much for me in the past. This could finally be my way to do that.

Would he accept it as that? Probably not.

And let's not forget about the panty-scorching asshole.

Honest to god, my kitty tingled every time that man talked.

Why are all the hot ones mega fucking dicks? Also, way out of my league. I wouldn't even know what to do if I got my hands on someone like him. It's been longer than I'm comfortable admitting since my kitty got some cream. What few exes I've had were the complete opposite of him. They'd rather spend their Friday night in front of a video game instead of between a random chick's legs.

I sigh, thinking about what it would feel like to have his beard brush against the inside of my thighs. Would it tickle? Or would it be just rough enough to leave a little scratch on the way up to suck on my clit.

No.

Absolutely not. We are not going there.

"Snap the fuck out of it, girl," I tell myself. He's an asshole, and you've sworn off all men for good.

Damn Zeke for having to have attractive friends.

ROLLING OVER IN BED, I hear a long groan that isn't coming from me.

Fucking Hades.

The man is a diva and definitely not a morning person. "I know, sweet baby. It's really early for us, but mommy has things to take care of," I coo at him while scratching that spot he likes right behind his ear—things that involve keeping a certain MC off my back. "Oh, is that the spot?" Hades' leg starts moving quickly up and down.

Throwing the fluffy teal duvet off, I grumble as my feet land on the scratchy wood floor. They need to be refinished badly, but one girl only has so much time, and honestly, DIY videos make things look way too fucking easy. I swear everything takes me five times as long as the person filming.

I slip on what I call my "dirty whore" leggings and a baggy t-shirt before heading out to the barn with a grumpy Hades trailing behind.

Sometimes, I think I'm hilarious with what I come up with. A few of my leggings have a bunch of holes, slits, rips, you name it, all over them from working in the barn. Some of them happen to be right up by my coochy, but you need to be at just the right angle to see that.

The first thing I do when I enter the barn is turn on the music. Zeke thinks I'm nuts, but I firmly believe that plants grow better with some kick-ass tunes. No one can tell me otherwise. It's all about creating the perfect growing environment.

A sigh escapes me as I look around at everything I have. I'm going to need a decent amount of time to come up with what they need.

Time I'm not sure they have.

A low rumble pulls me from my thoughts long enough to hear a bike coming down the driveway and to notice Hades' eyes are locked on the door, ready to go. As soon as I adopted Hades, I sent him to a training school. I spent a fucking fortune to make sure I had a dog that would protect me.

Which brings me back to who is here?

Only two people know where I live.

Yanking open the side door, my eyes narrow into slits as I see who it is.

The one person I would have been fine not seeing ever again.

The asshole.

"What the fuck are you doing here?" I bite out.

"Now, little hellcat. I don't think that's any way to greet your guest."

## 8

Cain

Goddamn.

I know I'm staring again, but those legs. Those fucking legs.

The little rips and tears in her pants give me a small peek at all that soft, milky skin I haven't stopped thinking about since she ran out of my office yesterday.

I know she's pissed I dropped by unannounced. Scotch doesn't even know I'm here. Didn't give me her address either. It took me calling in a favor from one of the prospects, Brock, — tech nerd turned biker. He did time in the Army, got out, and was looking for a new life to settle into. So, basically, I had him hack Scotch's phone to find out this little hellcat's address.

Shocked the shit out of me to find out she basically lives in my backyard.

Which brings me back to why I have never seen her before? I get Scotch wanting to protect her, but I haven't even seen her up at DD's, and I know I would recognize that face anywhere.

It's the eyes. She draws her makeup out dramatically, making her look like she's about to rip your dick off. They're the kind that are engraved in your brain as soon as you see them, and the kind that makes my dick twitch every time we make contact. I walk toward her, needing to get a glimpse of them. Never in my life have I seen someone with one green and one blue eye. They're so captivating that they almost make you unable to look away.

Fuck. What is happening to me?

I sound like a lovesick, pussy-whipped bitch right now. The guys would be riding my ass so hard if they could hear what was running through my head.

Her arms are crossed over her chest. I know that body language is supposed to warn me that this little hellcat is pissed, but all it's doing is pushing her massive tits up and giving me a better view of her impressive rack.

"Show me the goods, babe."

"Excuse me?" One of her eyebrows shoots up. I open my mouth to clarify, but she fires off before I get the chance. "I'm not one of your club sluts, *babe*. This is going to come as a shock to you, but not every girl takes her clothes off on demand."

It took everything in me not to burst out laughing. "The weed, babe. I'm here to talk about weed."

Her cute fucking mouth forms into an "O," and her arms drop down by her sides as it all clicks in her head. Fucking cute as hell.

"I haven't officially agreed. I said I would get back to you," she snaps. Such a feisty little thing.

"You really about to leave Scotch hangin' like that? Didn't peg you for that type, babe." That's when I knew I had her. Resignation passed through her eyes. Hook, line, and sinker.

"No," she whispers in defeat, turns around, and heads back into the barn without saying another word.

Taking that as my invitation, I follow the little hellcat's delectable ass into the barn.

**9**

Evan

I can feel his eyes on me as I walk over to the counters lining the front of the barn. When I had it built, I really wanted the barn to match the moody vibe of the house. With that in mind, I ended up with black countertops, a gold-pressed tin backsplash, and dark grey cabinets. It's a dream to look at, really.

"Got to say, babe. I didn't even know this place was here, and it's basically in my backyard. You own all the way back to the fence?"

The fence that he's referring to is an old wrought-iron fence that separates my property from the club's property. All the trails back there are overgrown from not being used in years, but they do lead to a gate—a gate that happens to be padlocked at all times. I figured by now some crazy kids would have cut it from temptation, wanting to sneak in and see what's here, but now it makes a lot more sense why that hasn't happened yet.

"Yeah." I can't help but take him in now that he's in my space, leaning against the counter like he owns it. I can't stand the sight of him, but I also can't look away. It's so infuriating. Damn him for looking like my fictional boyfriend come to life.

"Look, babe. I think we got off on the wrong foot yesterday. I was just a little surprised to find out that the 'Evan' Scotch was talking about is a woman. I know I can be a fucking dick sometimes, but I swear I didn't mean any harm. We've just had a lot going on, and I'm trying to figure some shit out. Can we start over?"

Hmm. So he's here for a peace offering.

I know firsthand that I suck at meeting new people. Especially in a tense situation. And I'm definitely fucking used to everyone who hasn't met me assuming that I'm a guy, so I nod. "Alright, I think we can do that."

"Hey. I'm Cain." Plastering on his panty-melting smile, he holds out his hand for me to take. Cain. Finally, a name for the asshole's face. Although I guess I can't call him that anymore, can I?

Looking between his face and his outreached hand, I sigh and take it. "Hi, Cain. I'm Evan." His name fits his rough-looking exterior.

That same sensation that happened in his office yesterday is back with a vengeance, lighting my whole body on fire. This time, I don't rip my hand away. I bask in the feeling. A part of me hopes I'm not the only one feeling this.

"Hi, Evan. So, what are we working with?" Cain asks, breaking the awkward silence that has settled in from me staring at him like a fucking weirdo.

God. I need to get a grip.

"I have some drying out now, some about ready for harvest, and a bunch of new plants I just got in last week. Like I said, I'm going to need a little bit of time," I explain as Cain looks around at my setup and nods his head.

The angle allows me to get a good look at the snake tattoo peeking out from his shirt collar. Part of the body is coiled around his throat, moving with every swallow and opening of his mouth, looking as if it's ready to strike. And damn, if that isn't one of the hottest tattoos I've ever seen.

I swallow as I try to move in a subtle way that still allows my thighs to rub together lightly—anything to stop this minor ache. "Is that okay? I'm not really sure what kind of timeline you're working with on your end."

"Yeah, it should work. I'm calling a meet with them, so I'll know more then," Cain says, a look crossing his face and making his eyes harden. Whatever mood we just had going on died.

"Um... well, not to add any more stress for you guys, but this is my livelihood. If I give you everything I grow, that kind of leaves me with no source of income." God, this is fucking awkward. No one likes to talk about money and finances. I have a little saved up where I would be fine, but that would mean putting a pause on my house. And why should I have to sacrifice my dreams for their fuck-up?

Cain starts chuckling.

Fucking chucking.

Like this is funny for some reason.

"You'll be more than compensated for your time, little hellcat." Cain smirks a knowing smile at me that has me going ramrod straight. The fuck? Is he implying what I think he's implying?

"Were you not listening to anything I said earlier?" I grit out through clenched teeth. "It's hilarious that you think any woman will just fall at your feet. Newsflash, asshole, you're not the only male on the planet that has the whole tatted silver fox thing going for him."

I didn't think it would be possible, but the stupid smirk is growing. What I wouldn't give to wipe it off his stupid, arrogant face.

"All I'm hearing from that, babe, is that you think I'm attractive." Cain winks as he heads back for the door, slipping on his black sunglasses before slipping through. "By compensation, I meant cash. We'll be in touch, hellcat."

Oh.

Who is the asshole now for assuming shit?

**10**

**Cain**

I know what I did was wrong.

I shouldn't have had Brock hack into Scotch's phone with orders to find anything he could on Evan. Not that I found out much- just your basic check-in conversations and obviously her address. But I can't get this little hellcat out of my goddamn head. And why?

In my 25ish years of having women in my bed, I've never gotten attached. Never had that itch for more. I always just slapped them on their ass on their way out and hoped I never saw them again. But doing that shit with Evan? That has my skin crawling. And why? I don't fucking know her. What I do know is once I have her, one time isn't going to be enough. I just have a feeling that she's going to be more than just an itch to scratch. More like a prickly thorn I'm going to have to rip out.

But now that I think about it, when was the last time I was even with someone?

Too fucking long ago, and that isn't like me. Like I said yesterday, I need to get fucking laid.

Scotch would lose his ever-loving fucking mind if he knew where I just was. If he knew the dirty thoughts that ran through my head when I saw her in those tattered leggings. It made me want to touch what little milky skin was visible and see just how close that hole would let me get to her warm, wet heat. And I fucking knew she was wet. She thinks I missed that little thigh rub, but I didn't. The kitten was just trying to ease its ache. Doesn't she know that only daddy can do that?

She can act like she hates me all she wants. She can't take back what I saw.

I PARK my bike just outside of DD's, short for Dirty Devils, and I'm relieved to see that Scotch's bike isn't here. Not that I owe that fucker any explanation. I just don't like lying, and omitting is in the same family when it comes to my brothers. I'd lose my shit if I found out one of them was doing this.

"Hey, Prez," Delaney greets me from behind the bar as I walk past and head toward my office. "You want your usual?"

I bought this place for the club as soon as I started it. Knowing we needed a way to funnel some of the cash, I figured a bar was an easy way to do just that. Delaney has been here since we opened. So far, she's been the only bartender who's been able to put up with us, seeing as she hasn't left. She isn't a club slut and is otherwise off-limits. "Please, and thanks, babe." It's the calm before the storm in here right now. The evenings are always fucking packed, but the hours before are usually pretty quiet.

I just begin going through the books that Ink, our club's treasurer, sent over when Delaney pops in with my three fingers of Jameson. "Hey, Delaney," I call, stopping her on the way out.

"Yeah?" She looks back over her shoulder.

"Have you ever heard Scotch talk about anyone named Evan?"

Now leaning against the doorframe, she focuses completely on me. "Not that I can remember. Why?"

"You know that's club business, babe. If you hear anything, let me know." Dismissing her, I grab my whiskey and take a long sip before getting back to work. I exhale as I feel the burn hit my throat. Damn, that first sip always hits just right. I must have lost track of time because the next thing I know, a pissed-off Scotch is busting in through my door without fucking knocking. "Can I fucking help you?"

"You just had to fucking go over there, didn't you? How did you even know where she lived? I told you I would keep an eye on her!" Scotch yells.

My face hardens at the same time Scotch must remember who the fuck he's talking to. I wave my hand condescendingly at the seat across from me. He doesn't say a word as he slumps down in the chair. Tension is thick and heavy in the air.

"You got it checked?" I wait for his tight-head nod before I continue, "I'm not going to apologize for what you think is over-stepping on this. I get that you view Evan as your sister, and this is more personal to you, but the bottom line is this is fucking club business. I needed to see with my own two fucking eyes that this girl is legit as you claim she is. It's not that I don't trust you. I do. You're my brother, and I wouldn't have made you my head enforcer if I didn't think you'd always have my back. But I have a lot of lives on the line, man."

A tense silence settles over us, neither one wanting to break eye contact first.

"I get it." Scotch finally gives in. "I don't have to like it, but I get it. She doesn't come before the club for me, but she also doesn't come after. You get me?"

"Yeah, I get you." I'd be just as, if not more, protective of her than he is right now, and I'm not looking into what that means right now. "If it makes you feel any better, I apologized for being a dick to her yesterday."

Scotch's eyes instantly narrow. "Never in my life have I seen you fucking apologize to someone. Why her.... Oh, you motherfucker. No. Fuck no," Scotch crosses his arms across his chest. "Evan is fucking off-limits. Especially to your ass."

"According to Evan, I'm silver fox material." I smirk as Scotch lets out a growl.

"If you fuck with her, brother or not, I'm coming for your ass. Evan isn't a club girl," Scotch growls out.

"Doesn't mean she can't be a willing participant," I retort, knowing just how to get under his skin as he storms out of my office.

I'm sure he can hear me laughing my ass off as he walks down the hall.

But what he doesn't know is that I have a feeling when it comes to Evan, I would be one step ahead of Scotch, ready to kill the motherfucker that had the balls to even touch her.

And well, we're just not going to dive into that thought either.

**11**

**Evan**

I haven't been able to focus since my little run-in with Cain earlier. It's like I can't think around that man. He makes my brain turn to mush, and I get so fucking mad at the same time, making me flustered. Which is bad. Very, very bad.

"Come on, Hades, babe. Let's head inside. Mama is hungry," I say as I start to head up to the house. Feeling my phone vibrate, I pull it out to see a text from Zeke.

> Zeke: Hey. You around so we can talk about what went down yesterday?

> Me: Thanks, but no need. Cain just left, and it's all good.

> Zeke: What do you mean Cain just left? When did you invite him over?

> Me: I didn't. I assumed you did.

Zeke: I definitely fucking did not.

What the fuck.

So Cain just thinks he can randomly show up on me like that? And more importantly, how did he know where I live if Zeke didn't tell him?

"Fucking bikers. They just think they can do whatever the hell they want," I grumble to Hades as we head into the kitchen. "You want a little treat, baby? Mama needs to go to the store to get some more food for us."

And maybe stop for a big juicy bleu cheese burger. Zeke can never shut up about the ones this one bar has in the city. As someone who is lactose intolerant with a disgusting case of IBS, bleu cheese is my weakness. Any cheese, if I'm being honest. Popping a few Imodium to, you know, combat the cheese, I check to make sure Hades has water and his show on-*yes, I'm that dog mom*-and head out.

~

IT TAKES a minute for my eyes to adjust to the lighting in DD's. I find an empty seat next to an older guy who seems like he's been here for one too many.

"What can I get for ya?" a short but curvy girl on the other side of the bar asks. Her round face gives her that innocent look, but you can feel the 'don't fuck with me' vibes radiating off of her.

"Double rum and diet, please." God knows I fucking need it after all the shit that has happened in the last two days. It's funny how one day you can go from simply existing to wondering what's happening.

"Sure thing. Menu?" Nodding my head, I look around and take it all in. This bar has a very similar feel to the one at Scotch's club's compound, except instead of random worn-down couches and stripper poles, there are actual tables and a few booths. A stage is set up in the corner, I'm assuming for a live band or something. After ordering my burger, I bring the glass to my lips and take a large sip.

"I haven't seen your face in here before, and I would remember a pretty little thing like you." The man next to me slurs and tries to do what I think is a failed attempt at a wink, but his eye just kind of stays drooped.

Ugh.

This is one thing that's wrong with society. A girl can't just be. There's always some man who thinks he's entitled to a piece of her.

Smelling the alcohol on him from where I'm sitting, my nose turns up. "I don't get out much." I give him a tight smile and turn my body slightly away from him, silently letting him know I want to be left alone.

"Another one?" The bartender asks as she sets my food down in front of me.

I open my mouth to answer yes, but a voice I unfortunately now know all too well sounds from behind me, cutting me off. "Put it on my tab, Delaney." His skull-tattooed hand reaches over my shoulder and nabs a fry.

I let out a long sigh as my eyes dart up to the ceiling. I swear I can't catch a break.

"I didn't notice you were here," I say, annoyance clear as I swat his hand away from my food.

"You wouldn't have, babe. I was in the office. But then I saw your sweet ass on camera and just knew you stopped by to brighten my day." Cain smirks while biting into the stolen fry.

And that's when it clicks.

DD.

Dirty Devils.

The name of their club.

Apparently, I need to tattoo 'dumb bitch' across my forehead for not putting all of this together way before I thought it was a great idea to come get a burger. Zeke talks about this place all the time, and I've never made the connection.

God, I'm an idiot.

"Trust me, the last thing I would do is go out of my way to see you." I can feel Delaney's eyes on us, assessing what I am to him. Maybe she's fucking him.

Cain's arms come around either side of me, caging me in. I can feel his body heat radiating off him, making the temptation all too great to lean back into it. To just get a little feel for the spank bank of what his hard chest would feel like.

"The whole sarcastic bitch act you have goin' only turns me on, babe. Makes me want to throw you over my knee and spank that attitude right out of you," he growls in my ear while lightly trailing a finger down my neck to where it meets my shoulder. A shudder runs through my body at the touch. I don't even have time to process what's happening because before I can even come up with a reply, he's pushing off the rail and sauntering down the hallway toward the right of the bar.

Damn, that man. I don't get like this. I'm flustered, which isn't like me, and I hate it. Hate not being in control of my emotions. And I hate that my body just can't seem to figure out how to act around him.

"Don't beat yourself up too much over him. He has that effect on all the women he comes in contact with," the bartender, whom I now know as Delaney, says in passing. Like I didn't already know he's the type that only has to snap his fingers, and someone is there asking how he likes his dick sucked.

And on that thought, I just don't want to be anywhere near here right now. I slide my burger basket to the creepy drunk guy next to me and signal for my tab.

I need to get the fuck out of here.

After trying to settle my tab only to find out she actually put everything I ordered on his, I left a twenty on the bar and got the fuck out of there.

I need to clear this Cain fog and get my head on straight.

BY THE TIME I get home, I feel no better than I did when I left the bar. Not even Hades, acting like he hasn't seen me in ten years when I walked through the door, cracked a smile.

My stomach growls as I pop the last bit of edible I had made the other day into my mouth before I lay out the ingredients for my famous beef Wellington. Declared famous by me and Hades, who swallows it without chewing. Cooking has always been meditative for me. There has just always been something about bringing random ingredients together to create a delicious dish. This is my form of therapy. Frustrated? Beat it out on the meat. Sad? Add your favorite alcohol to the sauce. A little buzz has never hurt anyone. I'm just finishing wrapping the beef in the puff pastry when I catch a flicker of light out of the corner of my eye, making me freeze.

What the fuck was that?

I move over to the kitchen sink and lean forward, eyes squinting as if that's going to make looking out the kitchen window into the pitch-black yard any easier. I know I smoke a lot, and sometimes, I do get into my head and hear and see things that aren't actually there. I won't go as far as to say that I'm a paranoid smoker, but there's always a tiny bit present with me. I just chalk it up to being the result of a shitty fucking childhood.

There!

I see the light again coming out from behind the barn. It almost looks like someone is walking around with a flashlight. What the hell?

My stomach is in my throat as I whistle for Hades and grab

my handgun from the kitchen drawer. I conveniently have a gun stashed somewhere in every room of the house—something Zeke insisted on when I bought this place. At the time, I never understood, but now I hate to admit that I get it. "Let's go, boy," I whisper quietly while motioning for him to follow me out the back door.

"Seek," I command quietly, silently thanking myself for basically selling my arm and leg for this type of dog training.

Hades doesn't hesitate before he's off sprinting in the direction where I last saw that stranger. It never ceases to amaze me how smart dogs are.

I quietly step off the back deck and make my way to where the grass and trees meet. Slowly, I creep along them, heading toward where Hades ran, trying to blend into the shadows. I inhale sharply, trying to suck my stomach in as much as possible. Like that will make me melt into the shadows.

My heart is racing so fucking fast from all of this. What if it's an axe murder? All the crime documentaries I've watched have taught me that a situation like this only ends one way. Assaulted in every shape and form before they choke you out and send you six feet under. God. I don't think I've felt this much blinding fear since my foster dad, drunk off his ass, was trying to bust down my dead-bolted bedroom door. Again.

Just when I think I'm going to throw up from it all, I hear Hades' "I'm going to fuck you up" growl. And that's when I start running at a dead sprint directly toward where Hades is. And by dead sprint, I mean a light jog where I start to regret my life choice of canceling my gym membership because I didn't think I needed it. There's nothing like the universe giving you a big "fuck you, I told you so."

I flatten myself up against the back of the barn's wall, my hand on the safety of my gun, ready to fuck someone up as I peek around the corner.

I wasn't quick enough, though.

A bike's engine quickly fires up as I round the corner, the trespasser speeding out from behind a tree where his bike must have been stashed, darting across my lawn and back up my driveway. "Motherfucker!" I yell.

"Hades, come!" I scream as he starts to give chase, but immediately stops and comes back to me. "Good boy. I'll get you a treat in a second."

I tried to get a good look at the person, but it all happened so fast, and they were wearing a black ski mask. Fucker.

What in the hell just happened?

During the entire time that I've lived here, I have never had someone come out here like that. It was pretty fucking obvious that they didn't want me to know they were here.

Only two people — well, three now know what is back here and what I do for a living. I guess that isn't true, is it? The whole club probably knows. Guys I haven't even met before.

An uneasy feeling settles in the pit of my stomach. It feels like an immense sense of dread. Like no matter what I do, something really fucked up is about to happen.

That could have been so much worse than what it was. This person was clearly looking for something. But what? My plants? You're not going to ride out of here with those on the back of your bike. Maybe what I have packed and ready to go? But even then, you still wouldn't fit that much in a saddlebag. Thank god they don't know that everything I have ready to go isn't kept in the greenhouse.

It's kept in the highly secured bunker I installed when I first moved in. It was a typical old, unfinished basement. And if someone got their hands on the plans for my house, that's all it would show. I fucking made sure of that.

Would the club double-cross me?

No, Zeke would die protecting me before he let that happen.

Would Storm rat me out? I'd like to say I doubt it, but our business arrangement isn't exactly legally binding.

You see, I just grow the product. But dealing? That's a whole different ball game that I want no part of.

There are too many risks and the possibility of a deal going sideways.

So once everything is ready, Storm meets me, buys it off of me, and does god knows what with it. Oh god. Is it him?

I met Storm at a bar I worked at right out of high school. He was your typical line cook/drug dealer. I couldn't tell you exactly how we got into business together. It kind of just happened. And when I finally had enough saved up to buy this place, it was kind of an unspoken agreement that we would expand slightly. I mean, why not? Money makes the world go round.

Hades follows me through the back door and sits in front of the fridge, waiting for his treat. I threw him his bone before quickly setting the alarm system and putting my handgun back in its designated drawer.

As I get ready for bed, all the possibilities of what could have happened to Hades and me run through my head. Hades snuggles up to my side and is out like a light, as if we weren't almost just murdered and made into someone's dinner. I envy his resilience because me?

I didn't get any fucking sleep that night.

**12**

**Cain**

Just when I thought I was tricking my brain into getting that little hellcat out of it, I see her sweet ass strutting across the screen from one of the cameras walking into my bar.

It's like whatever I do, I can't escape her.

My plan was just to ignore her. The only reason I should even be conversing with her is if it involves our little arrangement. So why do I find myself slamming my office door shut and marching down to where she's perched on a stool?

I saw the way drunk fucking Carl was staring at her, looking her up and down like he was going to have a taste whether she liked it or not. If he even so much as lays a finger on her, I'm going to snap it the fuck off.

That has me halting.

When have I ever been possessive of a woman? Fucking never.

I need to get laid or some shit.

Get my head back on straight.

That's a conversation to have with myself another time because all I can think about is touching her smooth-looking skin. It's all I've thought about since I found out Evan had a pussy. And tits. Glorious fucking tits.

I know she isn't aware that I just walked up right behind her. We need to work on that. She should always be aware of her surroundings, whether it's in a place she knows or not.

"Put it on my tab," I tell Delaney before I can even process the words.

Evan's scent must be getting to my head. The sweet smell of jasmine, gardenia, and warm woods hits my nose, and all I can think about is wanting to find out if she smells like that everywhere.

My body still has a mind of its own because before I know it, I'm whispering in her ear about how much her sass turns me on and lightly dragging my finger from the bottom of her ear down to the base of her neck. Just enough to have my fix.

I don't even think she's aware of the reaction her body has to me. The shudder that moves through her makes me wish we were alone so I could get a taste of that wet heat she has between those sweet thighs.

The attitude she continues to throw my way has my dick in a constant state of hardness. Normally, this wouldn't be a problem, but it seems like the fucker only wants the sweet raven with a side of purple-haired beauty. It's like as soon as he senses her presence, he's back to being 15 years old all over again. Begging for just a lick of attention. Literally and figuratively. He just doesn't know how to act around her.

Evan has quickly become a temptation I'm having a very hard time resisting.

Casting a glare towards Carl that has him inching farther away, letting him know what the fuck is up, I turn and head back toward my office. I almost made it to my door when I felt my phone vibrate in my pocket. Pulling it out, I see it's a text from Scotch.

*Call me.*

Picking up on the second ring, I hear, "Hey, Prez."

"What's up?" I say as I unlock the office door and step inside.

"You busy? You're needed at the clubhouse." That has my eyebrows raising. "Some uninvited visitors decided to stop by," Scotch says, his voice tight.

Shit. This can't be good.

"Yeah, I'm at DD's. Be there in 20." I hang up without even waiting for a response. Slipping on my cut, I make sure everything is locked up behind me before I slip out the back. The last thing I need is to get a whiff of Evan again and lose all of my fucking concentration.

PULLING UP TO THE CLUBHOUSE, I see Spider's bike, the president of The Reapers MC, a club a few states over who we happen to be in this fucking situation with, along with the other guys he brought with him, parked outside.

Fuck.

The door to the clubhouse slams behind me as I take in the scene. The air is full of tension you could cut with a fucking knife.

My men are flanked by Scotch, and Spider is in front of him as the two face off.

"What the fuck is going on?"

Spider turns his attention to me, eyes set in hard lines as he says, "What the fuck is going on is that our shipment got fucking jacked in the hands of you fucking pussies." I can feel everyone in the room stiffen, waiting for someone to strike first. "We fulfilled our end of the arrangement. You were supposed to transport it to the cartel, and somehow you fucks managed to fuck that up."

"Watch your fucking tone, Spider. You might be president of your club, but this is my fucking house you're standing in," I growl.

"You better fucking fix this shit. The last thing I want is the cartel sniffing around. We don't need a war right now," he growls back.

"What the fuck do you think I'm doing? I'm working on it."

"You just going to pull five hundred pounds out of your ass?

And that's when I lose it.

In the blink of an eye, I'm on him, my hands hauling him up by the collar of his cut, slamming him against the wall behind him. The sounds of guns being drawn echo behind me, but I only have eyes for Spider. "You're not going to come into my house and talk to me like I'm your bitch. If I said I'm fucking handling it, then I'm fucking handling it. You got me?" I growl, squeezing my hand around his throat.

"I got you," Spider chokes out.

Releasing him but not before giving him one last shove, I step back. Spider is rubbing his throat while catching his breath, glaring at me. Clearly fucking pissed that I just made him look like the little bitch he is in front of his men.

"Now, if you're done mouthing off, I can fill you in on what I have set in play," I say, waiting for a nod of confirmation from him. "We have another contact that we've talked to who can come up with the same amount that got jacked."

"Who is the contact?"

"That's something you don't need to know," I answer, feeling Scotch stiffen beside me.

If they got wind of Evan, Scotch would be out for blood, and I'd be right behind him, ready to fuck a motherfucker up.

"Bullshit. We need to know what we're dealing with."

"And if I feel like shit is about to hit the fan, I'll call your secretary." I smirk as my eyes slide to the scrawny bitch next to Spider. "We're done," I say at the same time the scrawny bitch lets out a growl. "Follow them out, boys. And make sure they get the fuck off of my property."

On that parting, I head towards the meeting room for church to wait for the rest of the guys. There's one thing that's not sitting right about their unexpected visit.

Just how did the Reapers find out about the jacked shipment?

~

"They leave okay?" I ask as soon as they start filing in.

"Sure." Repo gives me a knowing smirk.

"Cyrus fuck 'em up a little?"

"You know Cyrus," came my confirmation. I'm not even going to tell him to chill out. Those fuckers deserve it after showing up unannounced like that.

Cyrus has one outlet he uses to deal with any sort of emotion, and that's beating the ever-loving shit out of a sorry motherfucker. Can't say it doesn't come in handy. It's why I made him one of my enforcers. It took a little bit of training to get it under control, though. I can't have anyone just randomly beating the shit out of someone whenever something disrupts them. What would that say about the club?

So we met halfway, and he joined an underground fighting ring. He has a release, and I make a ton of money from betting on him. It's a win-win.

"Alright!" I yell, the talking quieting down as I wait for their attention. "Does someone want to explain to me how the fuck they knew about the shipment when I specifically said this stays between us for now?" Looking around, the guys are looking at each other like they haven't got a fucking clue.

"No idea, Prez. I know we had the prospects do clean up,

but I know they didn't leave anything behind. Repo supervised to make sure that shit got done right," Cyrus said from the seat next to me on my left.

An uncomfortable silence settled over the room as we all tried to think of any possible reason as to how the fuck this happened.

"You think it could have been Evan?" Ink asks, breaking the silence as he raises his hands in defense when the low rumble comes out of me. I'm sure the glare I shot him matched Scotch's based on the way his fist slammed down on the table.

"No, it wasn't fucking Evan."

Every single one of the guy's eyebrows shot up at the intensity of my voice.

"Alright... didn't mean no offense, Prez. Just trying to consider all possibilities."

"Well, if all of you say it wasn't you, and we covered that it wasn't Evan, I think it's safe to say something else is going on."

The solemn faces around me confirm my suspicions.

But who in the fuck would be stupid enough to double-cross me?

**13**

I haven't left my house yet.

I need to.

But I just can't make myself do it.

All of last night's events, combined with my not sleeping, have officially caught up to me. I'm a paranoid bitch right now. It's the worst feeling to feel uncomfortable in your own home. Like someone is watching your every move. I worked so hard to never feel like this again, and I'm pissed as hell that someone is taking that away from me.

I need to go outside and see if the guy from last night left any evidence or indication of what he wanted.

"Come on, Hades. Let's go outside for a second, okay?" I call for him as I slip on my shoes. Hades has been glued to my side since he felt my anxiety when he woke up.

I scratch his head, and he bounds out in front of me through the back door.

One question that hasn't stopped running through my head while I was tossing and turning all night is: How did someone on a bike get back here without Hades or me even hearing it? That just doesn't seem possible to me. I mean, yeah, I had rock music playing while I was cooking, but it wasn't so loud that I wouldn't have heard a bike pull up. Unless they cut the engine before they hit my drive and pushed it all the way back? I guess that's always a possibility.

My suspicions are confirmed when I see tire tracks with footprints next to them leading back to the barn. I follow the tracks to the barn's side door. Scratches are on the door and lock, as if he tried to pick it in a rush. So, the mystery man was trying to break in.

"Well, that's unsettling," I say out loud as I stare at the lock like it's magically going to give me all the answers I'm looking for.

How does anyone know what's inside my barn, though? It just doesn't add up. If you weren't close to me, there is no way you would even know what I have back here.

A feeling of dread comes over me. Part of me wants to chalk this up as a fluke thing, but I have a feeling I may need to involve Cain, which is the last thing I want to do. Staying away from that man is so high up on my list it isn't even funny.

"Check with Storm first. Then, if nothing comes from that, as a last resort, I'll see if Cain knows anything," I tell myself as I head back into the house.

The first priority is definitely getting some kind of security system set up out here. I guess I never thought I would need it, but here we are.

I SERIOUSLY NEED to start questioning my life choices. Storm's trailer looks like the one from Breaking Bad. I don't really know what I was expecting, but this wasn't it.

Reality starts setting in as I realize just how little I actually know about my "business associate." I use that term loosely because, well, doesn't the other person have to actually put money in? I guess Storm is more like my unofficial employee. Maybe I should invest in a beater car for these types of situations. Something that no one can trace back to me. Not that I ever plan on being in a situation like this again, but I probably have "Please rob me" stamped on my forehead as I climb out of my Mustang.

"I've got a gun!" someone that sounds a lot like a fucked-up Storm shouts from behind the trailer door.

"Don't shoot, you dickhead. It's Evan." I still find myself putting my hands up, unsure of what he's about to do.

"Evan?"

"Yeah, Storm. Evan. You know, your... friend?" I say with a wince. I don't even know what to call myself to him. That's how little we talk. A few moments of uncomfortable silence pass, as if he's trying to remember who I am, before I hear a lock being flipped over, and the door flies open.

Oh my god.

He looks rough.

Rough as in, 'I drank a bunch of Long Islands, took a Xanax, and don't remember the night.' His hair is sticking in every direction, not styled like that on purpose, but from the grease I can see from here. And if the smell I'm getting from 10 feet away is anything to go by, I don't think he's showered in a while.

Ugh. Fuck my life. Why can't anything ever go smoothly anymore?

"Why are you here? How did you find this place?" Storm rushes out before I can even get a word in. His body is wound tight as his left leg bounces up and down, his eyes scanning all over the drive and yard behind me.

Is he for real right now?

I texted him not even two hours ago, asking to meet up. I gave him a bogus story about wanting to talk about having more stuff to move, but really, I just want to feel him out to see if he knows anything about last night.

The impending dread I was feeling earlier is back with a vengeance.

"I texted you a couple of hours ago asking if we could meet up, and you sent me this address. You don't remember?"

"Oh. Yeah, right. Of course." He waves me in, his eyes still scanning quickly over the area behind me.

You know that feeling you get when you feel like you're being watched but don't see anyone watching you? That's exactly how I feel right now. The amount of times he's looked behind me has me turning around and doing a scan before I step inside.

The overwhelming stench that greets my nose has me inhaling sharply.

Holy mother of god. What is that smell? Looking around, trying to find the source but coming up with a million different possibilities for the cause because, let's be honest here, the place is fucking trashed. Imagine if a hoarder and the dirtiest person you can think of had a baby. That's what Storm's place would be.

Does he even know what a trash can is?

I can't see anything on the countertops because takeout containers are stacked up to the bottom of the cabinets. Random wrappers, papers, dirty clothes, and boxes are scattered all over the floor.

Oh god. Please tell me that isn't a used condom in the corner.

It's official.

I'm going to fucking throw up.

"So, uh, how have you been?" I ask, forcing back my gag.

"Oh, you know, the usual. I stay pretty busy with my contacts and the pussy that throws itself at me." He smirks a yellow-toothed smile that doesn't reach his eyes.

Ugh. Ick. He gives me the fucking ick.

I would have thought being back behind the closed door of his trailer would ease some of his anxiety, but his leg is still bouncing. As I scan him up and down, he almost seems more uncomfortable.

Is it because I'm in his personal space? I guess I haven't ever dropped by like this before. He doesn't exactly seem like the type to know what your standard social protocols are, considering he didn't even attempt to clean. This definitely seems deeper than that, though. Now that I'm up close and can really look into his eyes, I notice that he's high as hell.

"Have you had any issues with the product lately?" I cut straight to the chase. No sense in beating around the bush because I have about 5 good minutes left of breathing this disgusting fucking air. It's the kind of dirty that makes you want to leave and bathe in bleach.

"No." He shakes his head quickly. "No, not at all." If I hadn't already been focused on Storm, I would have missed how he refused to make eye contact and how his leg bounce seemed to pick up speed.

Well, well, well. I think I have myself a coked-out liar on my hands.

Fucking great.

"So no one has asked about where it's coming from or anything?" I cock my eyebrow at him.

"No," Storm gushes out too fast. Suspiciously fast. "Why would they? Weed is weed. People come to me because they don't want to pay the dispensary prices."

Holding my hands up, much like I did earlier when this cokehead threatened to shoot me, I say, "Hey, I didn't mean anything by it. I was just making sure." This seems to placate him because the leg bouncing slows slightly. "I was cleaning out the barn, and I found a few extra pounds. I didn't know if you wanted a little more to work with."

"Oh, yeah. That'd be great. I'll stop over later and grab it." He jumps up from where he's sitting on the couch, motioning me to the door. Hmm... so quick to have me leave. Suspicious.

There's not a chance in hell I'm inviting him back over to my place until I figure out what the fuck is going on. "No need. I brought it with me."

"You brought it with you?" he hisses, quickly moving to peek out the opening in the living room window blinds. They're closed, but some of the ends have snapped off. If you've ever lived in a cheap apartment, you know exactly what type of blinds I'm talking about.

"Are you looking for someone?" I finally ask after a few uncomfortable moments because this is weird. Really fucking weird.

"No. Of course not," he snaps while heading to the front door.

Obviously, that's my cue to leave.

Fine by me. I'm going to need to bathe myself in bleach from just standing in this fucking infested place.

"Let me know if you have any issues," I say as I close my trunk, and we switch bags. I may be stupid for not looking into Storm more before we started anything, but I'm not so stupid that I don't make him pay me up front first. If I didn't do that, I'd probably never see any fucking money.

Storm doesn't meet my eyes as he nods, still looking all over. "You head on home now, Evan."

I can't help but feel like something huge is about to happen as I climb into my car and leave.

The real question is what and when?

**14**

**Cain**

It's been a week, and we've made no progress on the missing shipment.

But it's Friday, and Friday means we party. I'm hoping the pussy and booze will lighten the mood around here for a little bit. We've all been on edge all week. I wish I could say mine was from the obvious, but it wasn't. Much to my displeasure, it has to do with a certain little hellcat.

My plan to get Evan out of my goddamn head is to find the first club girl that begs to suck my cock. I've lost count of how many times I've jacked off at the thought of tasting her sweet cunt. I can't stop thinking about all the ways I want to take her. Hard up against a wall. Bent over my desk in both offices so I can smack that sweet ass. On all fours, begging to be deep-throated, shooting my load down her throat.

"We ready to go for tonight?" I call to Levi, the prospect who is stocking the bar.

"Yeah, Prez. Brock is checking the sound system now."

Perfect.

It isn't long before the clubhouse is packed. The music is playing, and the booze is flowing. Seated on a couch in the far corner, I look around. We're pretty well known for our parties in the area. Fuck, anytime I meet up with Matteo, he tells me all the girls from the city can't shut the fuck up about them. Whenever a girl gets the itch of wanting to live a little on the naughty side, they usually end up here. Scotch has each arm wrapped around a couple right now while another grinds down on his lap. Hash has always been a little more reserved regarding the girls, but he's even chatting one up in the corner. Lord knows that man needs to get laid.

I snort. Like I'm one to talk.

At 40 years old, the thought of hooking up with a new girl every night has lost its appeal. It just seems like... so much work. The thought of having a woman I actually like warming my bed every night is what's appealing now. Someone who isn't just trying to get with you because of your patch. I can never say that out loud, though. The brothers would have my fucking balls if they knew I was even thinking about settling down.

"You look stressed, baby." A girl who has been hanging around the club recently, but I can't fucking remember her name, pouts as she slides up next to me on the couch. One arm sneaks around the back of my shoulders while her other hand slowly climbs up my chest until she reaches my jaw, lightly stroking it.

I turn my head so I'm facing her. "I'm good, babe."

"You sure? You don't look okay," she purrs. "I could take your mind off it." Her chest slides against my arm, making my eyes dart down to her overly inflated fake tits that are way too fucking big for her body. I might not be a huge tit man, but I have never been and never will be attracted to fake tits that look like they're going to fucking pop if I touch them. The skin on them looks tighter than my virgin fucking asshole.

"Nah, uh.." Ah, fuck. What is her name?

"Candy. My name is Candy," she fills in, her smile growing tight.

I snort. Of fucking course, it's Candy. How original.

My hand moves down to tap her ass. "I'm good, Candy. I think Trick needs some lovin'. He's had a long, hard day if you catch my drift." I wink.

"Oh, okay!" And she's off. Hopefully, to give my brother some of that sweetness.

I shouldn't have done that. I should have taken her up on her offer. That was my plan tonight, to get Evan out of my head, and I just can't fucking do it. At that thought, something purple across the room catches my eye.

A purple and raven-haired woman is staring right at me with wide eyes.

Fuck.

That's what's wrong with me.

**15**

Evan

I know I have to look like the biggest fucking idiot right now. But I can't look away, and that infuriates me to no end. Because why? I shouldn't care what Cain is doing or who he is with. Seeing Cain with that girl all up on him is just what I needed to bring me back to reality. I look nothing like that girl. Her hair is a fried bleach blonde, whereas mine is a rich violet with a black shadow root. One of her tits is as big as my head and so fucking perky that they look like they actually might touch her chin if she looks down. Mine are on the naturally bigger side, but they're definitely not about to touch my chin anytime soon. You would never catch me without a bra.

God, I hate that I feel so fucking stupid. Stupid for fantasizing about a man who would never want someone like me. Stupid for thinking his flirting had meant anything. I had no business entertaining any of it. My mind just kept playing into the fantasy of him not being a jerk after he apologized.

Fuck him. The last thing I need in my life is someone like

him. He would cast me aside in a heartbeat as soon as the next best thing came along.

"Hey, darlin'," a voice comes from my side, breaking my gaze I had locked on Cain. "I haven't seen you around before. Can I get you a drink?"

He wasn't bad-looking. He kind of had that Tom Hardy vibe going for him. You know, when his hair was a little longer on top? Styled and gelled but still has that messy look to it that every single girl in the world finds sexy as fuck. And that neatly trimmed beard that would give you just the right amount of roughness between your thighs to drive you crazy. Just add in a shit ton of tattoos and a few inches in height, and you have this man. I bet his piercing blue eyes get a lot of panties to drop.

"Uh, no thanks. I'm good." I smile politely, feeling a little on edge with so many people I don't know around me.

I wouldn't consider myself shy, and I think that's where people underestimate me. Just because I don't talk a lot doesn't mean I won't put you in your place if you cross a line with me. I just prefer not to socialize, and large crowds make me want to crawl into a hole and never come out. I'm the girl who won't leave her house for two weeks before she realizes it's been that long.

"Aww, come on. I'm sure a sweet thing like you needs to blow off some steam every once in a while. How 'bout we make that night tonight?" The swagger of this man is almost suffocating. But I've never been that girl. One-night stands and I have never really mixed. And even if I were going to entertain one, it sure as hell wouldn't be with anyone associated with Cain.

"I'm uh. Actually, I was wondering if Zek—" I start to say before I remember his road name. I seriously need to get used to the names. "Scotch. I mean Scotch. I'm wondering if Scotch is around."

"Scotch, huh? What about my brother is it you like? Cause I can assure you, whatever he does, I can do a million times better. With a few more fingers added." Tom Hardy winks as he holds up his hand and wiggles his fingers. A laugh bursts out of me as I feel my cheeks heat up because this man seriously did not just add into a normal conversation that he could finger me better.

"I knew I could get the pretty lady to smile. And holy shit, is it a sight to see. Come on, darlin'. As much as it wounds my ego, I'll help you find my brother."

Before I can thank him, he's off weaving through the sea of people on the makeshift dance floor, bodies grinding and dry-humping each other as I try to keep up. Realizing he stopped, I look around to notice that we are outside. A fire is rolling in the pit toward the middle of the yard. An in-ground pool with a connecting hot tub sits off to the left. The beach volleyball pit to the right has me arching an eyebrow. Tom Hardy must catch it because he sheepishly says, "What? You haven't lived until you've played strip volleyball."

Well, alright then.

"Yo! Scotch!" Tom Hardy yells toward the pit, making a lot of people's eyes turn on us. It could be the fact that he's shouting or, more so, that his arm is currently around my shoulders.

"This better be good if you're pulling me away fro—" Zeke yells while turning to look over at us and stopping once he notices me. He doesn't even hesitate before he's up, taking huge strides to cut the distance between us. "Back the fuck off of her, Ink," Zeke growls, earning a smirk from Ink. "What's wrong, Evan? Give me a name, and they're fucking dead."

Ah, so the Tom Hardy look-alike has a name. Fitting, considering the man doesn't have an inch of skin that isn't covered in a tattoo besides his face.

I can see it all start to click behind Ink's eyes. "So you're the infamous Evan?" he drawls, which earns another growl from Zeke. "Alright, alright," Ink says, backing away with his hands up, the smirk never leaving his face. "I'll leave you two to it. It was a pleasure meetin' you, darlin'. I'm sure I'll be seein' you around." Again, sauntering off before I can thank him.

"I'm so sorry, Zeke," I rush out. "I didn't realize you guys were having a party. Although I guess this is probably a usual night for you guys." I conclude as I look around at everyone. "It can wait until tomorrow," I assure him before trying to leave.

"Whoa, whoa, whoa. No," he says while grabbing my arm and turning me back to him. "You've never just randomly dropped in to talk to me before, so tell me what the fuck is going on, Ev."

"Um..." I start but stop. Everyone isn't watching us anymore, but you can tell they're trying to listen. I'm seriously regretting my timing in deciding to come to him with my little problem. They're bikers. Of course they're partying on a Friday night.

"Come on." Zeke starts dragging me behind him, picking up on my growing anxiety about the crowd around us.

"Yo, Scotch! Want a shot?" a random dude that is well on his way to being shit-faced yells from over by the bar.

"Later! A little occupied right now!"

I caught Cain's questioning gaze from across the room, darting between mine and Zeke's locked hands before I was pulled through the door that leads to the stairs.

"Alright, Ev. Tell me what the fuck is going on," Zeke says as soon as we are behind the privacy of what I'm assuming is his bedroom door.

"Really, Zeke. It's not that pressing. I was just stopping by to see if you could help me out with getting some sort of security system for the barn, maybe one with cameras."

"Why?" His tone had taken on a whole new edge. "You've lived there for years now and haven't said shit about it. Even when I forced you to install the one inside the house."

It was a fucking stupid idea to come here. Of course he was

going to read between the lines and not buy my simple explanation of just wanting some cameras.

"Oh my god. Can't I just want to upgrade my security system?" I exclaim, throwing my hands up in the air as I start to pace the room.

"No. You fucking can not. A —" he rumbled before getting cut off by his bedroom door bursting open, revealing a very angry Cain. His eyes quickly search the room before settling on us. I visibly see some of the anger leave his body when he notices Zeke and I are feet apart from each other.

Oh my god.

He thought something was going on between us. Did he seriously think we were fucking? Is that why he's so pissed off? Like he has any sort of fucking right after I caught him with the club girl in his lap.

Zeke shoots Cain a glare as he steps inside the room, closing the door behind him. "As I was saying, the only time a female needs more security than she already has is when she feels unsafe. Now, Evangeline. I'm only going to ask one more time, what the fuck happened?"

Cain's gaze shoots to Zeke as I cringe at him using my full name. He's really not going to let this go. So much for Cain seeming like he was starting to calm down. He looks as if he's ready to murder someone again. You would think Hades was in here because of the rumbling that's coming from that man's chest. "If you don't tell him what the fuck happened, I'm going to find out what the fuck happened. And you don't want me finding out on my own. What fucking happened?" Cain growls, body tight, fists clenched at his sides.

For once, Zeke doesn't even try to come to my defense. Clearly on Cain's side. I'm not easily intimidated, but it's a little fucking scary when you have two angry biker badasses growling at you.

"Okay, okay. Let's just calm down," I say as I try to placate them. It doesn't seem to be working if their stares are anything to go by. "Last night, when I was making dinner, I thought I saw a light from a flashlight or something through the kitchen window out by the barn. I wanted to make sure I wasn't losing my freaking mind, so I went outside with Hades to—" I get cut off by two growling bikers yelling at the same damn time.

"You should have fucking called me!"

"What the fuck, Evan? You don't go out there by yourself!"

"Do you guys want to hear the rest or not?!" I yell over them, waiting for them to shut up. "As I was saying, I grabbed Hades and my gun," shooting a pointed look at both of them so they don't think I'm a complete idiot, I continue, "before I went outside to look. I quietly commanded Hades to seek while I crept along the treelike because if someone was out there, I didn't want them to see me. By the time I got close, Hades was growling his 'I'm going to fuck you up' growl, and some random fucking dude started up a bike and took off across my yard," I finish on a big exhale. It feels good to get that off my chest, even if it's about to bite me in the ass.

"Are you fucking kidding me?" they both say in unison.

"You should have called me immediately," Cain growls. "I'm not fucking liking this," Cain says while looking at Zeke, who nods his head in agreement.

"No offense, but you and I aren't on terms of calling each other for help. I don't even have your number. It's also really none of your business," I say, crossing my arms across my chest, in turn pushing my boobs up. Cain notices the move because his eyes flare as he looks down.

"It became my business, hellcat, when you walked your sweet ass into my club and agreed to help us. No one fucks with one of our own." Cain drags his eyes back up to meet mine. The heat behind them only intensifies.

And damn if my body isn't betraying me by lighting up. My

nipples tighten as I feel heat pool between my legs. Cain's eyes flare as if he knows exactly how my body is reacting.

"Send Brock out tomorrow to look at what needs to be done," Cain tells Zeke, breaking our silent exchange.

I decide it's probably best to leave out the little tidbit about Storm clearly being on something and acting super sus. The two can't be related, right?

"On it. I'll pop out with him to see if that mystery dipshit left anything behind."

"And I want a man on her starting tonight. I know Levi's sober. I set him on watch duty." They continue on as if I'm not even here.

Oh, hell no. A random guy I don't even know will not be staying at my place.

"Um, hello?" I wave my hands in front of their faces. "I'm not having someone I don't know stay at my place. Don't I get a say in any of this?"

"No," they say in unison.

I'm really starting to regret asking for help.

**16**

**Cain**

The thought of something happening to Evan is a kick to the gut. I can't even think about it without my eye twitching, and I'm really trying hard not to think about why that is, but I can't help it. It's probably because the look on her face when she saw Candy in my lap is burned into my brain.

Once I got over the initial shock of seeing her ass standing in my club, I thought it was weird she was even here in the first place. Scotch would have mentioned she was dropping by. My suspicions grew when I saw a pissed-off Scotch hauling her back inside the compound toward our rooms. My body started moving before my mind realized what it was doing because the next thing I knew, I was climbing the stairs two at a time and barging into Scotch's room like I was trying to catch them in the act.

Part of me needed to be reassured that he actually thought of her as a sister. It's just hard for me to comprehend having someone who looks and acts like Evan in your life and not wanting anything more out of it. The other part of me wonders if they ever tried to be more. I can't say that I wouldn't murder Scotch if I found that the answer was yes.

Fuck, she's way too young and way too good for me, anyway. I've got to be at least ten years older. Fuck. Doesn't stop me from wanting to beat the ever-loving shit out of him if I caught his hands anywhere on her body. Brother or not. But what I saw when I charged through the door, ready to beat his ass, was the opposite of the image that had made its way into my head. Unfortunately, Evan still has me losing my fucking mind. Just in a whole new way that I didn't see coming.

How could she have some random fucking guy coming on her property and not say shit to us? She needs to learn that she's not alone on this. No one fucks with what's mine. It all seems too coincidental with everything that has happened, and I don't fucking believe in coincidences.

So here I sit, in my fucking office, twiddling my fucking thumbs like a dumbass, while a party is raging on outside, waiting for Scotch to come back with Levi. I told Evan to stay put in Scotch's room until I could confirm that a man would follow her home.

"Hey, Prez," Levi says as he enters my office with Scotch behind him, all too eager to please.

"I'm putting you on Evan. Wherever she goes, you follow. Follow her like a lost fucking puppy. Starting tonight. I'll be checking in, but I also want you to report in." The kid is looking at me like I hung the moon by giving him something more to do than just washing our bikes and whatever random bitch-work or errands we don't want to do ourselves. "Time to prove yourself, prospect."

"Absolutely, Prez. Let me grab a change of clothes, and I'll be ready to go."

I wait for Levi to leave the office before I turn to Scotch, but someone knocks on my door. "Yeah?"

Hash, my VP, appears. "What's going on? I saw Evan show up, and then you three are going upstairs." I give Hash a quick rundown of what happened as he takes the seat next to Scotch.

"I'm not likin' how this is all startin' to look," Hash replies as he reclines back in the chair.

"I'm not either."

"The only people who even know about Evan being involved with us is just our crew. I hate to say it, Prez, but this is looking more and more like there's a leak on the inside," Scotch says, face grim, which I'm sure is a reflection of my own.

Hash and I both grunt in agreement.

"That, or someone is double-crossing us. For now, I want this to stay between us. Levi doesn't know why he's watching Evan, and I think that's for the best right now." Levi's a good kid. If he keeps it up, he'll patch in.

"I'm going to have Brock go over to Evan's tomorrow to see about getting some cameras set up around that barn. I don't like that some motherfucker just thought he could walk up there and help himself with no repercussions." Both guys grunt and nod in agreement. "Whoever it is, is going to fucking pay for messing with one of our own like that."

"She holdin' up alright?" Hash asks.

"I think so. She seems more mad about Scotch and I intervening and taking over."

"Stubborn."

Scotch and I both snort in agreement.

That's the understatement of the year.

**17**

Evan

The kid they put on me looks like he isn't even old enough to drive.

It's downright insulting that they think I can't defend myself if anything were to happen. Like this kid is going to be able to save me. The last thing I need right now is someone following me around. Not to mention I have a lot of shit I need to do.

"The inside is a bit of a construction zone at the moment, and I don't have a bed in any of the guest rooms yet. Sorry." I throw him a sheepish look over my shoulder as I unlock the backdoor for us.

"I'm good with the couch, babe. Better, too." I arch my eyebrow at him because who in their right mind thinks a couch is better than a bed? "Just in case he comes back and tries to break into the house, I'll be able to shoot his balls off before he even makes it past the entryway."

He looks way too pleased at the thought of that. "Fucking biker dudes," I mumble to myself.

"Help yourself to anything in the kitchen. The bathroom is down the hall, first door on the right. I'll get you a pillow and a blanket," I say before I head upstairs, the steps creaking the whole way. It's one of the quirks of buying an old house that I haven't had the time to tune up yet.

A nice long bath is calling my name tonight. The need to decompress and take a minute to breathe is so strong. I hate feeling like my life is spiraling out of control, and there's no way to stop it. Ever since the day I agreed to help out the club, weird shit has happened. And not the good kind of weird. I've worked so hard for my stability. I'll be damned if some random fuckhead thinks he can come in and take that away from me.

I come to a halt just before I reach my bedroom. Would it be weird if I took a bath with a man downstairs whom I just met tonight?

For some reason, sitting naked in a tub of water with someone in my house seems weirdly intimate. Especially in this house, where you can hear someone breathing from the opposite end because it's so old. You know what I mean? Like they're just going to be sitting downstairs thinking about everything I'm doing. And if they hear the water splash? The thought alone makes me cringe.

I find the blankets and pillows I'm looking for tucked away in my closet. I completely gutted the linen closet by the bathroom in the hall and haven't opened the door since. Just another thing on my to-do list.

"I keep the alarm set at night, so if you need to step out for whatever reason, the code is 666420." I can't help but snort as I set the bedding on the couch. Life isn't worth living if you can't laugh at yourself along the way.

Only two people know the code: Zeke and the guy who installed it, and even they didn't get it until I told them. So I'm a little surprised when Levi starts laughing. "The devil's lettuce, right? 666 for devil and 420 for weed. That's a pretty good one."

"Yeah." I smirk. I don't know whether to be happy someone finally got it without me explaining anything or if I should be slightly concerned that I have the same sense of humor as a kid who probably isn't old enough to drink legally.

"Alright, well, I'm going to call it a night. Again, anything in the kitchen is free game. Help yourself to whatever. I'm sorry you're stuck babysitting me," I say as I start to head back toward the stairs, snapping at Hades to follow.

"Don't sweat it, babe. Prez just wants to make sure you're safe. Although I can't say I've ever seen him like this with a woman. You two a thing?" he asks, looking like he's trying to put everything together before he realizes what he just asked. "Ah, fuck. Please don't tell Prez I asked you that. He would have my ass, and I'm finally doing something other than being their bitch. Not that I don't enjoy being their bitch. I do. I know I need to earn—" he rambles.

"Levi," I cut him off. "It's fine. I know you didn't mean anything by it," I assure him. "It's already forgotten. But to answer your question—no, we aren't a thing. He's only being like this because I'm the only option right now." At those parting words, I finish the trek to my room, but not before I see the unsure look on Levi's face. Like he didn't believe a fucking word I just said.

Levi is already up and ready to go when I finally come down around 11am.

"Didn't know if I was gonna have to go up and put a mirror under your nose." Levi smirked, coffee cup in hand.

"Waking up before 10am should be illegal, and anyone that does is probably well on their way to being a serial killer if they aren't already," I grumble as I pour myself a cup of coffee over ice before grabbing the dairy-free creamer out of the fridge. I can't stand hot beverages. The feeling of hot liquid going down my throat and into my stomach makes me want to crawl out of my skin.

"Are you stuck with me today, too?" I ask after finally feeling that first sip of caffeine entering my bloodstream.

"Until Prez says otherwise. I'll probably get relieved when Scotch and Brock come over," he replies, scratching Hades behind the ear where he likes it.

I'm just about to tell him that he doesn't need to stay when I hear the faint sound of bikes coming up through the woods. No, that can't be right. Levi also hears it because he jumps out of his seat to go look out the back door as I move to look out the kitchen window. It's not long before I see Cain, Scotch, and Brock coming out of the far left trail.

Those assholes.

They cut the fucking gate.

"Where the fuck did they come from?" Levi asks while putting on his boots.

"The back edge of my property butts up against the end of the club's property. I realized that the other day when I found out that we're neighbors." I sigh. I should never have let Cain in on that little detail. Clearly, he thinks he can just do whatever the fuck pleases him.

"Hellcat." Cain smirks as I step outside to meet them, Levi following behind.

"Cain," I answer as I cross my arms across my chest.

"This is Brock. He's going to be the one installing the cameras." I nod my head toward him. He doesn't have a cut on either. He must be a prospect like Levi, just way older. I'd put my money on around my age. "Now, show us where the fuck you caught this guy."

Motioning with my hand to follow, I walk over to the side door. "I didn't see exactly where he was because by the time I got over here, Hades already had him moving. But I noticed a bunch of scratches around and on the deadbolt that weren't there before. Like maybe he was trying to pick it?" All the males nod their heads, and their faces harden, confirming my assumption.

"The ground was still kind of wet from all the rain we had, so I noticed footprints next to tire tracks from a bike, like he walked it up my drive. That's the only thing I can think of because I never heard the bike. I mean, I heard you guys coming up the trail from way back." I cut all three of them a glare. "Thanks for cutting the chain, by the way. But I would have heard a bike, you know?"

"My guess is whoever it was knew you were home and somehow knew where the barn was because it doesn't seem like they needed any help finding their way back," Cain said, hands on his toned muscular waist as he looked around, surveying everything.

"Prez is right, Ev. This seems more personal. I just can't tell if it's more personal toward you or the club. You okay?" Zeke asks while wrapping an arm around my shoulder. Before I can respond, a loud rumbling erupts from Cain, who looks like he's about a second away from skinning Zeke alive.

Smirking with his hands in the air as he backs up to where he was originally standing, Zeke says, "Sorry, Prez. You know she's the closest thing I have to a sister. I'll keep it in check, though."

Uh, what was that?

Deciding it's better to just ignore that little exchange for now, I answer Zeke, "Yeah, I'm alright. Just a little weirded out that someone has been scoping out my place. I don't like feeling like I'm being watched."

"We're going to catch the fucker, hellcat. And he's going to pay," Cain vowed.

"Thanks. I appreciate it. I have some work to get done, so

I'm going to leave you all to do whatever it is you're about to do," I say before I head inside the barn.

I keep things very clean around here. To avoid any sort of dog hair or really anything getting on the plants or bud, I had a shower installed in the barn. This allows me to clean off and change into my dirty whore leggings and tank. After securing my hair in a tight bun on my head, I make my way toward the glass door that leads to the plants.

"Want some help?" a voice I'm beginning to know all too well sounds from behind me. How did he follow me in here and I didn't even notice? For being so large, the man sure moves quietly.

"I'm alright, thanks. I know you have things going on out there." I wave my hand toward the door.

"It doesn't take 4 guys to install cameras, babe."

Sighing in defeat as I realize that I'm probably not going to be able to get rid of him like I wanted, I ask, "Do you have a change of clothes? You can't come in here with what you've been wearing all over the place."

"Always keep a change in my saddlebag, hellcat." The bastard has the nerve to smirk. I'm sure he fucking does keep a change of clothes. Probably so he can get whatever skank's cheap perfume off of him when he's done. I can't figure out why I'm getting so mad over some guy that isn't even mine. And I hate it. I hate it so much. But seeing Candy in his lap, climbing all over him, is burned into my brain. I never thought I was a jealous person, but in that moment, I was. Hell, I obviously still am.

"It's not for what you think, hellcat," Cain says softly. I open my mouth to try to say that it doesn't matter, and he doesn't owe me any explanation, but he beats me to the punch. "I never know what might happen or if I might be needed somewhere. Saves me some time to be prepared if something goes to shit."

He offered me reassurance without even asking.

And I liked that.

I liked that a lot.

And I hate that I like it.

"You don't owe me an explanation, Cain, but thank you," I reply just as softly. Even though I hate all the mixed signals I've been getting, I can't seem to work up the courage to ruin the moment. "There's a shower right over there if you want to rinse off before changing and coming in."

I don't wait for a reply before I enter the area with my plant babies, the glass door slamming shut behind me. It isn't long before Cain follows.

We work in silence. And by silence, I mean the only sound is the sexy, soothing sound of David Draiman playing in the background. What can I say? The man can sing and has songs for any mood.

I thought I was going to need to show Cain what to do, but he came inside confident as always and went right to work, starting on the opposite end from me. I guess gun-running bikers probably know their way around plants.

As much as I hate asking for help, I can't deny that it feels nice having someone here helping me. I've never had an issue with being alone, but the more I think about it, the more I think I might be a little lonely.

Before I know it, someone is banging on the glass, scaring the shit out of me. I let out a scream as I fall flat on my ass from where I was just crouched. I glare up at Cain, who is currently looking down at me, laughing, with his hand outstretched. "Relax, hellcat. It's just Scotch letting me know they're done."

Grabbing it, allowing him to pull me up, I grumble, "Right. Just wasn't expecting that is all."

The funny feeling that I got when I first shook his hand is still there. If anything, it's more intense. I close my eyes as I take a second to just feel it. A light shiver runs through my body as I open my eyes to find his intense gaze locked on mine. Part of me thinks that there is no way this is one-sided because he still hasn't let go of my hand. The only problem is that there is this little devil on my shoulder telling me he's way out of my league.

I'm the one to break the contact as I take a step back. I need to get a fucking grip.

"Let me go see what's going on."

I nod in response. Thankful for the minute alone.

I collect all the supplies we pulled out and start putting them away, deciding to deal with them tomorrow. I think the events of the last few days call for a little R&R.

A long, hot shower is calling my name since I didn't get the bath I wanted last night. I just hope I don't have a prospect following me around anymore. There are only two types of people in this world that you can feel one hundred percent comfortable doing whatever the fuck you want in your house without feeling awkward. Your significant other who you have already crossed that line with, or one of the 'I can lie around the house in the same clothes as the day before, hair unbrushed in a messy bun, face not washed, all while stuffing my face to anything I can get my hands on' friend.

The prospect is so far away from either of those things that he might as well be on a completely different planet. Nice kid, though. I just prefer him not to hear the splash of water and think I'm getting off.

I head outside just as I hear the bikes start up. Zeke flicks me a wave, followed by one of those head nods guys do before taking off back down the trail with Brock and Levi in tow.

Cain must have seen the questioning look on my face because he chimes in with his stupid, famous smirk that I swear is permanently stuck on his face, "You're stuck with me today, little hellcat."

Maybe today will be the day that I finally wipe it off.

**18**

Evan

"I don't need a babysitter," I snap. "Nothing is going to happen, and if it does, I'm a big girl. I can handle it. I never asked for any of this. All I wanted was some fucking security cameras!" I shout at him as I start walking toward the house, leaving him behind with a glint in his eye.

As I head upstairs, I hear the back door beep, telling me it opened. Of course he wouldn't just leave me alone. Grabbing a towel out of the linen closet in the master bathroom, I turn the shower on as hot as it will go, letting the bathroom fill with steam before stripping out of my clothes and stepping in. It isn't until the hot water is streaming down my front that I finally feel my shoulders slump, all the tension that has been building up is now slowly releasing. You know that feeling when the water is so hot, but your skin doesn't feel like it is, and you kind of zone out?

Yeah.

That's where I'm at right now.

Which is probably why I didn't hear my bathroom door

opening and why I didn't hear the sound of a cut, jeans, and a belt being discarded on the floor. And I sure as hell didn't hear the curtain being pulled back. Or feel the cool air hit my numb skin. It wasn't until I felt a pair of strong arms wrap around my waist, pulling me up against a hard, naked body.

Freezing in place, I ask, "What do you think you're doing?"

"Showering," he simply replies while reaching around me for my loofah and body wash. "Just relax, hellcat. I'm not going to bite." I can hear his stupid smirk. "Well, not unless you ask me to." He loads the loofah up with soap before working it into a lather over my shoulders, slowly working his way down my back. I move my neck to the left, stretching it slightly because, as much as I hate to admit it, this feels so good.

"Damn, I love this ass," he rumbles before grabbing a handful of one cheek with the unoccupied hand while the other massages the other half with the loofah. "Can't leave something this gorgeous dirty now, can we?"

Now would be the time to tell him to stop. To tell him this can't happen for the million reasons I'm currently blanking on. But I don't. I never indulge in anything like this. I'm just going to enjoy this for what it is. The rush of it feels too good to be ignored, and it's been so long since I've been with anyone. I know a man like Cain isn't going to want any strings attached.

So what do I do?

I lean back into it, grinding against his growing erection, earning me that deep, sexy rumble I'm growing to love. The loofah trails back up my spine, lightly running over my shoul-der. "Turn around, little hellcat," Cain rumbles in my ear, his breath whispering across my skin. Turning around to face him, I take in a sharp breath. The heated, predatory look in his eyes has me backing up until I can feel the cool tile of the shower wall against my back. The growl that erupts from Cain's chest has my lower belly tightening and my breasts feeling heavy and full.

"They're pierced." Cain's nostrils flare as he growls. Before I can respond, Cain is claiming my mouth, loofah long forgotten. Gasping at the roughness, he takes advantage by sucking my bottom lip into his mouth before plunging his tongue inside, exploring and claiming it as his all in one.

A moan escapes me as I run my hands up his arms until I reach his strong, broad shoulders. Shoulders that feel like they could hold the weight of the world, just so you'd never fall. When I reach his neck, I switch to only my fingertips, lightly trailing them down his chest, through the rough hair he doesn't trim, down to his abs that I feel behind me. They definitely don't disappoint. They are more of a thick dad-bod type, which I absolutely loved. The chest hair makes everything that much better. The coarse feel of it against my skin sends a shiver running through me.

Deciding to test my limits, my fingers continue their trek slightly lower until I'm wrapping my hand around his thick, hard cock. And holy shit, is it thick. His sharp inhale is the only encouragement I need to give him a long, hard stroke.

Sweet mother of fucking hell.

He has to be a solid 9 inches. My core tightens at the thought of him pounding every inch deep inside me. Going deeper than any man has before. A long, low growl erupts from Cain as he rips his mouth from mine, roughly kissing and sucking down my neck. Teasing at this point, kissing everywhere but where I need him. My nipples harden as my breasts start to feel so heavy and achy, begging for his touch. I'm not left waiting as Cain roughly grabs one with his hand.

"They don't even fit in my hand." Cain groans while pulling away from my neck, bouncing his hand slightly, feeling the weight of them. "Do these pretty nipples need to be sucked?" he asks as he pulls on the peaks, messing with the small silver bar that's running through each nipple before kneading them again.

"Yes," I breathe, writhing against him, needing his mouth on me.

"You think you've been a good girl? You think you deserve this?" he asks, his face inches from my breast. I can feel his heavy breathing on my nipple, making it that much more sensitive. This is my own personal form of torture.

"Cain," I whine, borderline begging and squirming against his touch.

"Only because you begged so nicely." My head slams back against the shower wall as he roughly licks and sucks. "We can't have this one feeling left out, can we?" he says before diving on the other. My hands find their way to his head, gently tugging on his hair as I feel one of his hands leave my breast, traveling lower before it's just above my slit.

"Yes," I breathe out, thrusting my hips up, demanding. God, I'm so wet. So embarrassingly wet.

"You shave this pretty pussy, little hellcat?" he asks, voice rough.

"Yes, I was going to shave last night, but I felt weird with Levi in the house," I barely get out. Why is he asking this now? I need him to get down to business, not ask stupid questions. A rumble of approval erupts from his chest before he slides his finger along my slit, feeling how wet I am. "That's a good girl. This is my pussy, and I'll kill any motherfucker that even thinks about it." Another surge of wetness coats his finger, earning me a groan before he starts gathering as much of my juices as he can and rubbing it on my mound as if he's lubing it up.

"What are you doing?" I exhale as my hips try to follow his fingers.

"I'm going to shave my pussy," he says as he reaches over to grab my razor that's hanging on the wall, and two fingers dive into my pussy to grab more cream, making me cry out at the intrusion. Finally.

"Fuck, little hellcat." He groans, closing his eyes just for a moment before opening them and meeting mine. "I can't wait to feel this tight cunt around my cock." My walls tighten around his fingers at that. "You like that idea, baby? The thought of my thick, hard cock stuffing this tight cunt?"

"No." I whine at the loss of his fingers as he pulls out, my hips following them on instinct, searching and wanting the release I've been chasing. "I mean yes. Yes!" I cry out.

"Shh. You'll get it, little hellcat. But first, I need to take care of my pussy," he says as he rubs the evidence of my arousal he scooped out of me with his fingers around, making sure every inch of my skin is coated. "Spread your legs for me," he says as he lightly taps the inside of my thigh. A shudder runs through me in anticipation of what's to come. I spread my legs just before the hand unoccupied by the razor rubs circles around my entrance. My hips start rotating, trying to follow.

"Hold still," he orders. I obey instantly, wanting whatever he's willing to give me. I'm rewarded by him roughly shoving two fingers in, increasing the pace as he pumps them in and out before he takes the razor and lightly drags it up toward my stomach.

"Oh my god." I gasp.

This has to be the most erotic and intense feeling I have ever felt. The combination of his thick fingers working me and the tingly glide of the razor has me clamping down, my body trying to keep Cain inside of me.

Another swipe, and I feel that familiar sensation start to build. My walls grow even tighter around his fingers. It's so close I can taste it. If I had a clearer head, I would be embarrassed by how immense this orgasm is about to be. I just need a little more.

Cain rumbles as my legs start to shake. "You're close, but not quite there yet. Want to know how I know? Because this cunt is mine. And because it's mine, my cunt doesn't come until I tell it to."

Just before his last swipe of the razor, his thumb finds my clit. "Come, little hellcat," he demands. My walls clench his fingers so tight he can barely move them as I come crashing over the edge with his name on my lips.

"So soft and pretty. I love hearing my name on your lips when you come," he mumbles against my lips, his fingers lightly pumping in and out as I come down. I let out a whine as he removes his fingers. "I know, little hellcat. I know." He coos as he wipes my juices on my mound again. This time in a soothing way.

I reach for his dick as he pulls away. Before I can catch it, a hurt look takes over my face before he answers softly, "This was just for you, little hellcat. There will be plenty of other times when you can return the favor." He places a light kiss on my lips and winks before stepping out of the shower, leaving me alone under the spray that is now lukewarm as all the events of what just went down hit me at once.

Oh my god.

What the fuck just happened?

I basically just let some random guy who I think is a major fucking dick, hot, but a fucking dick, finger-fuck me against my shower wall and shave my pussy.

I'm not that girl.

I've had one one-night stand my entire life, and I hated myself afterward. I know some people love them, and hats off to you, sister, but it's just not for me. I need some sort of connection before wham, bam, thank you, ma'am. And what if Zeke finds out?

Oh my god. Zeke.

It's okay. We didn't go all the way. I'll just walk out of here and act like nothing happened.

"When you're done freaking out, babe, I'd like to go get some food," Cain calls from my bedroom, snapping me out of my panicked thoughts.

"I'm not freaking out," I shout back, irritation clear in my voice before I reach down and turn off the now-cold water.

I sigh as I wrap the thick, fluffy bath towel around my body. I may not have ninety percent of my house done, but you bet your ass that I went all out on fancy bath towels. The fabric on your skin makes you feel like you're staying at a five-star resort.

Looking at my flushed cheeks in the mirror, I can't help but think, what in the hell did I just get myself into?

**19**

**Cain**

Something in me changed during that shower.

I don't know what came over me, but as soon as I heard her turn the water on, I found myself stripping down and joining her. Half of me expected her to kick my ass out. But when she leaned back into me?

Fuuuuck.

I knew I was done for when I saw that her nipples were pierced. A man can only take so much. And that was the hottest thing I've ever done. And I've been with a lot of women, women who live life on the wild side and love to fuck and party with no shits given. I've even been to sex clubs and gotten my kink on there. But never in my life have I gotten my kink on with someone I felt a connection to. The razor thing was a first. I've never felt possessive of a pussy before, but once I felt it clench around my fingers, I knew it was mine.

My Ma always told me that one day I'll meet the game changer and stop whoring around, finally giving her some grandbabies. And I'm starting to think she was actually fucking right. Everything becomes less exciting in your forties. It never once crossed my mind that something was just missing.

My little hellcat can act like she doesn't want me all she wants, but she can't deny the way her body responds to me as soon as I get my hands on her. Or how her tight cunt sucks my fingers in, begging to be fucked. I thought I was going to black out when she wrapped her hand tightly around the end of my dick. Never felt something so soft before. She's enough to bring a man like me down to his knees. And that's saying something.

I knew she didn't believe me when I told her that this was just about her. I meant every fucking word I said. In the shower, I realized that I needed to prove to her that I'm serious about this. I also need to clear things up about fucking Candy.

I look up as I hear her exiting the bathroom. Her cheeks are still flushed from her orgasm. God, she looks gorgeous. I can't wait to see what look I'll put there when she finally takes my cock.

She stops dead in her tracks as soon as she notices me. Her alarmed eyes are glued to me lounging on her bed. "Oh. You were serious? About getting food?"

"I never joke about food, hellcat. You've worked me up an appetite. What type of man would I be if I didn't feed you?"

"Uh, the kind that gets off and leaves?" She says, looking even more confused than before.

"Did you see me get off? Feel my cum spurt all over your gorgeous tits and soft belly?" Her face turns crimson at that. I never thought a girl blushing at something sexual would be cute, but it is. So fuckin' cute.

"No," she rushes out. "I offered and yo—"

"And I said it was about you. Which it was, babe. I'm just yankin' your chain. Put on some clothes and let's go eat. We can talk over food." I cut her off before she could spew any more bullshit. I can see the doubt swirling in her eyes. The unanswered question of what I'm doing shines bright.

And if I'm being honest with myself, I don't even really know what the fuck I'm doing. I just know that I feel like there is something worth exploring here. Will that mean she's my old lady? No clue. But I'm about to find out. Let's just hope Scotch doesn't try to skin my ass alive in the process once he finds out what I'm doing with his baby sister.

Evan finally reappears from her walk-in closet dressed in black skinny jeans with rips all over them and an oversized crewneck sweatshirt that says "No Thanks."

"Ready, little hellcat?"

"I don't know. Am I?" She gestures towards her outfit. "You never said where we're going."

"DD's. I know you like the food. I know I like the food. And it's safe territory with all the weird shit that's been going on." Seemed like a win-win to me, but Evan seemed to tense up a little when I mentioned we were going to DD's. "That okay?"

Hesitating, as if about to say something else, she responds, "Yeah, that's fine. Let me just let Hades out real quick before we go."

"Keys, babe." I hold out my hand, waiting for them after she locks up the house. I've been itching to get a feel for her Mustang since I saw it at the clubhouse.

"Uh, you're not driving my car." She snorts.

"I think I proved earlier that I know my way around a hood. I'll have her purring sweet for me." I wink.

Seeing that she wasn't going to win this one, Evan drops the keys in my hand with a glare that instantly makes my dick hard and a warning to be careful before she slides into the passenger seat. But not before I slap that ass.

God, I'll never get sick of watching that ass.

I feel the adrenaline tingle through my whole body when I push the start ignition button, and the engine rumbles to life. Out of the corner of my eye, I notice Evan trying to discreetly rub her thighs together. "Get you hot, babe?"

"No." Liar.

It's cute my little hellcat doesn't think I know that she's trying to release some of the ache. I would be a fucking liar if I said my dick wasn't getting even harder at the purr of the engine, the feel of the black leather, and her scent surrounding me.

I think I've got myself an adrenaline sex kitten on my hands if she's already ready to go again, and all it took was this car coming to life.

"Buckle up, babe," I say as I back out of her driveway, throwing it into drive and putting the pedal to the floor.

We made it to DD's in record time. If I had to choose between a cage and my bike, I'd pick my bike every time. However, this little hellcat and her ride were seriously making me reconsider, especially now that I know how hot she runs.

Fuck. How is she single?

A woman like that deserves to be worshiped every day. She has no clue what she just got herself into with me—no clue she just tied herself to a man that will kill whatever motherfucker puts his hands on her. Fuck, even looks in her direction.

"Stay put," I say before opening my door and walking around the hood until I'm at her door, pulling it open and outstretching my hand for her to grab.

What a fucking gentleman I've become. I wouldn't be caught dead doing this to some bitch in the past. If the guys could see me right now, they would be laughing their asses off.

I clock the stares we're getting as Evan and I walk through the bar with my hand on her lower back to the circular booth that's always reserved for the club and me. The gesture wasn't lost on the guys looking. I made sure I made eye contact with every single motherfucker that had the balls to watch.

Yeah, she's off-limits, shithead.

Delaney clocked us as soon as we came in and set my drink

down seconds after we were seated, looking expectantly at Evan for her order.

"She'll take a rum and coke, Del."

"Menus?"

I nod my head, and she's off. I feel Evan's narrowed gaze on me. "What?"

"How did you know that's what I wanted to drink?"

"I pay attention, hellcat. It's what you were drinking when you were last here, and it was on your bar cart in your dining room. Along with tequila, but I figured you weren't ready for your clothes to fall off so soon." I wink, throwing my arm around her shoulder and pulling her flush against me.

"What are you doing?" Evan hisses, her back ramrod straight.

"What does it look like? We're having a drink and are about to have some food. You know what you're getting?" I ask; no sense in making her freak out more when I don't even know what the fuck I'm doing.

Seeming to accept that answer, she replies softly, "I want that bleu cheeseburger I ordered last time but didn't get the chance to eat."

"Whatever you want, babe." I smile. When Delaney returns with Evan's drink, I place our order of two bleu cheeseburgers.

We just settled into a comfortable silence, each taking a few sips of our drinks and watching the live band for the night get set up. A strange feeling settles over me as I realize I like this. I just like sitting here with her. Hell, I like just being around her in general. And that fucking scares me.

"Well, well, well. Don't mind if we join you, do ya?" An all too familiar voice comes from my right. I turn to see Hash, drink already in hand, with Scotch not far behind him, drink in hand as well, except his hard stare is locked on my arm around Evan's shoulders. I feel Evan tensing again as they approach, and I don't fucking like it. I just started getting her to relax around me and enjoy herself.

Hash plops down in the booth next to me while Scotch sits beside Evan. "Are we interrupting something?" Scotch asks, glare still in place as his eyes dart between Evan and me.

"Just treating Evan to some food after a rigorous afternoon of trimming." I smirk while looking at Evan, whose face is currently as red as the ketchup bottle on the table. Who knew I would be trimming more than one type of bush today?

"He helped me trim some plants today," she says while glaring at me. They don't know that I trimmed my hellcat's pretty little pussy. They don't know how wet she got with each stroke of the razor. How hard her pussy clenched when I played with her clit.

"Well, let's get this fucking party started! Del!" Hash yells toward the bar, breaking me from my thoughts of Evan's pussy. "Round of shots for the table!" Turning back to face us, eyes set on Evan, he asks, "You okay with whiskey, babe?" Her grimace has him yelling back toward Del, "Make one a tequila!" Hash wags his eyes at Evan. "I know all the ladies love tequila."

"Tequila's good." She smirks at him just as the live band starts up. Del is around a minute later with our shots and gone as quickly as she came. I raise an eyebrow toward Scotch, who has taken his glare off Evan and is now locked on Delaney.

"To a banging fucking night with our new friend, Evan!" Hash raises his shot glass to cheers against ours. I tap mine once on a table for good luck before bringing it to my lips, enjoying the small distraction the burn brings.

I think this is the first time I've seen Evan genuinely smile. She's relaxed a bit since the guys joined us. Unexpected and slightly unwanted, but if my girl is enjoying herself, then I could give a flying fuck where I'm at.

Wait, my girl?

I like spending time with Evan and having fun, but to claim

her? I like being able to control my environment, and this has me spiraling. The reason I do not have attachments is because it saves a lot of headaches. It's not easy being an old lady to a one-percenters. And honestly? I've never found someone I would want to go through headaches for. I need some space to clear my head from this shit.

"I need to get some stuff done in the back. You good with the guys?" I gruffly ask, my change in tone making her frown.

"Uh, yeah." Does she sound hurt? Shit. I have too much on the line right now to worry about feelings. Like who the fuck jacked what we were transporting and killed two of my men. I can't let it distract me whether she is or isn't upset.

I slam the rest of my drink while meeting Hash's questioning gaze. I nod my head toward Evan, signaling him to watch over her. Only when I get a nod in confirmation from him do I head on back without a word or a backward glance.

**20**



He seriously just left me.

Leaving me looking dumbfounded, like the idiot I am.

After everything that happened today, I thought his attitude toward me had changed. At least, it seemed like it had, right? There was the whole shower thing, and he seemed so different afterward. I knew I should have listened to my gut. It seemed so weird that he was suddenly all over me and so nice in a way that seemed too good to be true. It was completely out of character for a man like Cain, and I should have realized that.

"You good?" I look over to see Zeke and Hash watching me closely as I pick at my burger that Del had just dropped off before taking Cain's to the office or wherever the hell he went, I guess. So much for taking me to get food. I guess I thought that meant we would actually eat together.

"Yeah, I'm alright. This is all just a bit overwhelming. You know I barely leave my house. Sitting in a packed bar on a Friday night isn't exactly the norm for me," I reply, hoping he doesn't catch on to my lie. Small fib, if you will. I mean, it's half the truth. I really don't get out much, and large crowds give me a shit ton of anxiety, but really, I'm mostly sad about the change in Cain.

He seemed to accept my answer, though, because he nods his head before turning back toward the band.

You know what? Fuck Cain. Fuck him and the high horse he rode in on. I can't believe he just left me here like this. And I can't believe I let that piece of shit shave and finger fuck me. And then that motherfucker has the audacity to bring it up in front of everyone. I know they don't literally know, but it's still fucking embarrassing.

Reaching into my pocket, I pull out a fifty, which should be more than enough to cover my food, drinks, and tip. I throw it down on the table. "I'm going to head out."

"Don't think that's a good idea, darlin'," Hash says, shaking his head as he brings his drink to his mouth.

"And why not?" I snap.

"Prez wants us to keep an eye on ya. He would have our ass if he found out we just let ya leave."

"Well, boys, this clearly seems to be a foreign concept to you, but I don't need a keeper."

"Come on, Ev. Just wait for Prez to finish, and he'll take you home," Zeke pleads, knowing I'm not one to be told what to do. All of these men in my life can just fuck off.

"Fine. I need to use the restroom," I say before I slide out of the booth without waiting for a response.

Praying there's a back door I can slip out of, I duck into the bathroom on my way in that direction, just in case they're both watching me. I quickly check my social media profile to buy some time and make it look like I'm actually using the bathroom. After a few minutes, I quietly open the creaky bathroom door, looking both ways to make sure I don't see a face I know, and I put my plan into motion.

"Ah ha!" I cheer to myself as I spot the backdoor that I was hoping would be there. Quickly walking out and heading in that direction, I pass a closed door that I assume is Cain's office.

"Jokes on you, fucker." I flip off the door before pushing the back door open, the cool nighttime air calming my flushed skin. I laugh at the thought of him possibly having to ride bitch on the back of one of the guys' bikes since we drove my car here.

Walking around the back of the building, I pass two different couples fucking up against the wall, both watching the other. I know it's rude to stare, but I can't seem to look away. I always thought it would be hot as hell to have someone watch. I never found that person with whom I felt comfortable enough to do that with, though. But do I need comfort? I let some guy I've only known a week finger fuck me while he shaved my pussy in the shower. I think comfort might not be needed.

One of the girls' moans is getting higher and more breathy, but I can't stay for the finale. I can't risk the guys realizing I'm not coming back. But I'll be damned if I let some guy like Cain yank me around like I'm on a chain. I'm not a fucking dog. I won't be waiting for you to tell me to come when the mood strikes. Figuratively and literally.

Beeping the locks on my car, I slide into the driver's seat and fire her up, hoping I can make it home before they notice I left. It isn't until I'm parked in my driveway that I come to the conclusion that I might have fucked up.

How do I know fucked up? Because my headlights are shining on my front door. My front door is currently ajar. I rarely use that door. I can't even remember the last time it was open. It's basically a decoration piece at this point.

"Okay. Okay," I whisper to myself. Do I call the cops? I don't really want to wait if it's nothing. I should call Zeke, but I kind of ruined that one by sneaking out. "It's okay. I'm a grown-ass woman. I got this," I tell myself. I need to check on Hades, anyway.

Oh my fucking god! Hades!

I quickly grab the switchblade I keep in my glove box before throwing my car door open and rushing up to the door.

Wait.

I probably shouldn't just bust in here balls to the wall, right? I mean, what if the psychopath who broke in is still inside?

"Please don't let this be how I die," I whisper to myself before slowly pushing open the door enough that I can quietly slip through. I've seen enough crime documentaries to know it's a very real possibility that this is how I'll go.

Looking around, I don't see anything out of place except for the dirt tracked in by whoever broke in.

How fucking rude. You're going to break into my house *and* get it dirty?

I slide along the entryway wall in stealth mode until I can peek around and look into the kitchen like a lurking cat.

All clear there.

Continuing to creep along, I check the dining room, living room, and formal sitting room, which I turned into a library. They're all clear, too. No sign of anyone.

What the hell? Where is Hades?

I dash up the stairs and quickly check all the rooms, only to come up empty-handed. It isn't until I'm headed back down that I hear the unmistakable whine of my baby that makes my heart stop and my stomach drop.

"Hades?!" I yell, sprinting the rest of the way toward the whine that keeps coming from the downstairs bathroom that's just off the kitchen.

I don't think I've opened a door so fast in my life before I'm being tackled and licked by a freaked-out Hades.

"It's okay, baby. It's okay," I soothe. "Are you okay? Let Mama check you over." I run my hands along his body, checking for any cuts or scrapes and coming up with nothing. Thank god. Someone would seriously find themselves fucked up if anything had happened to him.

Finally calming him down enough to let me up off the floor, I flip on the switch for the kitchen light.

I scream and freeze as I notice the spray-painted writing on the far back wall of the living room, which is still only drywall.

*If you know what's good for you, bitch, you will stop associating with the Devils. This is your only warning before you get what's coming to you.*

Oh my fucking god.

Is that a threat? Did I just get threatened? This is all too fucking much for me to deal with right now. I bring my hands to my head, wrapping in my hair as I start to pace.

Someone had just broken in and vandalized my place.

Wait a minute, how did the alarm not go off?

Whipping my phone out of my pocket, I try to sign on to the cameras that Brock installed, only to find them offline.

"Please tell me this isn't happening right now," I say just as I hear a bike turn into my driveway. I flip off the light before diving into the kitchen, grabbing the gun out of the kitchen drawer, making sure to stay out of the moonlight coming in through the window above the sink as I walk back through to the living room, trying to peek out the front window to see who it is.

I can't see the bike well enough in the dark to recognize it. I really need to get the floodlights fixed. Hades lets out a low growl, clearly on edge, just like me. I jump as I hear heavy footsteps coming up the back steps before they pound at my backdoor, yelling, "Open the fuck up, Evan! I'm about to spank your ass so hard for making me ride bitch on Scotch's bike like some club pussy bitch."

Holy fuck.

It's Cain. A very pissed-off Cain.

And for some reason, I'm not even mad that he's being a dick after the shit he pulled back at DD's. All I can feel is relief. I can feel the tears coming from the adrenaline of fear that's been coursing through me, starting to crash as I sprint toward the backdoor, unlocking and yanking it open in record speed.

"You bet—" Cain starts to growl before I cut him off by throwing my arms around him, shoving my face in his neck, tears freely flowing now.

"What the fuck, hellcat?" Cain asks, instantly wrapping his arms tightly around me. It isn't until I feel the security of his arms that I realize how badly I'm shaking. "Talk to me."

"What the hell, Ev?" I hear Zeke coming up behind Cain, concern clear in his voice.

I look up, and his face instantly turns to anger at the sight of my tears. "Tell me who the fuck I'm killing," he says before walking past us into the house. "What the fuck, Evan?!"

Cain pulls back slightly, leaving his arms still around me as he shoots a questioning look my way before dragging me inside to see what has Zeke freaking out.

Oh shit.

Maybe I should have been the one to tell them.

# 21

**Cain**

"If you know what's good for you bitch, you will stop associating with the Dirty Devils. This is your only warning before you get what's coming to you." I read aloud the words spray-painted on Evan's living room wall. "What the fuck?" I turn towards a still-shaking Evan, who is standing back and off to the side.

"Start talking now," Scotch and I growl at the same time.

She starts to open her mouth, but I cut her off, "And you better not leave anything out. I'm getting the vibe you've been keeping some things from me, little hellcat. And I'm not fucking happy," I say through clenched teeth, trying my best to keep my anger in check but failing miserably. It doesn't help that I'm still pissed as hell that she left me at DD's, knowing damn well all the brothers rode in.

"I didn't do it on purpose. I just didn't think you needed to know every little detail of my life," Evan snaps, her hands going to her hips.

My lip twitches at seeing my little hellcat come back to life.

Seeing her all shaking and scared makes me want to kill someone, but a second of that lip? Yeah, that makes my dick hard. Nothing seems to keep her down for long. That's a quality I admire.

God, it's fucking hot, but now's not the time to be turned on.

"How bout we decide what is and isn't important regarding what the fuck is going on?" I say, getting enjoyment out of watching her irritation grow.

"I'm going to tell you only because of the recent events that have taken place. Not because your bossy ass just busted in here making demands."

"Well, don't let me stop you."

Evan shoots me a glare that if looks could kill, I'd be dead. Or have no balls. She'd probably do it in some fucked up way too. She doesn't know how much that turns me on. It makes me want to fuck the glare right off of her face.

"I decided I didn't want to stay at DD's anymore." I don't miss the look that crosses her face, letting me know it was clearly my fault she didn't want to stay. And damn if that doesn't sting. "And Hash and Zeke wouldn't let me leave because apparently you went all caveman and decided I couldn't leave on my own even though you left me." She pauses as she raises one eyebrow in emphasis at me. "I may have lied to them about going to the bathroom and slipped out the back," she finishes all innocently. As if she didn't just take ten years off my life when I heard she was missing.

"Making me ride bitch on the back of Scotch's bike, and let's not even mention the fact that you completely disobeyed me," I growl. I don't think I've ever met a female that can make me want to fuck her and kill her at the same goddamn time.

"I'm sorry, *disobeyed* you? I know you're older, but I didn't realize that made you my dad."

"If you want to call me daddy, little hellcat, all you have to do is scream it when you come on my cock." Her glare deepens, but the effect of it means nothing when I can see the heat flaring in her eyes.

Does my little hellcat have a daddy kink?

"God, will you two fucking stop? You're going to make me throw the fuck up before I even find out what's happening," Scotch says, looking like he's about to be sick. I'm not gonna lie; I forgot he was here.

That's how intoxicating she is. And as much as I hate it, there seems to be jack shit I can do about it. "My bad, brother."

"We're having that conversation later." I nod, knowing it was coming eventually. I decided in my office tonight that I need to sit him down and let him know I plan to see where things go and let them play out.

"Are you two done seeing whose dick is bigger?" Evan cocks an eyebrow at us. "I'd like to continue."

I motion with my hands like she needs some grand fucking gesture to get to the goddamn point.

"As I was saying, I slipped out the back to leave so no one would see me. When I got home, I noticed that my front door was slightly open, and I know we didn't leave it like that when we left. I barely use the front door. So, I grabbed the switchblade from my glove box and went to check it out."

I hold up my hand, stopping her from continuing. "So you see that someone obviously broke into your fucking house, and your first thought is, 'Hey, let me go investigate by myself' and not call someone for help? Jesus fucking christ. What if the fucker was still in here?!"

"Don't talk to me like I'm a fucking idiot, Cain! I was worried about Hades! Zeke knows I can —"

"Whoa, whoa, whoa," Scotch interrupts. "Don't fucking bring me into this. Sorry, Ev, but I'm on Cain's side. You should have called me as soon as you saw the door was open. A 250-pound man isn't going to be taken down by a little switchblade. You, of all people, should know that. You could have been seriously fucking hurt," Scotch says, sounding almost as pissed off as I am.

I'm not going to lie. It makes me feel fucking jealous about how close these two are. I hate feeling jealous. Something serious has gone down with them. I'm not stupid. I'm very aware that all of my brothers have a past. I'm just wondering how much Evan's and Scotch's intertwine.

"I know. And I'm sorry, okay?" She sounds so defeated. "My only thought was making sure Hades was okay."

"Just make sure it doesn't happen again." Scotch gives in.

Evan nods before continuing, "So I came inside, noticed whoever broke in brought dirt inside. Like, I get it's a construction zone, but do you have to be so rude on top of being an asshole by breaking in?"

Is she for real right now? Some fucker just vandalized her house, and she's worried about a little bit of dirt? "Evan!" I bite out. "Can we get to the point?"

"Right. Sorry. Where was I..." she trails off, lost in thought. I get it. Shit like this is fucking overwhelming. But my control is about to snap if she doesn't tell me what happened. "Oh, yeah! So, I tried to be as quiet as possible because I didn't know if they were still inside. I cleared the whole house but didn't find Hades, and honestly, I kind of forgot about him once I got inside. I was too worried about someone popping out of the shadows, you know?"

Scotch and I both nodded because we did. If you weren't used to the shadows, they would swallow you whole.

"So anyway, it wasn't until I came back down from checking upstairs that I heard him whining. It was coming from the bathroom down here. So, obviously, I let him out. He was totally fine, though. It was then that I turned the kitchen light on and saw what was on the drywall in the living room. I tried checking the cameras that Brock had installed, but it said that they were offline, so I had no luck with that. Then you two showed up. That's all I've got."

"Thanks for finally spitting that out. Appreciate it," I say, trying to lighten the mood a little because if I'm being honest, I'm fucking pissed.

Someone had the audacity to break into her house. No one fucks with us, and I'm sick of motherfuckers thinking they can.

I shoot Scotch a look, and he nods in agreement.

All of this shit, two of our prospects getting killed, a jacked shipment, someone casing Evan's barn, and now a break-in to try to warn her off?

Yeah, it's all fucking connected. And none of this is sitting right with me.

"Wait a minute," Scotch breaks the silence while looking right at Evan. "Hades is trained."

"Yeah..." Evan confirms while shooting him a look that says he's stupid for stating the obvious.

"He's trained, Ev. So why the fuck is there no blood or anything? You telling me a dog that's trained to protect just let a random person break in and lock him in the bathroom?"

Holy shit. He's right.

"Holy shit," Evan whispered as if she couldn't believe it. "That fucking motherfucker!"

Before I can even ask what she's thinking, she storms off, grabs her car keys off the counter, and heads toward the back door.

"Whoa, hellcat." I grab her arm, stopping her in her tracks. "I think there's more that you aren't telling us. Now would be a good time to go over that with us and not take off like a bat out of hell after god knows what." Evan's eyes lower into slits.

"I'm really trying to have patience here, Ev, but it's wearing thin. It's been a long fucking week, and I just need you to be honest with us so we can keep you safe. I don't know what I would do if something happened to you after I asked you to help the club." Who knew Scotch could be such a voice of fucking reason.

I've watched that motherfucker cut off a dude's hand and shove it down his throat without even blinking. It works, though. I can tell he got through to her because the arm I'm holding loses some of its tension. And damn if that doesn't make me jealous.

I want that power over her. To make her feel safe and at ease. To make her calm down in a situation like this. But why? I'm not that fucking guy. The guy that does feelings or deep shit.

"Fine," she sighs before turning back to face us, making me release her arm. "I may have suspicions about who was scoping out the barn. I did—"

"What?"

"Are you fucking kidding me?" Scotch and I both yell at the same time.

"I didn't have any concrete evidence! I'm not in the business of accusing innocent people! I still don't really have any!" Evan yells back, throwing her hands up in the air.

And there goes my dick again. Damn that sass. It's going to be the death of me.

"How 'bout we decide that, babe?" I fire back, battling between being horny as fuck and wanting to strangle her for withholding shit. "Now, tell us everything you know, or think you may know, or are suspicious of. Every little thing that made you question your gut."

"Alright," she snapped. "So before I came to you guys about the guy on the bike, I went to talk to Storm."

Who the fuck is Storm?

Judging by the growl coming from Scotch, this can't be good. "What did I tell you about meeting that piece of shit by yourself?"

"Who in the fuck is Storm?" I ask before Evan can respond.

"He's basically her middleman. Will sell to whoever needs it or sometimes dispensaries that are running short on what they've got. They feature Evan's stuff a lot, too," Scotch answers for her, looking no less pissed.

My eyebrows shoot up because now I'm impressed. Who knew this little hellcat was balling out like that. Explains this big ass house and nice ass car. Even if the house is a construction zone that I'm pretty sure she shouldn't be living in.

"I don't get a good feeling about this guy, Prez. I can't put my finger on it, but I've never been able to read him. I try to make sure I'm available for when she meets him in case he tries some sleazy shit."

So that's where he goes when he disappears for half a day randomly with the excuse of 'I have shit to do.' It's all starting to click now. But if Scotch doesn't trust the guy, then I sure as fuck don't either.

"Why did you go to Storm before us?" I ask, getting the elephant out of the room.

"Because the more I thought about it, the more it didn't make sense. I don't talk to people. I don't have friends. So for someone to know what's out here? There are only two people who could have told that to someone. Zeke or Storm."

Fuck. I hate that she's right.

"I thought you said that Storm didn't come out here? Thought you and Scotch would meet up with him at a mutual location?"

"Yeah, but he knows where I live. There were a couple of times Zeke wasn't around to go with me, so he came here to pick up. I figured if something was going to happen, I wanted it to be in a place I know like the back of my hand, and Hades would be here."

"Don't," I say to Scotch as he palms his face. I can already see the guilt setting in. Like he thinks this is all his fault. "This isn't on you, man."

"He's never been inside anything. When he came, I had everything ready to go outside the barn. So he doesn't literally know exactly what I have goin' on in there, but it doesn't take a fucking genius to put two and two together."

Fuck. She's right again.

"It's possible, but it doesn't explain breaking into your house and spray-painting a warning on your wall like a little fucking bitch." I'm starting to get really fucking pissed again.

In my world, if you want to give someone a warning, you do it face to face like a fuckin' man. Break a few fingers, fuck his bitch, whatever. What you don't do is break in and leave a note like you're fucking pen pals.

"Right. So, this is the part where I felt like something was a little off. I decided I wanted to feel him out, thinking that in the process, I would be able to eliminate him from my very long list of possible suspects." She snorts.

"This isn't fucking funny, Evangeline," Scotch growls.

"Oh, come on! I'm just trying to lighten the mood. Anyway, he texts me and tells me to meet at his pla—."

"Please tell me you fucking didn't," I growl, looking at her like she's grown an extra head. Has she lost her goddamn mind?

"I did." And there goes my last little bit of control

"Have you lost your fucking mind?!" I explode. Scotch is on his feet, stepping between us.

"Get a lock on it, Prez."

I would never lay hands on a woman, but holy shit. I can only deal with so much right now. If she even thought this Storm guy had anything slightly to do with it, why would she think it's a good fuckin' idea to go over to his place?

I'm trying to calm down.

I really am.

But all I can think about is everything that could have

happened to her while she was there. Beat the fuck up. Raped. Murdered.

I've never felt rage and possession like this over a woman.

"Stop talking to me like I'm a fucking idiot, Cain! Do you want to hear what I have to say or not? Because I don't owe you anything," she hisses, doing that little head bob women do when they're extra pissed and throwing sass.

"You don't *owe* me?" I say as I push Scotch's hand off me, stalking toward her until I'm inches from her face. "Was it not my fingers you just came on hours ago in the shower? Was it not your pussy I shaved while you clenched my fingers? Was it not my dick you were fucking grabbing like you'd die if you didn't feel it pounding in you?"

Yeah.

I went there.

And judging by the "Jesus fucking Christ" I heard from behind me and the look I was currently getting from Evan, two people are not happy about it.

"Did you really just go there?" she yells, her voice going up an octave.

"Yeah, hellcat. I did."

"Just because you gave me a quick, mediocre orgasm doesn't mean I owe you shit. This isn't a Desperate Housewives episode. You don't see me begging for it. Any fucking guy down at DD's can give me the same, if not better."

"You're signing a death wish to whatever motherfucker you try that with in my bar, babe. I'll cut his fucking hand off if he touches what's mine," I growl, trying my best not to lose my shit, but she has me seeing red. The thought of another man touching her gives me a murderous rage that I haven't felt in a long time.

"What's yours?" She rears back. "I'm not yours. I've never been yours, and I will never be yo—"

I can't listen to her spew bullshit anymore.

I grip both sides of her face with my hands and roughly kiss her. She gasps in shock, giving me the opening I need to dominate her mouth with my tongue. It only takes a few seconds for her to get over the shock before she kisses me back just as roughly. Her tongue battles mine and swirls before I bite and pull on her bottom lip.

"I can't decide if I want to beat the shit out of you for messing around with the closest thing I have to a sister or throw up at this PDA," Scotch rumbles from behind us, making me pull away slightly.

Still holding her face in my hands, I place a light kiss on her lips. "We'll talk about this later, okay?"

Heat still flaring in her gorgeous mismatched eyes, she quickly agrees, "Okay."

"If I promise not to lose it again, can you finish telling us what you have to say?"

She takes a minute to look between Scotch and me before she nods. "As I was saying, I said I would meet him at his place. As soon as I knocked on Storm's door, he sounded super paranoid and freaked out. Like he didn't know who was on the other side even though we had just made plans to meet, you know?"

"You think he was on something?" Scotch asks what we are both assuming.

"I didn't until he opened the door, and then yeah, I'd say he was definitely on something. His eyes were bloodshot, and he smelled so badly of stale alcohol. Like to the point where I thought I was going to throw up."

I wince because I've smelled that smell many fucking times, and I swear it stays in your nostrils for days.

"What was really weird, though, was that he wouldn't make eye contact. And the whole time I was standing in the doorway before he invited me in, he was scanning his yard behind me—almost like he was looking for something or someone."

"Did you see anyone?" No one is that paranoid unless they think they're being watched.

"No, that was the thing. I didn't see anyone, but I also couldn't shake the feeling that someone was watching me. You know what I mean? Like that weird tingly feeling you get at the base of your spine." Scotch and I both nod because we did.

"I couldn't really figure out if he was making me feel that way with how paranoid and jittery he was acting, or if someone was actually watching me in the bushes like a creep or something." She wraps her arms around herself while reliving the memory as if it still made her uncomfortable.

And no one makes my girl fucking uncomfortable. "Well, I think it's time we have a chat with our new buddy Storm," I say as I crack my knuckles while turning to face Scotch. "Text Hash and tell him church first thing in the morning. Have him let the brothers know."

"I'm staying here tonight."

22

Evan

Of course he is.

Because why would the universe be in my favor?

"You okay with this?" Zeke asks me quietly as I walk him to the door.

"Yeah, we need to talk about some stuff, anyway." It was bound to happen, eventually.

"I'm fucking pissed he went there with you. Everyone in the club knows that family is off-limits unless you ask. And he definitely didn't ask permission to fuck around with someone's sister."

"I'm sorry that it feels like this was all happening behind your back. It wasn't like that. This all just sort of... happened. And honestly, I don't even know what is happening."

Zeke releases a deep sigh. "I know. But that doesn't mean I'm still not going to have his ass for going there. What? Don't give me that look. Prez or not, he knows the rules. I'll check in tomorrow, Ev. Call me if you need me." I hug him goodbye before shutting and locking the back door.

"Are you hungry?" I ask while walking back into the kitchen, seeing Cain sitting on one of the bar stools at my island.

"I could eat." He grinned. "Like your place, babe. Don't think I told you that when I was here before."

"You didn't, but thank you." I smile as I put some potatoes in a pot of water on the stove. "I know it looks like a construction zone right now, but when I'm done, it's going to be the Victorian gothic home of my dreams—whenever that is." I laugh.

"Who's doing the work? I know most of the guys in town."

"Ah, no one. I mean, not no one, obviously. It's just me. Do you want a drink?"

"You have whiskey?"

"I think," I say, setting down the package of ribeyes I just took out of the fridge, ready to head over to the bar cart to check before Cain holds up his hand.

"I got it, babe. It's the least I can do since you're cooking for me." He pours three fingers worth of whiskey for himself and a glass of wine for me without even asking.

"Thank you," I say, somewhat surprised, while taking the wine. I give him a questioning look because how did he know this is what I wanted?

"The bottle looked like you had set it out to drink soon." I hate how observant he is because, damn, if he isn't right. "So, back to your place, you're really doing all of this by yourself?"

Nodding my head, I say, "Yeah. I know it seems overly ambitious, and sometimes I want to pull my hair out and sell the place, but when one thing comes together, it makes it all worth it. Plus, when I'm done, I can say I did all the renovations myself. Cool, right?"

"Yeah, hellcat. That's pretty fucking cool. If you ever need any help, let me know," he says before taking a swig of his whiskey.

"I could actually use a recommendation for an electrician," I tell him, turning my attention back to seasoning the steaks. "Sometimes the light switches turn on, and sometimes they don't. I tried watching some electrical videos on how to fix it, but I'm kind of scared of electrocuting myself."

"Brock. He used to do a lot of electrical work in the army. I'll talk to him tomorrow about stopping by."

"That would be great! Do you know what he charges?"

"Hellcat, you aren't paying him shit. If he needs to buy anything, the club will do it. We need to move some cash around anyway."

"It'll be a cold day in hell before you start paying for my stuff like that. I don't care if you need to make it look like you have money going somewhere. I said I'd help you guys with whatever you need, but I'm paying for what needs to be done here."

"We'll talk about it later," he responds, almost like he's just letting me entertain the idea.

"Um... no, we won't. Are you even listening to me?" I ask as he gets up off his bar stool and comes up from behind, wrapping his arms around me.

"Nope. I tune you out when you start spewing bullshit," he rumbles in my ear.

His scent surrounds me, almost overpowering the garlic-infused oil I poured into the cast-iron skillet. The smell of oak mixed with a hint of lavender invades my nose, wrapping me in comfort. All of my senses are heightened as his beard brushes against my neck, and his breath tickles my ear.

"Well, that's rude." I'm starting to lose my train of thought. I was getting mad at him. Why was I getting mad at him?

Oh, yeah.

"We're not talking about this later. We're going to talk about this now," I reply while preparing the asparagus for the pan.

His deep sigh whispers across my neck as he pulls away. "Alright, little hellcat. We'll talk about it now."

I can't help but feel anxious as he walks over to grab the open bottle of wine and a fifth of whiskey, bringing them to the island and topping off our drinks.

"I was a dick earlier. I had a lot to think about, and it messed with my head. I apologize. It's not an excuse to treat you like you don't exist. I won't do it again."

Hold, please, while I pick my jaw up off the floor. Two apologies in the same week? Maybe hell really has frozen over.

"I like that you didn't just lie down and take it. But if you ever leave me stranded somewhere, making me ride bitch on the back of a brother's bike again, I'm going to take you over my knee and spank that ass 'til you're just about to come. Then I'm going to stop and not let you touch that pretty pussy until I say. Got me?"

You see, the thing about me is that when someone gets an attitude with me, I naturally have to match that, if not top it. Challenge accepted. "No, I don't 'got you,'" I say as I throw my hands up, using air quotes. "If you're being a dick, I have every right to not stay, especially if you refuse to talk to me and abandon me."

"I just said I won't do it again," he says, jaw clenched.

"We'll see," I snap before turning back to the stove to check on the potatoes. Seeing that they're done, I drain and return to the pot to get the excess water out. That's the trick to the perfect mashed potatoes—that and using a potato ricer. Trust me—it's a game-changer. Lump-free every time.

"Woman," he growls, trying to demand my attention.

"Don't 'woman' me, Cain. I don't even get what you want from me. You're hot one second and cold the next. And honestly, it's exhausting. I get you're not the relationship guy, so why are you even here?"

"Because I can't get you out of my fucking head," he says,

jaw tight, like finally admitting it out loud bothers him that much. "And believe me, I've tried."

"Well, isn't that just the sweetest thing I've ever heard?" I say with an eye-roll. "Every girl wants to know someone is only with them because they want to forget about them but can't. Get real. I understand this bothers you, but I'm not exactly sure how it's my problem." Maybe it's because I can't get you out of my head, either.

"Sorry I'm not giving you flowers and fucking chocolate, but this isn't exactly a territory I'm used to being in."

"Let me make it easy for you then. There is no flowers and chocolate territory for you to enter," I say as I start plating up the steak, mashed potatoes, and grilled asparagus.

"There's going to be my version of it. What does that look like? I don't have a fucking clue. All I know is I can't get you out of my head, and until then, you're stuck with me."

I pause while setting his plate down in front of him because, once again, he's made me want to punch him in the face. "Are you seriously saying you want a relationship with me until I'm out of your head?"

"I'm still not really sure what I want, Evan. I just know that until you're out of here," he pauses as he taps a finger to his temple, "no one better touch you."

"Are you high? Because it sounds more like an infatuation. You just need to get it out of your system. And unfortunately, what happened earlier was a fluke for me. I'm not a fling kind of girl. None of this is yours."

"Damn, this is the best steak I've ever had. You always cook like this?" Cain says, finally taking his first bite. He doesn't give me a chance to respond before he talks again, "Well, you're in luck, little hellcat. Because all of you is, in fact, mine. I'm thinking I want to give this exclusive thing a shot. The thought of some pencil dick having his hands on you makes me want to murder someone," he says as if it's the simplest thing in the world.

"That's it?"

"Yeah, hellcat. That's it."

Sighing as I set my fork down, I say, "I just don't see how this is going to work. You're used to club girls hanging off of you. You can literally have your pick of any girl you want. I don't see you being exclusive. It's not that I don't trust you or anything; I just know you're used to a certain way of life. I'm not in the business of making someone change who they are."

"What if I want to change?" He's looking me dead in the eyes now. "I don't like bringing up past exploits, but it's been a minute since I've even thought about being with a club girl. That shit you saw with Candy wasn't what it seemed. Yeah, you saw her climb into my lap, but you didn't hear me telling her to go find someone else. That I wasn't interested."

"Why would you do that?" I swallow, suddenly all too nervous that I am going to hear an answer that I really don't want to hear. This is starting to seem a little too real now.

"Have you been listening to me? I know I'm speaking English. It's because I can't stop thinking about you. And I don't know... something about being with another girl that wasn't you just felt wrong."

"But you haven't even been with me!" I squeak out.

"I might not have had your pussy clenching my cock, but I liked it just fine when my fingers were buried in that sweet heat." This man and his way with words.

"Is that my grand romantic gesture?" I ask, knowing my cheeks are now the same color as my wine.

"For now." He smirks while taking another bite of steak.

Taking a bite of my own food, I start thinking all of this over.

Do I really want a relationship right now? Despite not

having any friends, I still have a lot going on. I spend all of my free time working on my house.

And there's the Storm drama. Because what the hell is up with him? I don't know how to cut ties with a middleman like that, even if I wanted to. How do you find a new one and know if they have connections?

Can I trust what Cain says about wanting to try to be exclusive? But he also doesn't know where this is going, so what does that even mean? I'm not about to be yanked around. The thought of him being with someone else makes me see red. I never considered myself a jealous person until I saw him with Candy.

"I can see the wheels turning over there. Want to share?" Cain says, snapping me out of the rabbit hole my thoughts were going down.

"It's just been a long few weeks."

"So this isn't about you and me?"

Setting my fork down and leaning back against the barstool, I sigh and answer, "It's part of it. I guess I'm just getting mixed signals from you. I know you don't know where this is going to go, and I get that, but it's the whole 'you don't know what to label it, but want to be exclusive' thing." Pausing to take a sip of my wine, I add, "And the Storm stuff is starting to eat at me."

Cain sets his fork down and grabs his drink, taking a long swig before turning fully to me, giving me his full attention. "How about this? I like you, and I think you like me. Let's just see where this goes. If we decide we want it to be more serious, then we'll talk about that when the time comes. In the meantime, while exploring what this is, we are exclusive to each other."

I nod because, honestly, that takes a lot of pressure off. I don't have to second-guess whether he's with someone, and I actually have time to figure out what the hell I want.

"As far as the Storm thing goes, I don't have much to say until I chat with the fucker. How'd you meet him?"

"I got a job as a server right out of high school, and Storm was a cook. He was your typical 'I'll sell you what you need after work' type of line cook, and we just kind of hit it off in that sense." I paused to think about it. "Honestly? I don't really know him much more than that. Our conversations have always been around what we're dealing with."

"Good."

"Good?"

"Yeah, good. It won't matter if I beat his ass for making you feel uncomfortable."

On that, I roll my eyes because, really?

"You all done?"

It takes me a second to realize he's talking about my food.

"Oh, yeah. I'm all set." I reach to grab his plate before he smacks my hand away. My 'what the fuck,' expression has him laughing.

"You cook, I clean." My eyebrows shoot up to my hairline because who is this man? "I may be a biker hellcat, but my Ma did try to raise me right. Only a quarter of it stuck." He smirks while grabbing my plate off the island. "Go sit down and relax; I'll finish up here."

I'm so used to doing everything on my own that I almost feel sort of awkward having someone clean up after me. Grabbing my wine, I head over to the couch in the living room. The warning that's graffitied on the wall just staring back at me.

One positive is that I haven't really touched this room except for the new drywall that was put up. So it's not like there's really any money lost.

I think this is the room I'll focus on next. My kitchen is nearly complete except for a few small finishing touches. I wanted to maintain a dark vibe, so I made sure the cabinets stayed black. I paired that with a gorgeous black reflective backsplash and modern Victorian-style appliances that are such a dark gray they look almost black, but aren't. My style is kind of hard to find things for, but I tend to have a lot of luck hitting up estate sales. That's how I found the gorgeous chandelier I have hanging above the island in the kitchen. The lights are in the shape of a circle and look like actual candles are lit when they are on. Darker glass pieces dangle from that, creating the most beautiful reflection of light. I got it for a steal, too. I'm pretty sure Zeke thought I was crazy when I called him, begging him to pick it up for me.

I then decided to accent the area with plants, gold knobs, and handles. And by plants, I mean cactuses and aloe plants because they're the only thing I can keep alive. I tried a few snake plants because everyone in online plant groups said they're so easy and require little light. One girl told me that you would basically have to try to kill it for it to die. The joke's on me, I guess, because I tried to keep it alive, and it died within two months of me having it.

"Kind of looks like you have one of those abstract modern art pieces on your wall that everyone loves," Cain says, interrupting my thoughts and making me realize that I zoned out while looking at the mess.

I let out a laugh. "Yeah, it kind of does. I was just thinking about how I will start on this room next." He sits beside me on the couch, grabs my legs propped up by my side, and places them across his lap. "I'm getting kind of sick of walking on plywood. It's not a good look for my guests." I joke.

Cracking a smile, he replies, "Looks pretty fucking fancy to me. You have any idea of what you want to do with it?"

"I'd like to continue on with my moody vibes. I'm obsessed with anything gothic or Victorian, obviously." I point out the obvious while waving my hand around. "I'm thinking of some teal shades with black, white, and gold?"

He nods his head as I talk it out. "That's all you, hellcat. I can see it now. One of my brothers does flooring on the side. I'll tell him to stop over so you two can discuss your options."

"You don't ha—" I start before I'm cut off.

"What did I say earlier? It's no sweat off anybody's nose, and it's a great way to generate cash for the club. It's a win-win in my book, babe."

"Are you always this bossy?" I ask before sipping my wine.

"You'll get used to it."

I let out an embarrassing moan as Cain grabs my foot and starts massaging the arch with his thumb, pressing in all the right spots.

Heat flares in his eyes at the sound, pressing his thumb in that perfect spot again, earning a longer moan this time.

"I can't wait to hear that noise when my cock is buried deep in you."

I choke on my wine because who just says things like that mid-conversation? I've never been with a man like him. All one-hundred percent alpha and so sure of himself. His air of confidence that he carries is just enough to assert his dominance and control in every situation he's in without coming off like a cocky douchebag. I can see why he's the president of a one-percenter motorcycle club.

His tone commands your attention.

And damn if it doesn't make my pussy quiver.

And damn if I don't love that too.

**23**

Cain

"You tired?" I ask softly. Her head is starting to do that little bobbing thing when you're starting to doze off but are also trying to fight it.

So fucking cute.

She made me face a lot of things that I haven't wanted to think about tonight.

I hate that I have that douchebag Storm to thank for it. I'm ninety percent sure he's the fuck face that broke into her place. And I hate that I wouldn't have come to terms with wanting to see how things play out with her if that didn't happen. The rage I felt when she was shaking in my arms was nothing like I've ever experienced. I want to hunt down and murder anyone that makes her feel like that.

I smile as Evan does another little head bob. When was the last time I smiled? I can't even fucking remember. She does that to me.

Makes me feel shit that I've never felt before. And that scares the shit out of me.

I watch one more head bob before I lightly drag my finger along the arch of her foot until I reach her toes. I've never been attracted to feet before, but hers look sexy as fuck. The skin is so soft and milky, like she just put lotion on. Her toenails are painted black, making her skin seem even more pale and fragile.

I peek over at her to see if she's woken fully back up yet.

She hasn't.

All that's running through my mind is 'taste, taste, taste.' Just one little lick and I'll be satisfied. I raise her foot off my lap, meeting it halfway with my mouth before I take a deep inhale and let out a quiet groan.

Fuck.

Even her feet smell like that citrusy jasmine and cedar scent.

Before I even realize what I'm doing, my mouth lightly kisses her big toe. That light kiss just fuels my urge for more. Taking it a step further, I gently suck her big toe into my mouth, lightly grazing the skin with my teeth and swirling my tongue around the tip.

A startled gasp has me looking up, meeting a pair of very heated, mismatched eyes.

Ah ha, so my little hellcat has a thing for feet?

"What are you doing?" Evan breathes out, but doesn't move her foot.

"What does it look like? I'm tasting this milky skin," I reply before going in for another suck, this one longer, a little rougher, tongue moving a little faster. Every little moan and sigh just eggs me on until her breath comes in and out in short, heavy gasps. Like she can't get enough.

I take her whole toe in my mouth, lightly biting at the base, dragging my teeth along the skin as I slowly pull my mouth away, earning a long moan from Evan.

And that's all I can take before throwing her legs off my lap in one quick swoosh.

"What are yo — Oh!" She startles, and I quickly pick her up off the couch and throw her over my shoulder, heading for the stairs. "Cain! Put me down!" she yells as her fist pounds on my back, making me groan as I picture them being her nails raking down my back.

Slapping her gorgeous ass, I climb the stairs and make my way to her bedroom. Once inside, I toss her down on the teal, fluffy duvet. The contrast of the deep teal color against her skin makes my dick grow harder, straining against the zipper of my jeans.

"You're looking at me like you want to eat me." Evan laughs as she stares up at me, eyes matching the heat that has my dick hard as a rock. Glad the feeling isn't mutual.

"I'm gonna eat something." I wink before climbing onto the bed, placing my legs on either side of her hips so I'm straddling her. My hard dick brushes against where she wants me the most, making her hips jump up, searching for that friction that I know she's craving.

Her arms wrap around my neck before pulling my face to hers. I give in, crushing my mouth to hers, not giving her a chance to react before I shove my tongue in her mouth, taking control. She lets out that long moan I've been waiting to hear since I first sucked on her toe as I grind my dick against her wet heat.

"You achy baby?" I rumble and nip my way across the bottom of her jaw, to her ear, and down her neck, sucking at the base that I discovered in the shower that she likes, earning me an arch of her back.

I groan, feeling her full breasts push against my chest. I can't take it anymore. My hands are under her shirt, lifting it up and over her head before I pull the cup of her bra down.

"Fuck, hellcat," I growl. Seeing her pierced, hard nipples

staring up at me makes my cock just jump a little. "Another time," I say to myself as I massage the girls.

"What's another time?" Evan breathes out, arching her back even more as I roughly suck on her tight nipple.

"Me titty fucking these fuckin' tits," I rumble as I play with the silver bars running through each bud. "These alone are enough to bring a fuckin' man to his knees. Too bad no one else will ever find out what these pretty babies look like because they're mine," I claim before roughly biting the other nipple and pulling.

"Cain, please," she whines, hips searching and grinding against my cock, trying to ease her ache.

"Easy. You'll get it when I'm ready to give it to you." Using a firm grip, I press her hips back into the mattress.

Daddy's here now, little hellcat.

**24**

Evan

My hands frantically find their way to the hem of his shirt and yank hard. I'm desperate to get it off. Desperate to feel his skin flush against mine. Desperate for the connection.

He gives me this, yanking his shirt off in one swoop like all the guys do in the movies. I barely even register the move because all I can think about is having my turn to explore. I trail my fingers over every scar, tattoo, and mark that makes up Cain. I want to commit every inch of him to memory and savor what his weight feels like on me, how his skin feels against mine.

I scratch my nails lightly down his chest, making a shiver run through him. I feel empowered because I did that. I have that effect on him. I start to pull his belt through the loops when he stops me, making me look up at him in question.

Did I misread where this was going?

"I get to play first, little hellcat." He devilishly smirks at me before undoing the button on my jeans and roughly pulling them down my legs until I can kick them off the rest of the way with my feet.

Cain sharply inhales as he notices the tiny little black scrap of lace I have on. "Jesus. Are those even panties? I can see your slit."

"Yes," I breathe, thrusting my hips up toward him, begging for any kind of contact to help ease the ache. "I only wear thongs."

His eyes flare, and he lets out a low growl from deep in his chest—a sound I'll never get tired of hearing. In one quick motion, Cain snaps the thin material and rips it off me.

"Hey! It might not cover much, but those are still expensive," I whine. I need more than deep growls and ripped panties.

"I'll buy you more," he replies before his face dives toward my core, inhaling deep. "I knew you'd smell sweet." He rubs his nose along my slit, slowly driving me insane as he inhales one more time. "Yeah. You smell like mine."

My hands quickly find their way into his hair, roughly pulling and yanking every which way as his tongue finally runs along my slit.

"Yes," I hiss as his tongue explores, circling my entrance before sliding back up. My hips have a mind of their own as they start thrusting up, needing more of everything. His firm grip on my hip pushes it back into the mattress, holding me down.

Damn, if that doesn't make me feel owned.

I gasp as he roughly sucks my clit into his mouth while two thick fingers shove deep inside without warning, not waiting for me to adjust before quickly thrusting in and out. The ache is slightly relieved, but it isn't enough.

I need more.

He knows I need more.

"Cain," I whine, trying to thrust out of the hold he has on my hips, chasing that small build I can feel starting. He lets out a low chuckle before I feel empty at the quick loss of his mouth and fingers. I hear his belt hit the hardwood floor, making my eyes fly open, shooting straight to his hands that are drawing his zipper down.

I can't help but lick my lips as he slowly pulls his jeans down, seeing he's gone commando, and damn, that's so hot.

"You want this dick?" Cain growls while gripping the thick base and slowly giving himself a pump.

My eye catches a silver glint with the motion, zeroing in on the base of his cock. Holy shit. Is that...? "Are you pierced?" The words are just above a whisper because this man is my fantasy come to life. How did I not notice that before? I guess, in my defense, I was a little shocked and overwhelmed when everything was happening.

"Yeah, little hellcat. I can tell by that drenched pussy that you're into it. Now be a good girl and spread those sweet thighs for daddy. I want to look at what I'm about to claim."

My breathing increases as a sound I've never heard before slips out of me at him saying he wants to claim me. I can feel myself getting wetter by the second as I spread my legs. I know I'm glistening.

"Fuuuuck." Cain pumps his cock faster. "You're drenched for me, babe. You think you deserve this?" He tugs at the head, making it weep.

"Yes," I say, licking my lips. All I want is his cock. "Gimme. It's mine."

"You claiming it?" he rumbles

"If you get over here and fill me, yeah, daddy. I'm claiming it."

Cain growls while climbing on the bed. I hear the tearing of a wrapper before he's back over me on the bed. I watch as he guides himself to my heat, the tip of him rubbing up and down my slit, coating his cock in my juices before he finally presses the head against my entrance. "Eyes," he demands. "I want your fucking eyes on me when I enter my pussy for the first time."

My eyes shoot up to his. His heated green ones feel like they see every little part of me. This type of feeling is something I've only read about in books. Never in my life did I think I would experience it. He inches forward, the head of him being sucked in, making me gasp as he groans at the same time.

"Fuck, you're so goddamn tight."

The sensation makes his control slip as he slams forward to the hilt. I feel a slight sting from how long it's been since I've last been with someone. How can one motion hurt but feel so good at the same time?

"You okay?" Cain asks, his voice tight as if it's taking every ounce of control he has to not let loose and pound into me.

"Yeah," I breathe. "It's just been a minute, and you're huge."

"You can take it," he rumbles as he pulls out slightly and pushes back in. "Feel how good you're taking me." I try to thrust my hips up, needing more of everything, but he has me pinned down by his body.

He slowly pulls out, inch by fucking inch, until only the head is the only thing being gripped by my pussy before he slams back in. The pace he's set is just enough to drive me to the edge but not quite enough to push me over.

"Cain," I whine on a gasp, feeling so full but so empty.

"What do you need, little hellcat?" he asks as he thrusts in, picking up the pace. "I'll always give you what you need."

"You." I gasp. "I need you."

His control snaps as he starts hammering in and out. The stud at the base of his cock brushes against my clit every time, sending little tingles down my spine. I can feel it starting to build as he picks up the pace. His eyes are glued to my tits that are bouncing violently from the thrusts.

"Oh my god!" I cry as he places a hand on the inside of my knees, spreading them wide open and sliding me up on his muscular thighs, allowing him to adjust the angle, hitting that spot that you pray every guy can find. The one that instantly makes your eyes roll back into your head and your toes tingle.

"It's not God fucking you," he growls before roughly sucking my nipple into his mouth, swirling his tongue around the bar through it before quickly tugging it and releasing it with a pop. "It better be my name on your lips when you cry out." *Thrust.* "My name on your lips when you scream." *Thrust.* "And my name on your lips when you come on my cock." *Thrust.*

Holy fuck. It's right there. I clench down hard on him, about to explode.

"Let go," he growls as the last bit of his control slips, as he slams in and out of me. "Come on daddy's cock, little hellcat"

On command, I explode around him, his name on my lips, head thrown back, vision going black, my walls spasming around him so hard he has to force his dick back in as the force of my orgasm tries to push him out.

"Fuck, fuck, fuck," Cain chants as his orgasm slams into him, thrusting his dick all the way in as he fills the condom, collapsing on top of me as we both try to even out our breathing as we come down. His weight feels like the warmest blanket, making me wish we could stay in this position forever.

"Let me up, babe," he says as he lightly pats my ass. "Need to deal with this condom."

I let out a little mewl as he slips out, the loss of him making me feel empty. I already know I'm going to be feeling him tomorrow.

"I know, baby," he says as he runs a hand through my hair before lightly placing a kiss on my lips. I never thought I would ever be able to describe Cain's eyes as soft, but right now, he looks so relaxed and unguarded. Another wall around my heart shatters, knowing I put that look there. He's slowly wedging his way in, and that scares the shit out of me. It's unexplored territory.

I watch him saunter to the bathroom until he disappears, hearing the water turn on. A moment later, he's standing at the door, leaning against the doorframe. "Damn, I love the look on your face right now. And if I were fifteen years younger, knowing I put it there would make me hard as a rock again, but I need a minute."

A laugh burst out of me because that was the last thing I expected him to say. That's one thing I'm growing to love about him. He's the most unexpected thing that seems to be making me the happiest right now. "It's been a minute for me. I'm going to be feeling you tomorrow."

"Oh yeah?" he asks as he pushes off the door frame, walking around to the side of the bed closest to the door and climbing in under the duvet. He takes a second to settle himself with one arm under the pillows supporting his head before he uses the other to drag me to him. "Get under." I slide my butt up on the bed so I can pull the duvet back and climb under and cuddle in against Cain. I never pegged him for a cuddler. When was the last time I was even held like this?

"Stop."

"What?"

"I can hear your wheels turning. What set you off now?" he asks, lightly running his fingertips along the Medusa tattoo on my upper arm.

"I just wasn't expecting you to be a cuddler."

"I'm not."

I lift my head back to look at him. "Um... then what are we doing?"

"Shit's different with you, Evan. You can either keep freaking out and playing stuff up in your head, or you can be okay with the fact that you're the first woman that gets this from me."

What? Did I just hear him right?

I must have died and gone to heaven because, oh my god. Another chip just fell, making the wall around my heart a lot less stable, and that's scary as fuck. That giddy feeling you get when you're in the honeymoon phase of your relationship is settling in the pit of my stomach as I really process what he just said, relaxing into him more. Feeling me relax more into him must have given him the assurance he was looking for because he continued on, "So, how long has it been?"

"How long has what been?" I ask as I trace circles on the skull covering his hand.

"Since you've been with a man, hellcat." Oh. Of course he picked up on that little bit of information. I purse my lips together because I don't want to say it. It's honestly kind of embarrassing—embarrassing as in I'm surprised he didn't find any cobwebs down there.

"Babe."

I remain silent, hoping he picks up on the vibe that I'm pleading the fifth.

"Evangeline." He shakes my shoulder lightly. Ugh. He just had to use my full first name.

Sighing, I give in. "It's been a few years." I bury my face in the crook of his neck to hide my embarrassment. I mean, who just wants to openly admit that? Especially to a guy that they're into. Hi, I'm basically a born-again virgin.

A low rumble vibrates against my cheek, making me look up and see Cain's eyes flare. "I never thought I would find something like that attractive, but it's fucking hot." I throw him an eye roll. "I'm serious. I like that I'm the first man that's touched you in a long time. The first man to get you to light up like that. It's making my dick hard just thinking about it. I never considered myself to be possessive, but I'd kill any fucker that even looked you the wrong way, Evan."

Cain settles down lower on the bed, curling his body around me before patting the mattress and calling for Hades to hop up. "Now, let's go to sleep. I have to get up for church in the morning."

I went to sleep that night feeling like the safest girl in the world.

**25**

**Cain**

Last night was the first night that I've ever spent with a woman. And by spent the night, I mean actually slept over. And damn, if that wasn't the best night of sleep I've had in a long time. She was cute as fuck when she woke up too. All grumpy and shit. Reminded me of a cute little feral cat. Mean as fuck until they got their cream, or in Evan's case, the cream comes in the form of caffeine. I think I helped take the edge off by waking her up with my mouth on her pussy. She sweetened just enough to not bite my head off before she got her fix.

And that meal she made me last night. I don't even know the last time I had someone cook for me. Hell, I can't even remember the last time I had dinner with a woman. Did that count as a date? Do I need to take her out? Girls like that shit, I think.

I take a long drag of my cigarette as I change my thought process to how I want this meeting to go. Honestly, I don't even want a meeting. I want to go over to that fucker's house and beat the ever-loving shit out of him until I have the answers I want. Unfortunately, that's not how it works in the club. I need a vote. I feel like they'd back me, though. Ink seemed to really take to Evan in the first three seconds of meeting her. That's the kind of impact she leaves on people.

Rubbing the cigarette butt in the ashtray that's on the picnic table outside the clubhouse, I head inside for church.

"Alright, you fucks!" I yell as I pound my gavel on the table, quieting down the brothers. "I had Scotch call this meeting because we've had another issue arise."

The smiles instantly disappear from their faces, all of them straightening in their seats.

"Scotch and I stopped by Evan's last night, and some fuck thought it was okay to break into her place and vandalize it."

"Are you fucking serious?" Ink growls. "Is she okay?"

"Yeah, she's okay. Was a little shaken up, but she's made of tough shit."

"How bad is the damage?" Hash asks.

"Not too bad. Just need to replace the lock on the front door and redo some of the drywall. Whoever did this spray-painted a threat on her wall, warning her away from us."

"How in the fuck does someone know she's working with us?" Trick asked, looking like he's ready to murder someone.

"That's the million-dollar fucking question. I think that the person who was scoping out her place the other night and the shit that happened last night are related and, somehow, also related to us."

"I don't believe in coincidences like that. I agree with you on it," Hash says, looking deep in thought.

None of this makes any fucking sense. If Evan already had a bunch of enemies and people after her, I'd assume other scenarios, but the girl is a hermit. I haven't even heard her mention friends' names.

"You think it has something to do with the jacked shipment

and two of our prospects getting killed?" Ink asks, drawing all the attention to himself. "What? You can't tell me you haven't thought of it." He shrugs. "We need to look at every angle as a possibility."

"She doesn't have any idea? I doubt it's the Reapers. This screams amateur. Or someone scared to do it face-to-face," Trick says, looking no less pissed off.

"Scotch and I talked to her last night, and she thinks it might be the guy who sells for her. Scotch has met him a few times and doesn't get a good vibe from him."

"I think he's worth looking into. If Ev thinks something is off with him, then I believe her. I never liked the son of a bitch anyway," Scotch says as the other guys nod their heads and think everything over.

"Alright, let's vote. Do we pay this fucker a visit or let it lie and see what happens? Hands for a visit?" Looking around the table, I see every brother's hands raised. Hell yeah. "Looks like we're paying this bitch a visit." I grin, and cheers erupt.

What can I say? It's been getting a little fucking boring around here.

"Scotch, you're coming with me since you've met him before. I want a familiar face with me. Cyrus, I want you to come too. Just in case shit goes south and we need a little more muscle." The dude gets off on cutting off fingers. I'm in no position to judge. We all have our kinks. Some are newer than others based on how I sucked on Evan's fucking toes last night. Just thinking about it is making my dick hard. That's the last thing I need. My head needs to be in the game and not thinking about how sexy my little hellcat looks while she's under me.

Trick's shoulders sag. "I always miss out on all the fun stuff."

"You were the one who beat the shit out of the drunk piece of shit that was drugging drinks at DD's. Didn't even give me a chance with him." Hash crossed his arms, looking equally put out.

"I need you two to stay back at the club with the prospects in case the Reapers decide to stop by uninvited again. You don't need to wait for me to give them a message if it happens." Meeting Trick and Hash's eyes, I see hope flare that they actually stop by. Crazy fuckers.

"Let's ride out." I bang the gavel on the table while the brothers cheer.

I'm TAKING up the lead with Scotch and Cyrus on each side, hanging slightly back as we cruise down the road on the way to Storm's. I'm trying to contain my rage because, you know, innocent until proven guilty and all that shit. The only promise I'm making is not to kill him unless I find out he's behind this.

My lip curls up in disgust as we turn into the drive at the address that Evan gave us. It's even farther out from Ravenna Heights than we are—just a single trailer on a lot in the middle of nowhere.

I'm pissed as fuck that she came out here alone. It's in the middle of nowhere and in the woods to boot. This fucker could have killed her, and no one would be around to hear her screams.

"You think anyone's home?" Cyrus asks as soon as we cut the bikes.

"Good fucking question." There isn't even a car here. "You guys see any movement through the blinds?"

"Nope," Scotch replies. "God, this place is a fucking dump. It smells like piss, too."

He's not wrong about that. Judging by how the grass in the yard is almost up to my knee, it's clear he doesn't take care of this place. I can only imagine what the inside looks like. "This place looks like a trap house and a hoarder's house had a baby."

Cyrus grunts in agreement as he walks up the front steps.

He pounds his fists on the door, only to be greeted with no response. Of course, he's conveniently not home.

Cyrus turns his head, pressing his ear to the door while Scotch and I keep our eyes glued to the windows in the off-chance we catch a peeping tom.

Cyrus shakes his head, letting us know that he isn't hearing anything, before reaching into his back pocket and pulling out his lock pick. He picks it in under 30 seconds, and we're in. I pull my Glock out of my waistband and signal to Cyrus to let me lead.

I slowly push open the door, quickly scanning the area and coming up clear. I nod my head toward the door down the left of the hall, telling one of them to check out that room as I move through the kitchen and the living room.

Scotch comes back, shaking his head. "It's all clear. His drawers are thrown open as if he were leaving in a hurry. Clothes all over the fucking place."

"I don't know if that means anything. It doesn't look like he's cleaned since he moved in. This place fucking reeks like a dirty hooker's pussy." Cyrus grimaces as he looks around at the moldy dishes on the counter and table and old beer cans scattered on the floor.

"I think Evan was right about him being on something," Scotch says while pointing to the broken glass pipe on the coffee table.

This guy is living in filth. The longer I stay in here, the angrier I get again that Evan thought it was okay to come here on her own. That shit is not happening again.

"You guys thinking what I'm thinking?" This doesn't look good, but at the same time, it isn't adding up to anything.

"If you're thinking that he split in a hurry, then yeah, I'm thinking what you're thinking," Cyrus says, while Scotch grunts in agreement. "The question is, who is after him that made him leave like that? You think Evan would know?"

Shrugging my shoulders, I answer, "No fucking clue, but I doubt it. She made it sound as if she didn't really know him outside the arrangement they had going on. Just an old coworker turned associate. They never hung out outside of this."

"I feel like if Evan knew him on a level more than what she's saying, she would have mentioned it," Scotch agrees.

"Let's get the fuck out of here and fill Hash and Trick in. Lucky fuckers missed out on this fucking shit hole," I say, heading toward the front door. I don't even make it down to the last step before gunfire erupts out of nowhere, aiming right for me.

Quickly jumping back up and into the trailer, I slam the front door shut and dive behind the paper-thin wall that separates the kitchen from the entryway. A few shots have penetrated the cheap siding, hitting the couch and the other side of the trailer since this piece of shit is only 14 feet wide.

"Everyone okay?" I yell over the shots. They definitely have a semi-automatic.

"We're good!" Scotch yells, crouched behind the coffee table he overturned.

"What's the plan? I've got two clips on me," Cyrus yells just before the firing stops.

Raising my pointer finger to my lips, signaling for them to be quiet, I slowly creep toward the edge of the front window. A few of the blinds have the ends snapped off already, creating a tiny opening, which I try to look out of without being noticed..

Darting my eyes all along the tree line of the front yard, I come up blank.

What. The. Fuck.

I start to stand to my full height when laughter outside has me freezing. It sounds like he's coming closer, but I can't tell for sure. I make eye contact with Scotch and Cyrus and notice they have the same look in their eyes. What are we going to do?

There's nowhere to hide in this small piece of shit. And it's three against however many with bigger guns than we have right now.

This will be the last time I underestimate this stupid fuck.

"Boss will be very pleased to know we just killed the Dirty Devils' Prez."

What accent is that? It sounds so familiar, but I can't place it.

"Who were the guys with him?"

"Do not know. Do not give a fuck. Let's go talk to Boss."

"I'm getting real sick of doing his bitch work."

A smack sounds out as if the one guy smacked the other. "Do not talk about the Pakhan like that."

Fuck.

I look over at Scotch and Cyrus, who are sharing the same as me. Because why in the fuck are the Russians on my territory, and how did they know I was coming to talk to Storm?

**26**

Cain

We waited until we were sure they left, not knowing if they had more power with them. We're not ones to hide and cower, but we're also not eighteen anymore. We know when we're outnumbered.

"How in the fuck did the Russians know we were going to be here?" Scotch growls as we walk back to our bikes.

"No fucking clue. None of this makes any sense. I don't want to talk about it out here, though." It's too open, leaving us vulnerable. I scan the surrounding woods. I can't shake the feeling that we're still being watched. These woods have eyes, and I don't like that. Evan did say that she had the same feeling, though, didn't she?

I nod to Scotch and Cyrus to watch their backs as we start up our bikes and head back. None of this is sitting right.

Trick is already out front by the entrance to our clubhouse, smoking a cigarette.

"Well?" he asks as soon as we cut our engines.

"Inside," I growl as I prowl in. "Brock! Levi! Outside,

watching the gate. Now!" I yell as I head straight to the bar, pouring myself a glass full of Jameson and downing it in one swallow.

"What in the hell happened?" Hash asks, eyes wide, knowing I only drink like that when shit is fucked up.

"We got shot at by the Russians, and I'm pretty fucking sure they think that they killed me."

Silence. That's what I'm met with before the guys lose their fucking minds, shouting questions at me at the same time.

Holding up my hand to silence them, I say, "We still don't really know much. He wasn't home, but they knew we were coming unless it was just really good timing. We broke into look around, and it looked like he had left in a hurry. He's into some shit. I just don't know how his shit ties to us."

"If he was gone, why would the Russians be there waiting?" Hash asks, taking a seat at the bar.

"Good question." I shrug, trying to wrap my brain around all of this.

"You guys shoot back?"

"No. They had bigger toys than we did, and it was just us against that. We weren't prepared for that kind of fight, so we just laid low until it played out, and the idiots thought they killed us without even checking."

"Can't blame you there," Ink says, getting beers out for everyone.

"It's almost as if they knew we were coming."

"What do you mean?" Trick asks, and everyone's eyes move to me.

"They could have shot at us when we first got there, but they didn't. We scoped out the outside, knocked and waited, picked the lock, and checked out the inside. They didn't open fire until I was halfway down the front steps," I say, staring almost too deeply at the bottle of Jameson like it's going to give me all the answers.

"The shooters also knew it was us. They specifically said the Dirty Devils' president. I wish we could have seen their fucking faces." Scotch slams his beer down on the bar, and an eerie silence settles in the room. Tension is at an all-time high.

Hash breaks the silence by clearing his throat, making everyone's eyes jump to him. "You don't think Evan tipped Storm off that you guys were coming?"

A low growl erupts in my chest because there is no way. No fucking way was it Evan.

Hash raises his hands in defense. "I didn't mean any disrespect, Prez. I'm just trying to look at it from all angles."

"Evan isn't a fucking rat," I say between clenched teeth.

"It's just a little weird that you said it looked like this guy left in a rush. Like maybe she tipped him off. And he tipped off the Russians because he's involved with them somehow."

Fuck.

I hate that what he just said sounds like a real possibility. Without another word, I grab the Jameson bottle by the neck and head to my room.

Is Hash right? Would Evan do this? I didn't think she would be the type, especially after last night. She just seems loyal to her core. Scotch even vouched for her, but Hash's theory makes the most sense right now. Someone tipped these guys off.

"Fuck," I say out loud to no one but my bottle of Jameson before taking a big swig as I sit back on my bed and lean against the wall.

Feeling my phone vibrate in my pocket, I pull it out to see it's a text from Evan.

Evan: Hey, you!

Me: Hey

> Evan: I was wondering if maybe you wanted to
> hang out tonight?

> Me: Can't. Got shit going on.

I take another swig as five minutes pass with no response. I know I'm being short, and she probably thinks I'm back to being a dick. Maybe it's best this way. A one-percenter president has no business getting attached to a woman. Let alone a woman like Evan. There's too much risk on both sides and too much to gain from the other turning on each other.

They say you can't find answers at the bottom of a bottle, but I'm damn well going to try.

Too bad those gorgeous blue and green eyes haunt my dreams.

**27**

Evan

Cain: Can't. Got shit going on.

T hat's it.

That's all he said.

He's back to Cain, the asshole. Not the Cain that was in my bed last night. And that hurts. And I hate that it hurts.

"Something's going on, Hades baby," I murmur while scratching his head.

We're currently lying in bed. After the chaos that has consumed my life, I felt like having a lazy day. Everyone has their own way of relaxing, but I find the best way is to binge eat with an assortment of drinks, curl up in bed with a good book, have music or a show playing in the background, and never move. If I do move, it's to take a bath. I basically become a potato—a very satisfied potato.

I was secretly hoping that Cain would want to come over and be a potato with me. My ideal dream date is a day in bed doing all of the above with dessert afterward. The kind that comes in the form of a massive cock.

I guess I thought things had changed after our talk yesterday and him staying the night last night. I can't say that I'm not disappointed that it feels like we're back to square one. Even through the hurt, I think I just kind of... expected it.

I deserve answers, though. If he got freaked and decided that he's changed his mind about letting things play out, then fine. I'd rather it end now before it goes too far and before I won't even want to do business with him because I won't be able to stand to look at his asshole face. But I deserve to know what the hell happened today.

Hades perks up as I throw the covers off myself. "I'm going over there, and he's going to tell me what in the hell is going on." I throw on a pair of leggings and change out of my old t-shirt for a bra and low-cut tank top. Sliding on my Vans, I head out. "Be good, baby," I tell Hades, blowing a kiss in his direction.

I decide to drive over to the clubhouse. I could walk through the connecting trails, but I don't need the extra time to stew in my anger. I'm pissed-off enough.

Levi opens the gate for me at the clubhouse, greeting me with a friendly smile. The others are a different story. I don't even have one foot out of my car before Hash prowls toward me with a scowl.

"Did Prez invite you here?" he growls.

Uh... what the hell? "No. He didn't. I wasn't aware I needed to be invited if I had something I wanted to talk about."

His arms are now folded across his chest. "You might have a nice pair of tits and spread your legs without him asking, but if I find out you're behind this, we're going to have a fucking prob-lem. Scotch's sister or not."

I rear my head back at his response because where in the

fuck did that come from? And did he just basically call me a club whore?

I climb out of the car and stand, facing him and looking directly into his eyes so that he knows he can't talk down to me, and give him a glare to rival his. "I don't know what your problem is. I don't even know you. And I really don't appreciate you basically calling me a whore. Now if you'll excuse me, I have shit to do that doesn't include looking at your patchy beard that you still can't fill in as a grown-ass man." Shoving past him, I head inside, not waiting for a response after the growl that ensued.

"Hey, Ink." I smile at him, seeing him lounging on one of the couches. He looks up and gives me a quick smile that doesn't quite reach his eyes.

"Hey, Darlin'. Whatcha doin' here?" His gaze is on me, looking skeptical. What is up with everyone looking at me like that?

"I wanted to talk to Cain. Is he around?"

Ink's attention is already back on his phone when he responds dismissively, "Should be in his room."

Well, okay then.

I don't even bother asking which room is Cain's before heading up the stairs. I just reach the top when I see a guy I remember seeing at the party the other night.

"What are you doing up here?" he asks, eyes guarded and his tone matching.

"I'm looking for Cain. Ink said he was in his room."

"Last door on the left."

I can feel his eyes on me as I walk down the hall until I reach Cain's door. I turn my head to look at him, still standing in the same spot, watching me. I raise my eyebrows at him, silently asking, 'Can I help you?' while I pound on Cain's door.

I mean, honestly, why is everyone here acting like I'm enemy number one?

I raise my fist, ready to knock again, but the door is yanked open, and a very angry Cain is now staring back at me. "What the fuck are you doing here?"

"I wanted to talk."

"Can you not fucking read? I told you I got shit going on."

I look down at the bottle of Jameson he has in his hand, hanging by his left side.

Okay, so something definitely fucking happened then. Cain's drinking away said problem while the other guys are acting weird as hell. I swear these guys are more emotional than me when I'm riding the red dragon. But no way is this asshole shutting me out if it has something to do with business.

I push my way through the opening between his side and the doorframe on the right. "Goddamnit!" he yells as he turns to face me. "Don't make me throw you out of here. I don't give a shit if you're Scotch's sister."

I cock my hip out to the side as I cross my arms under my boobs, making them push up as I look him up and down. I didn't miss the way his eyes immediately shot to my cleavage. And I definitely didn't miss the flare in them, either.

"You're not going to throw me out of anywhere until we talk about what is going on," I say calmly. I think that's the best approach to get the answers I want. You can't fight fire with fire. Unless that fire cheats. Then, by all means, cut his dick off. "If you want me gone after that, then fine. I'm gone."

I don't miss the low, frustrated growl he lets out before he slams his bedroom door shut. I take a second to look around at everything. They say a person's room is their most sacred space. It lets you in on little secrets and quirks they would never tell you—lets you see their true personality. And Cain's room was definitely all Cain.

It has a darker vibe but is kind of bare at the same time. He has a basic black comforter and black drapes on the window that look like they are probably the blackout kind. His walls are what make the room feel bare. He has one poster of a pin-up girl straddling a Harley that looks 20 years old. His dresser in the corner is home to the TV, and there's a desk on the other side that looks like it serves the same purpose as my clothes chair in my room. Everyone has that one spot where they pile clean clothes that they don't feel like putting away.

"You have 30 seconds to start talking before I throw your ass out," he rumbles, not moving from his spot in front of the door.

This man and his attitude are really starting to test my patience. Taking a deep breath to control my urge to knock him out, I decide to get comfy by sitting on his bed, leaning up against the wall.

"I want to know what in the hell is going on. You were fine when you left my place. I know you went to talk to Storm. And now, all of a sudden, it seems like you've done a complete 180 towards me. So please, fill in the gaps," I say in a tone that sounds extremely calm to my ears compared to how I'm feeling right now as I flick my hand out.

"When did you tell Storm I was coming? Right after my dick was in you?"

Are you fucking kidding me?

**28**

Evan

My head jerks back as if he slapped me, the back of my head hitting the wall hard, making me wince. "What?"

"I want to know why you tipped him off that we were coming! Because when we got there, his ass was nowhere to be found, and then we ended up getting fucking shot at! Was that your end goal? Take me out, and you get to keep the money you're making from us? Or did someone else pay you to give them our location? Who are you working with?" He fires off question after question, not giving me a chance to answer as he stalks toward me.

"What?" I breathe out. He can't seriously think I sold him out. Sold Zeke out.

"Tell me you fucking sold me out!" Cain screams in my face that he's now inches from, so close that I think I felt a little spit hit my cheek. The veins in his neck are bulging from how tightly wound his body is.

And that's when I snap, slapping him right across the face.

"I didn't fucking sell you out, you asshole!" I scream back.

He lets out a roar before slamming both palms against the wall, framing my face and making me jump. "Then how did they know I was there?!"

"I don't know!" I scream. "I don't fucking know!"

"What the fuck is going on?" Zeke bursts into Cain's room, the door bouncing off the wall. His face instantly hardens as he takes in the scene in front of him. "Get the fuck out of her face, man."

Cain pushes off the wall and faces Zeke. "This is between Evan and me. We'll talk later about you thinking you own this fucking place and can barge into my room."

Zeke's eyes bounce between me and Cain. I give him a stiff nod, letting him know that I'm okay. "I didn't fucking forget. I just don't like that I can hear the way you're talking to her sitting at the bar. You need to check that shit. She didn't rat us out. Show her some fucking respect." He turns to leave but stops just before he's out the door. "Just scream if you need me, Ev." And on that parting, he's gone.

Cain walks over and closes his door again, this time softer.

"Look, Cain. I don't know what you're talking about, but I didn't sell you out. I can show you my phone or whatever you want, but I didn't do it," I say in a softer tone from my spot on his bed that I haven't moved from. "The thought of you and Zeke getting kill—" I cough, trying to choke back and hide the tears that are threatening to fall from my eyes. "The thought of you and Zeke getting killed is something I never want to think about."

Cain stares at me from his spot by the door, lost in thought. He may be looking at me, but he isn't looking *at* me.

"Cain?" I ask softly, making his eyes dart to mine, breaking his train of thought. "I swear I didn't do anything."

He holds my gaze for a long time before finally breaking his silence. "I believe you." He sighs, sounding resigned and looking slightly defeated.

"Come here." I pat the open spot on the bed next to me.

Once he's settled in, I reach my arm up until I can touch his head, lightly running my fingers through his messy hair and massaging his scalp. "You okay?"

He sighs deeply before responding, "I'm okay, little hellcat. I'm sorry for how I just acted. I know I scared you, but you know that I would never hurt you."

I can't even begin to describe the relief that runs through me when he uses the nickname I've grown to love. "It's okay."

"No, it's not okay. I should have talked to you about all of this first. Some of the brothers just got into my head, and it spiraled from there. And that's on me. But I never want you to just sit back and take it. That shit ain't right. You, of all people, don't deserve to be treated like that. I promise I'll check it next time until I discuss it with you."

Another piece of my wall just chipped away. I can't believe he's apologizing. Again. "Do you want to tell me what happened?" I ask softly, still lightly massaging his scalp.

"Basically, what I yelled at you earlier. I don't even know. We got there and could tell he wasn't home, so we went inside to look around. The place was trashed." He paused to tilt his head up so he was looking at me. "I'm pissed at you for going there by yourself. I was mad before, but once I saw it with my own two eyes- babe, what in the hell were you thinking?"

"I don't know. I guess I was just thinking that I've known him for years, and it would be okay. I also didn't picture him living in a place like that, you know? He just never seemed like he would be that dirty."

"You never really know someone like that, babe. Especially when it's a fucked-up situation. Just don't do it again unless you have me or a man with you."

"You're not going to follow me around every second of my life. I'm going to have times when I need to meet up with someone or do something without you."

"If this goes where I think it's going to go, then yeah, you fucking will."

"Let's just agree to disagree, okay?" I say, hoping to get him to drop it for now. My emotions are spent for the day. "Tell me what else happened."

"This stays between us, yeah? Technically, this is club business, and I shouldn't be telling you any of it, but since it kind of involves you, I'm going to let that slide." I nod my head even though he can't see me, waiting for him to continue. "Good. So when we were leaving, I wasn't even two feet out the door before they started firing on us. We couldn't see who it was or where they were, so we just waited it out inside. Felt like a little bitch not being able to face them, but I didn't want to die on you either." He smirked.

Smirked.

Like the thought of dying is funny.

"I'm just joking, little hellcat." He laughs. "Anyway, after the firing stopped, we heard some guys outside with Russian accents. They left, and we followed soon after, and now here we are."

My mind is running a mile a minute, and none of this is making any sense. What is Storm doing with the Russians?

Wait a minute... "How did that lead to you and the whole club thinking I sold you out?" It's downright insulting, honestly.

"I don't know. Hash got into my head when we were discussing it when we got back. It was the only explanation that made any sense as to how the Russians knew we were there. He knew I was inside, hellcat."

"I would rather pull every single fingernail out one by one before I sold any of you out. I hope you know that."

"I know you would." He smirks. "That's very touching."

"So I guess that explains why Hash ambushed me at my car and why Ink acted like I'm the number one enemy." I get they were trying to protect their president and brother, but it still hurt how fast they turned on me, even if I barely know them.

Cain stirs under my arm, sitting up and stretching out his back before he pulls my legs onto his lap and massages my feet again. This might be my new favorite way to relax.

"I'll talk to them. They shouldn't have treated you like that until I had talked to you and let them know what was up. Again, that's on me, and I'm sorry, hellcat," Cain says sincerely as he rubs up to my ankle.

"No, it's okay. I get it. They're protective of you, and they should be." I moan as he rubs just the right spot. "I like that you have that."

God, I can't get enough of this man's hands on my body. I turn my body so I'm facing him, allowing him to have more access to both of my legs.

"You have it too, babe. I don't want you to think that we all wouldn't have your back like that. We just need to set a couple of things straight. Everyone is on edge with what's been going on."

I know he's trying to make me feel better about everything that just happened, but all I can think about is him sucking on my toes the other night. I'm getting turned on just from picturing him bending down right now and lightly sucking on them.

I wonder... I start to move the foot that he isn't massaging over the outline of his cock, which is tucked slightly down the side of his left thigh, before I continue, "I know. Zeke would do anything for me, and he has in the past. But you and I are still seeing where this goes, so please don't chew them out. Their loyalty should be with you."

"What are yo—" he starts to ask just as I rub my foot over the head of his cock, cutting him off mid-sentence. "Oh, fuck."

Grinning, I do it again, but this time, I go farther toward the base, earning me a deep intake of breath. It's so thick and hard. I imagine him weeping at the slit just from my contact. Knowing that I can get this reaction out of him makes me feel so empowered. Like I have the control to bring him to his knees.

"Take it out," I say demandingly. His eyes fly up to meet mine, eyebrows slightly furrowed at my tone. Will he let me have control?

Cain hesitates for a beat before taking his hand off my foot and unbuttoning his jeans. He lifts his hips up slightly so he can pull them down just past his hips, making his cock spring free. The pubic piercing glints at me, just begging to be caressed.

It's such a turn-on that he doesn't wear boxers. The thought that I can just unzip his pants and touch his dick at any given moment makes my inner walls clench.

"It's out, little hellcat. Now, what are you going to do with it?" he rumbles.

And damn if I don't feel that rumble in my pussy.

"I'm going to play with it, daddy," I breathe as I take my foot and lightly rub at the base of his cock, just shy of touching the two silver balls staring up at me.

"Be careful, baby. Payback is a bitch."

"There won't be time for payback if you're begging to get inside."

That earns me the growl I absolutely love. I finally give him what he wants, lightly rubbing my big toe between the two balls before dragging it up along the velvety flesh until I reach the head of his cock. A soft moan escapes me. The silky feeling under my feet is almost too much to bear. I shiver as his cock jumps as I circle the head, making it weep at the contact.

My toe drags the wetness around, using it as lube to circle again before I start trailing back to the base, this time on the underside. Back and forth with light, short strokes until I reach his balls. A growl releases from Cain at the contact, making his control snap. My time in charge is done, and he's over me in a flash, pinning me to his mattress with my arms above my head, and a startled gasp escapes me.

Almost instantly, my hips are searching, needing some friction to ease this ache. The ache that only his dick can satisfy.

"You feel that, little hellcat?" he asks as he pushes his stiff cock into my covered core.

"Yes." I grind my hips up, feeling his hard cock press into me.

His lips slam down hard on mine, wasting no time as his tongue plunders in, demanding the dominance that he already knows he has. I meet him thrash for thrash, suck for suck, and bite for bite. His growl runs down my throat, making my insides quiver.

"Please," I whine as I try to pull my wrists out of his hold. I need to touch and explore, to feel his skin against mine.

"Please, what?"

"Let me touch you."

"Only because you asked like the good girl you are."

A moan slips out at the praise as he releases my wrists. His hands immediately go to the end of my tank, pulling it up. I lift up slightly, raising my arms to help him out. He wastes no time reaching around my back and unhooking my bra before yanking it off.

"Goddamn," he groans as he fists both of my breasts. "I'll never get tired of looking at these fucking tits."

I let out a loud moan as he dives on one, sucking my nipple in his mouth roughly. My hands shoot to his head, threading through his hair, tugging as he gives it a little nip. His tongue swirls around the hard point, playing with the silver bar as he does so, sending a tingling sensation down my spine.

I tug his hair hard before I trail my hands down his back, lightly scratching my nails as I go. I trail my pointer fingers from his lower back around his waist until I reach the front. Grabbing the waistband of my leggings, I try to pull them down before I'm stopped.

"What do you think you're doing?" Cain rumbles.

"I want these off." I basically beg at this point.

"What did I say about payback being a bitch?"

"I learned my lesson. No more teasing." Okay, now I'm actually begging. "I promise. Please."

"Mmmmm," he rumbles as he trails his lips down my stomach. "I don't think you have yet." He inhales deeply, taking in the scent of my arousal. "Is my pussy wet for me?"

"Yes." I thrust my hips up to his face.

"I don't think I believe you. I think I better see for myself." He slides a hand inside my waistband and runs a finger down my slit before he thrusts in with no warning.

"Finally," I moan out as I arch my back at the welcome intrusion. It's gone before any of the aches I feel can be eased. His hand exits my leggings, and my eyes shoot open in time to see him sticking the finger that was just inside me in his mouth.

"Goddamn, little hellcat. You taste like sin and perfection, all wrapped in one." He growls. "You taste like mine."

It's game on from here. Using my feet, I push his jeans down the rest of his legs until they are around his ankles, kicking them off with my feet. His hands are flirting with my waistband before he yanks my leggings and panties down in one swoop, and I rub one foot along each ankle until I can fully kick them off.

Finally, the feeling of his skin on mine is one I'll never grow tired of. The weight of his body on mine. The feel of his delicious chest hair brushing against my smooth skin. His hands roaming, kneading, and rubbing as he goes. It's unmatched. The sudden need to taste him is overwhelming. Using all my strength, I push up on his shoulder. Catching him off guard, he rolls with it so he is half on his side but still slightly over me.

"What's wrong?" he asks, looking startled.

Instead of answering him, I push on his shoulder again, making him lay fully back before I assault his neck by sucking and licking it. It earns me a groan and a grab of my ass that gives me the confidence I need to continue my assault. As I kiss my way down his chest, I thread his fingers with mine. His hands squeeze mine tightly when he realizes where I'm headed.

"You going to suck daddy's thick cock, little hellcat?"

"I'm going to suck *my* thick cock." Before he can even respond, I take him in my mouth to the hilt, making me gag. I don't let up, though, letting the tears flow from my eyes as I get used to the intrusion.

"Shit," he hisses out as a hand grabs my hair.

I haven't been with a ton of guys in my 28 years, but I have sucked a few dicks. I never really felt the driving need to do it. It just always seemed like something I needed to do out of obligation. Like, 'Hey, thanks for going downtown, dude, let me just suck you off real quick' type of thing. No real effort was ever put into it. I was only focused on getting them off as quickly as possible so it would end. And I sure as hell have never swallowed. If I wasn't into sucking you off in the first place, why would I want any of that inside of me?

It's different with Cain, though. I want to get him off in the best way possible. I want to rip every moan, groan, cuss, and shout out of him. I want to be the one to bring him to his knees. Literally and figuratively. And for the first time in my life, I want to swallow everything he's willing to give me.

Hearing his hiss spurs me on, and I relax my throat so I can take him deeper. Pulling back so the head is at the opening of my mouth, I hollow my cheeks out, sucking hard on it while swirling my tongue around the tip. One hand is playing with his balls, while the other is playing with the little silver bar at the base.

"You're sucking daddy so good, little hellcat." He groans, tipping his head back, his neck and the veins alongside it straining. It's full-on nasty now. Spit is dripping down my chin and down his cock and balls as I work him faster. And, fuck, if it isn't the hottest thing.

"Fuck. I'm close, baby." His hips are now thrusting, going deeper down my throat.

I wonder what he would do if I just...

"What are you — oh fuck!" he shouts as he explodes down my throat. My hand that I had on his balls is now massaging his taint. I swallow every last drop, lazily licking his cock as the tremors rack through his body. Popping him out of my mouth, I look up at him, satisfied with what I see. He looks completely relaxed and sated. A complete one-eighty from when I arrived.

"Damn, baby. You continue to blow my mind," he praises as he hauls me up so I'm straddling him. "I think this needs to be a daily thing. You know, for good health."

"For good health?" I laugh.

"Yeah. I've heard it's good for your skin," he says, looking sheepish. "You know, that was a first for me. Never had someone touch my taint before, and I sure as hell never thought I would be into it, but I don't think I've ever come that hard in my life."

There's that feeling again. The fact that I was just able to give him something no one else has? It's unmatched. I kiss his lips and whisper against them, "I'll let you in on a little secret, too. You're the first guy I've ever swallowed with."

A low rumble starts in his chest and makes its way up his throat and out. "You saying I'm the first guy to mark you in that way?"

"Yup," I say, popping the p.

"You can't say things like that to me. Now I've got to fuck you."

"I would be offended if you didn't." I nip his bottom lip before I'm flipped on my back, and he's motor-boating my tits.

I can't help but think this is who I want to spend the rest of my life with.

**29**

Cain

Something is tickling my nose.

I inhale deeply, taking in that familiar scent—the same scent that has quickly become my home. Opening my eyes, I smile.

Evan is sprawled out on top of me with her face tucked into the corner of my neck. Hair wild and scattered all over my chest and beard. Only the top sheet covers my favorite ass in the world, leaving her back exposed.

What I wouldn't give to wake up like this every day.

I still can't believe what an asshole I was yesterday. I probably would have lost her if Evan hadn't been so stubborn and determined. Lost this scary feeling of home that I'm growing to love. I have a feeling it would have been the biggest mistake of my life. I'm proud of her, though. I like that she didn't take my shit lying down. If she's going to stick around with me, I need someone who can put up with this life. It's not always crazy. We party hard and live life to the fullest, but it tends to go from zero to one hundred in thirty seconds when it gets tough. I need someone by my side that can handle it. Face it head-on with me.

Feeling Evan stir, I lightly place a kiss on her forehead before trailing my fingers up her spine, and she starts to squirm. "Mmmm." She lets out a little moan while snuggling in closer, tucking her leg in between mine and her foot under my calf. "Too early."

"It's almost 11." I chuckle. My little demon in the morning.

"Too early," she mumbles back.

Tapping her ass, I say, "Come on, little demon. We have to get up and search for Storm. I want this shit taken care of today."

"Ugh." She flops over. "Stupid Storm. When I see him, I'm going to rip him two new assholes. One for messing with me and one for messing with you."

"I can't wait to see it, hellcat." I'm sure my dick will be hard the entire time. Of course, I don't tell her that. She doesn't need a reason to be even more crazy than she already is. Even if I do love it.

I head to the bathroom first, leaving Evan to wake up a little on her own. After my first morning with her, I understand now that she isn't someone who just wakes up and springs out of bed. You're just asking for the demon to charge with that.

I shower and trim my beard before exiting the bathroom, finding Evan in the exact same spot that I left her in.

Damn, if that isn't a view I want to see every day.

"Shower's all yours, babe."

"I didn't even bring any clothes," she grumbles. "I wasn't expecting to stay."

"What did you think was going to happen?"

"I planned on reaming your ass and storming out in the wake of my fury. What a waste of a glorious dramatic exit."

A deep laugh burst out of me. "I would have loved watching

your dramatic ass strut out of here, but unfortunately for you, I kissed it and made it better."

"Unfortunately." She smirks.

"We'll talk to the guys and set it straight that you're not in on this, and then we'll swing by your place so you can change."

"Or I can just go home and change while you talk to the guys."

"What about 'you're going to have a man on you at all times' did you not understand?"

"I didn't have one yesterday." And now she's throwing sass. I quickly glance down at my cock, commanding him to stay soft. I know firsthand how much he loves her tone right now.

"And that was before I got shot at," I throw back. We're in a stare-down now, but this time, she keeps her mouth shut. "What? No smart-ass response?"

"Not when it comes to the safety of lives. I'll allow it. This time." She shoots me a quick glare before climbing out of bed. "Blah. I need caffeine."

"Come on, little demon, let's get your fix before you burst out of the flames from Hell."

"Ha. Aren't you so funny? I don't know why you're joking about it. I think your kinky ass would like it. You could be my demon daddy," she says as she exits my room.

"I see everyone has kissed, fucked, and made up?" Cyrus smirks as he appears in the doorway two doors down from mine. "Could hear the show from all the way down here. Bravo, Prez." He claps.

"Oh my god!" Evan snaps. "I'm not loud, so it wasn't me you were hearing. It was probably Zeke. He's never with the same girl twice."

I cough, trying to cover my laugh. "I hate to break it to you, hellcat, but I'm sure the guys could hear you over the music in the living area. You're a screamer."

"I am not!" She screeches, and Cyrus bursts out laughing. Her cheeks are the color of my henley now.

I snake an arm around her waist, pulling her close before whispering, "Don't be embarrassed. It's hot as fuck knowing every single man in here knows that I'm the one owning that pussy."

That earned me the eye roll that I love so much.

"Down, boy," I say to my dick.

"What?" Evan asks, looking confused.

"Nothing." I smirk and swat her on the ass. "Let's go, babe."

Silence settles over the kitchen as Evan and I enter. Hash's murderous stare is aimed right at her. You could cut the tension in the room with a knife. Evan is so tense against me, and I can tell that she's preparing for a fight.

"What in the fuck is she still doing here?" Hash sneers, looking at Evan as if she should be six feet under. Scotch tenses at his tone, ready to step in to defend Evan. Even if I didn't fully believe Evan after last night, and I do, Scotch's reaction right now would have sealed the deal. He is ready to turn on a brother for his sister, whom he never even questioned was in the wrong. That speaks volumes to me.

"Easy," I say firmly as I hold my hand up. "Evan had nothing to do with what happened yesterday."

"What? She sucked your dick good enough for you to believe that?"

"Watch your fucking mouth," I growl. "I'm only going to say this once, and I shouldn't even have to say it, but you treat my girl with fucking respect."

"Yes, Prez," he grits out. I can see it in his eyes that he doesn't believe it yet.

Ink is still over by the fridge, eyes darting between everyone, unsure of what side to take. I know he has a soft spot for Evan. I'm hoping that wins over whatever shit Hash has been saying.

"Evan and I talked it out last night," I start to say before I'm cut off by Cyrus laughing his ass off again.

"If 'talk it out' now comes in the form of the headboard thumping and some hips rocking, then I'm all for finding a lady." The shithead winks.

Scotch slaps him on the back of the head before I get the chance. "Ow! What the fuck, man?"

"That's my fucking sister, you sick fuck."

"Doesn't mean I can't appreciate the lovely symphony I heard last night."

I don't even have to look at Evan to know her face is right back to that red shade. "Alright, alright. Do you fuckers want to hear what I have to say or not?" I wait a second for them to settle down before continuing. "Evan and I talked it out last night, and she didn't tip Storm off." I cut a look at Hash. "Even if she hated me, which she doesn't," I smirk at Cyrus and Scotch, "she wouldn't want anything to have happened to Scotch. My theory is that Storm is in debt to some serious people and ran based on that."

"That still doesn't answer how the Russians knew you were there." Scotch says.

No, it didn't. And that's the part I'm stuck on. "Unless this was all just an 'in the wrong place at the wrong time' situation. Maybe they saw Cyrus, Scotch, and me go in, and we just didn't see them. One of the guys could have recognized our cuts and received the orders to take us out."

"Mikhail has made his interest known in wanting our territory," Hash reluctantly says, looking lost in thought.

"Maybe he figured now was his time to make a move since you three had no backup. Surprise attacks make our world go round," Ink adds.

"That's not how that saying goes, you dumbass," Scotch says.

"It's how it goes in my world. You know I love to fuck shit up." The fucker smirks.

Shaking my head, trying not to laugh, I continue, "I think that's what happened. But I want to know what Storm is involved with. Anything new on the shipment?"

All the guys shake their heads, looking as pissed off as I feel. "Nope. It's weird as hell, too. No one seems to know anything. I'm not getting a good feeling about any of this, Prez," Trick says from his spot at the table.

"I have an idea," Evan speaks for the first time since entering the kitchen, making all eyes shoot to her like they forgot she was standing next to me. "What if I text Storm asking to meet up again? I could see what he's been up to and where he's been."

"Absolutely fucking not."

"And why not?" She sasses back, hands on her hips, making my dick semi-hard. Damn this woman.

"Wait a minute, Prez," Trick interjects. "She might be onto something. We could flush him out this way. He isn't going to come out for any of us alone."

Oh, hell no. "We are not using Evan as bait," I growl. "We don't know what he's on, who he's with or in debt to, and we don't know what he will do. He's clearly fuckin' spooked enough to be runnin' now. I'm not putting Evan in the middle of that."

Evan places her hand on the upper part of my arm, trying to calm me down, but it isn't working. "Think about it, Cain. I can tell him I have more ready for him to sell and have him meet me at my place. It wouldn't be suspicious because he has met me at my place a couple of times in the past."

"I'm not letting this nasty fucker breathe your air, Evan. This isn't up for negotiation."

That earns me a glare. Here we go. I can tell she's rearing up to give me sass.

"This isn't up for negotiation? Did you bump your head in the shower this morning? Because I know I didn't just hear you say something involving my life isn't up for negotiation, Cain." She snaps, narrowing her eyes at me.

"You tell him, girl!" Cyrus cheers her on, earning a glare from me. The fucker is supposed to be on my side.

"You're not helping." I glare at him before turning back to Evan. "I don't want you to get hurt. I'm just looking out for your safety."

"I don't mean to butt into this lover's quarrel, but I think Trick is onto something," Hash says.

"I think we need to use this to our advantage," Evan says. "Storm doesn't know anything about the layout of my property. Even if it was him scoping out the place the other night, he only had time to look around the barn."

"Where are you going with this?"

"I'll text him and ask him to meet me at my place, preferably near the barn. You guys can be waiting out of sight for him when he comes. Since someone cut the chain, you can use the trails that connect the property." She shoots me a look that tells me she still isn't pleased about that. "If he tries anything, you guys would be right there."

I hate that this plan has merit. "I don't like this."

"One of us can even be hiding in the barn, Prez. You know if he so much as touches a pretty hair on her head, we'll cut his finger off." Cyrus grins. His favorite pastime.

"Fine. But if anything happens, I'm killing the fucker."

**30**

Evan

“Hey.”

I turn around as I walk to my car and see Hash approaching me, looking sheepish.

“Hey. Everything okay?” I ask, trying not to let on how wary I am of him now.

“Yeah. Ah... I mean, not really.” He shoves his hands in his pocket and looks around at everything but me. “I wanted to apologize for how I treated you yesterday. And this morning. I shouldn’t have said what I said.”

“It’s okay, Hash. Water under the bridge.” I smile.

“No, it’s not okay. I shouldn’t have jumped to conclusions like that. I was just trying to look out for Prez and the club’s best interest. It’s not an excuse, but I just wanted to tell you I’m sorry.”

“Don’t ever apologize for defending Cain or your club. You’re all family, and that’s what family does. I love that you guys have found that. Loyalty is so hard to find these days.”

“Are you really trying to sneak out of here without a man on you? Was I talking to a wall last night?" We both whip around to see a very unhappy Cain prowling toward us.

"Damn," I mumble to myself.

Hash snorts. "Sorry, babe. You knew you weren't going to get out of here like that."

Rolling my eyes, I say, "Yeah, yeah, yeah. A girl can dream, though."

Cain's eyes are moving between Hash and me, trying to feel out the situation.

"We're all good, Prez. I'll be seeing you around, Evan." Hash nods before heading back into the club, leaving me out here with Mr. Grumpy Pants.

I open my mouth to tell him I'll be fine at home by myself, but he beats me to it. "I sent Levi over to your house. He should already be there, waiting for you."

"I didn't see him leave," I say while looking around.

"You wouldn't. I sent him along the trails. We don't know if Storm dropped your name and where you live to anyone, and I don't want him being seen."

"And you don't think this is all a bit much? I mean, I haven't even texted Storm yet."

"No. I'll see you tonight." He frames my face with his hands and places a kiss on my lips. This one is different from all the others. It's not rushed or rough from being caught up in the heat of the moment. This one is more soothing, like he knows how deep down I'm starting to freak the fuck out. Like he's trying to reassure me that everything will be okay because he's going to make sure of it. And damn if that doesn't make my cold heart flutter. "Be safe," he says as he pulls away before heading back into the clubhouse without a backward glance.

I can't help but smile at the thought that someone actually cares as I get into my car.

Just as Cain said, Levi was waiting for me on my back deck, and as much as I hate having a man on me, I'm glad it's Levi.

I've grown to like him being around. For being so young, he seems so mature for his age. But then again, aren't all of us who have gone through shit at such a young age?

"I didn't keep you waiting long, did I?" I ask as I climb out of my car.

"No ma'am. Just got here before you did. I don't think Hades is a fan, though," he says while looking at the house just as Hades starts barking again.

"Okay, first, never call me ma'am again. I'm 28, not 60." I laugh. "And second, he just needs to go out."

I barely have the door open an inch before Hades sticks his nose in the open space and yanks it open himself. He pays no mind to Levi as he runs around the yard and does his business.

"See? I think he's getting used to you. I know he's scary-looking, but he would never hurt you—unless I tell him to." I smirk before calling Hades to come and head inside. "Make yourself comfortable. I need to shower."

"Sounds good, Evan," Levi says as he settles on the couch. Hades hops up next to him, swatting him with his paw and demanding pets. "We'll be right here."

I RELEASE a long sigh as I climb under the hot spray. I didn't realize how much tension I was carrying around in my shoulders until it started melting away. These past few weeks have been extremely overwhelming.

And that's an understatement.

I went from living a calm and peaceful life to complete chaos with a guy who seems to have just barged his way in. As much as I like the life I have created, I didn't realize something was missing until Cain.

Growing up in foster homes made developing real connections with people hard. Everyone was out for themselves, and honestly, what's the point when you know you'll never see them again? I'm lucky that I met Zeke. I don't think I would have survived all of that without him. I envy the family he's found in the club. Even as an outsider, they make you feel like you're one of them. The loyalty is nothing like I've ever seen. Yeah, Zeke and I are loyal to each other, but in my lifetime, I've learned the larger the group, the more fake it is. Everyone will act like they're so close, but really, they're all secretly broken off into pairs, talking shit about the first person they can, trying to get ahead in any way possible.

Shaking away my spiraling thoughts, I lean my head back as more tension washes away as the hot water hits my hair. I stay like that until the water runs cold. I turn off the water and reach for my towel before pausing.

What is that pounding noise? Is it coming from my house?

I freeze outside of the bathroom door, trying to listen. It sounds like it's coming from the living room. "Goddamnit, Levi. I told you to just chill out," I grumble as I rush to find clothes and quickly brush my hair. "I can't even shower for 30 minutes in peace without something going on."

Before I know it, I'm rushing down the stairs, ready to rip him a new asshole for interrupting my me-time. "Levi! What in the hell are you doing? When I told you to make yourself at home, I didn't me—" I come to a halt in the living room as I take in the scene in front of me.

I can't stop staring at Cain, who currently has a tool belt slung around his waist. He traded his Henley for a tight white tee that shows every thick ripple and dent. My eyes are glued to the way it clings to his biceps, the way that tendons are slightly showing and flexing—the kind every hot guy on the planet has.

Who knew a tool belt could be so sexy?

"Hey, babe," Hash says, snapping me out of my trance as he walks by me with chunks of cut-up drywall in his arms and a tool belt around his waist.

Cain and Trick are lining up the new pieces, getting ready to screw them in.

"What are you doing?" I breathe out, still in shock.

"What the fuck does it look like, hellcat? We're fixing your walls," Cain responds, still not looking my way.

What a way with words he has.

"I see that, but why? You guys don't need to do this. This is way too much."

"Just accept it. Your place got trashed because of the club, and we're fixing it."

"The store had a few different shades, so I just got them all so we didn't need to go back." I turn to the back door to see Zeke coming in with six different gallons of paint.

And there I stood, dumbstruck. I hadn't been upstairs for forty-five minutes, and they were already here working on my house.

"You good?" Zeke asks while setting the gallons of paint down on the floor.

"How did you know what color to get?"

"Cain said teal. And knowing you, I went a little darker with it." He pauses as he takes in my stunned face. "Is this not the color you wanted?"

"No, no... It's good. Darker is good. Perfect actually. Thank you." I swallow down the lump that's forming in my throat.

I thought Cain was just asking questions the other night, so I didn't start spiraling with everything that had happened. As a distraction. You know, to keep it from being awkward. What guy wants to deal with a girl freaking out?

I didn't think he had actually listened.

And I definitely didn't think he would remember any of it.

I cough, trying to recover from the emotions swelling in my chest. "You can just leave it there, Zeke. I'll paint the living room this week sometime when all of this has blown over."

"No way, babe. We'll have this taken care of." Hash winks as he walks back inside, heading toward Cain and Trick.

"If you guys insist, then I'm paying you back for all the supplies, and I'm paying you hourly for working."

That earned me a growl from Cain. "Don't fucking insult me, babe."

I open my mouth to tell him that I'm not insulting him, that it's just all too much, but Zeke cuts me off, "Just accept the help, Evan. I know you're not used to it, and that's partly my fault for not bringing you into the fold sooner, but this is what family does," he says lowly so only I can hear. "And now that you and Prez are... whatever you and Prez are, it makes this even more of a priority. So just go outside and do whatever you need in the barn. Levi will be with you."

I nod my head as I take out some burgers for tonight before I head outside. If they're going to be working on my house without letting me pay them, the least I can do is feed them. Being in the barn will be good. There's just something about being around my plants that brings me a sense of peace.

And I'd like some peace and quiet while I text Storm.

**31**

Evan

Hades is already outside, sunbathing in his natural element. Dogs don't realize how easy they have it. No responsibilities. No bills. No one breaking into their house.

"Are you okay watching him? I'm going to work in the barn for a little bit." I ask Levi, who is lounging on the back deck.

I thought I would feel overwhelmed by having my house overtaken by a bunch of broody bikers, but if I'm being honest, I love it. I've been waiting for this feeling all my life—the feeling of having someone there whenever you need them. Yeah, I've always had Zeke, but it's not the same. I never wanted to bother him more than I had to. He would kill me for thinking that.

I guess I've just been waiting for the feeling of family. And for the first time, I'm just hoping it lasts because I know first-hand that good things never last.

"Yeah, we're good, babe. Just gonna chill right here. Holler if you need me," Levi says as he kicks his feet up on the little black cast-iron outdoor table that I found at an estate sale.

"Will do." I wave as I head into the barn.

Deciding it's best to get the Storm situation over with, I shoot him off a text.

> Me: Hey, I've got some stuff for you.

There. That doesn't sound suspicious, right? I'm one hundred percent overthinking this. I say this to him all the time. It's going to be fine.

I jump as my phone vibrates in my pocket. "Get a grip," I mumble as I pull it out. I open the lock screen at lightning speed.

> Storm: Yeah? Tell me when I can get it.

> Me: Tomorrow? At my place.

> Storm: K. Will that guy be with you?

I freeze. Just staring down at my phone.

He's never asked that before, and Zeke is almost always with me. So why is he asking now?

> Me: Maybe. I'm not sure. Is that a problem?

Good. That's good. There's no way he's onto me.

> Storm: Yeah. I don't want anyone I don't know in my business.

Since when was that an issue? We've had this arrangement for years, and now he doesn't want someone else in his business?

I hate that Cain's right. Something is up with Storm.

> Me: Alright, I get it. I'll make sure that it's just me here.

He doesn't make me wait for a response.

> Storm: Noon work?

> Me: Yup. See you then.

I let out a sigh of relief as I pocket my phone. I'm glad that's over with. The thought of being alone with him makes my skin crawl. It never used to be like this. I mean, yeah, I always thought he was a little scummy, but he was what you would expect from your basic line cook drug dealer. He could clean up if he wanted to, but for some reason, he likes looking like he showers once a week.

TIME FLIES by as I work in the barn, and before I know it, it's almost 5. I put everything away before heading up to the house, checking around for Levi and Hades as I head in, but they aren't outside anymore. As I step onto the back deck, I hear rock music playing throughout the house, and I smile. Is this what home feels like?

"Hope you don't mind we helped ourselves to your booze," Cain says as I step inside. He's at my side by the next time I blink, nabbing me around the waist and pulling me in for what I thought was going to be a quick kiss.

Instead, he's nipping at my bottom lip, making me gasp in surprise before his tongue slips inside my mouth, roughly tangling with mine. I get lost in the kiss. My body has a mind of its own as my arms wrap around his neck, pulling him closer. I can feel every hard inch brushing against my body, making my nipples peak into hard points, begging to be played with. It isn't until I hear the catcalls around us that I remember we aren't alone. Cain chuckles against my mouth as he feels me tense against him.

"You can greet me like that anytime, hellcat," he says against my lips before pulling away and smiling down at me.

I can feel how red my cheeks are as I look around at all the guys scattered across my kitchen and dining area.

"I'm ready for ya, darlin'." Ink smirks from the bar stool he's perched on, arms wide open in waiting.

"Ready for what?" I ask while furrowing my brow.

"My lovin'. It'll be sweeter than what Prez just gave ya."

I don't even get a chance to respond before Cain smacks Ink on the back of the head.

With a roll of my eyes, I ask, "Are you guys hungry?"

I was answered with a bunch of grunts, which I assume means yes in biker talk. "Alright, I'm going to make some burgers. Does that sound okay?"

"Babe, you don't need to feed us. We can just go to DD's."

"Absolutely not. If I can't pay you in money, then I'm going to pay you in food."

"A woman after my own heart," Ink declares while dramatically throwing his hand over his chest where his heart is.

"Get your own girl," Cain growls, placing a hand on my lower back, squeezing the side of my hip in a possessive move.

"Alright, alright. I get it, Prez. Evan is yours," Ink gives in.

Oh. "We're just see—" I start before Cain cuts me off.

"You want to see your new living room?"

"You finished?" You can hear the excitement in my voice. I've been spending so much time finishing my kitchen that I didn't realize how much the unfinished living room was bringing down my mood. It made the house feel so much less homey. Wait a second... "How did you know what shade of teal to go with? I never said which one I liked before I left."

Cain chuckles. "I'm going to pretend not to be insulted that you think I don't know by now that you would have picked the darkest shade. It fits my moody little hellcat the best."

He sounds so proud of himself as he leads me into the living room and holy shit. My jaw drops. The color is everything I've been dreaming of. I can see myself putting the finishing touches on and everything flowing into the perfect moody vibe. The black-and-white checkered rug I've had my eye on will look so amazing in here.

"Thank you," I whisper, the stupid tears brimming in my eyes again. "I don't know how I'll ever repay you, but thank you."

"No need to thank me, babe. If we go in the direction I think we're goin', this will eventually be my place, too. Can't only have my woman's sweat put into it." He places a kiss on my forehead before heading back into the kitchen where the guys are.

I'm frozen in my spot because he really just dropped that bomb on me and walked away like he didn't just rock my world. He says so much and so little at the same time. Cain isn't the type for grand romantic gestures. I'm starting to wonder if taking care of me is his love language.

And you know what?

A girl could get used to that.

**32**

**Cain**

The expression on Evan's face when she saw the living room was completely painted will forever be engraved in my brain. I feel something that I've never felt before. I feel full of pride. And yeah, I've felt this feeling with the club but never with a woman. This brought a whole new meaning to the word. It makes me feel like maybe I am enough for her.

I wish I could take one hundred percent of the credit, but I can't. Right after Evan left the clubhouse, Hash stopped me on my way in and said he wanted to take care of the damage that was done as a way to make it up to her for being a jackass.

And I was all for that.

We have enough shit going on to worry about that I don't want to have to worry about my girl and a brother being at odds.

I freaked her out when I said that if we go the distance, I'll be living here, too. In all honesty, it just kind of slipped out. She hasn't said shit when I call her mine in front of the club. I'm taking that as a good sign.

Once we put up the new drywall and started painting, I had a lot of time to think. It freaked me out at first that I could picture myself fitting right in here, watching the game on the couch and watching Evan make us dinner at the island.

Fuck, I already feel at home.

Evan just has that way about her.

"I'm hungry, woman!" Cyrus yells to Evan from his seat, snapping her back into reality.

"Sorry! I was just admiring your handiwork." She winked at him as she walked into the kitchen and took out the burger to make patties.

"You got a grill, babe?"

"Ah... no. I can cook and bake, but I can't grill." She lets out that laugh that I'll never get tired of hearing. "I tried to grill turkey burgers once, and as soon as I put the meat on the grill, the burger just fell through the slats. That was the end of my grilling career." Good thing she'll never need to learn now that I'm here.

"I texted Storm while I was outside."

All the guys stopped talking as soon as they heard the fucker's name.

"And?" How do you just drop that out of the blue and not say anything more about it?

"He was... weird. I asked him if he wanted to meet up here, and he was cool with it," she says while setting the last burger in the pan to cook, clearly avoiding telling me the part about why she thought he was being fucking weird.

All the guys' eyes are narrowed on her, picking up the same thing I did.

"How was he weird?"

"He basically said he doesn't want Zek— I mean Scotch."

She shoots Scotch a sorry look. I know it's been hard on her to catch on to his road name.

"Babe, as long as it's just us, you can call him whatever the fuck you want. In front of outsiders, it's Scotch, alright?"

Evan nods her head before continuing. "Right. He said he no longer wants Zeke with me whenever we meet up. He said that he doesn't want someone he doesn't know in his business." She pauses as her brow furrows. "Which I get, but... it's never been an issue before. It's not like Zeke tries to pry into his life. He doesn't even talk to him."

I share a look with the guys that they know all too well.

I have a bad feeling shit is going to hit the fan.

"Does he know your name?" I ask Scotch.

"Nah, I doubt it. I think I've maybe said ten words to this dude over the span of a few years. I always just hang back and let Evan do her thing."

"Does he know that you're part of the club?"

"It's possible. I never took my cut off when meeting up with him, but I was also never close enough for him to confirm whether I was part of one or not."

There's only one explanation then. "Someone has tipped him off."

"It wasn't me." Evan snaps before anyone else can get a word in. "I barely knew anything about you guys until Zeke said he needed help."

"We know it wasn't you, babe," Hash says, relaxing Evan's shoulders. You can tell she's still thinking the guys think she has something to do with all of this.

"Someone had to have tipped him off. Otherwise, why all of a sudden, after years of meet-ups, would he be uncomfortable?" Ink asks.

And isn't that the million-dollar question? Unless... "What if he wants to get Evan alone, and this actually has nothing to do with us? That would explain why someone was checking out her place."

"Doesn't explain the threat, though," Trick adds.

"Fuck." I lean my elbows on the counter on the island and scrub my hands over my face. None of this makes any fucking sense.

"Well, you guys will have your chance to get some answers because I told him Zeke wouldn't be there, and he agreed to come tomorrow," Evan says with her back to me as she plates up the burgers, giving me the perfect view of her ass that I wish I was bending over-the-counter right now.

"I don't like the thought of you being alone with him," I growl.

"Down boy. We talked about this earlier. We'll be waiting for him," Scotch says with a glint in his eye.

I know that glint. I've seen it a million times. It's why he's my head enforcer. This bastard will be begging for mercy by the time we're done with him.

**33**

Evan

I'm cleaning up the kitchen as the guys say their goodbyes. One by one, they file out the back door. And by goodbyes, I mean a couple of nods as a thanks for dinner while they slap Cain on the shoulder in the way all guys do. No one knows why they do it. It's like it's ingrained in their DNA or something. Ink let me know that if Cain wasn't keeping me satisfied, I knew where to find him, earning him yet another smack on the back of the head. I'm really growing to love that guy.

It isn't long before I hear all of their bikes fire up and fade away in the opposite direction of the road. If they continue to want to use the trails to get here, I will need to clean them up and make them a little wider. It would be nice if I could turn them into a one-lane dirt road.

I'm wiping off the counter when I hear the door shut, and I look over to see Cain sauntering in, bag in hand.

"Did you, the king of no strings attached, pack an overnight bag?" I tease.

"There were only no strings attached because I was holding out for a rack like yours." He winks as he presses his body up against my back, wrapping his arms around me and pulling me in tight before moving my hair to the side and placing a light kiss on the spot on my neck that he knows drives me wild. A shiver runs through me as I feel his breath whisper across my skin, leaving goosebumps.

"I let Hades out for you," he says softly against my neck. "I know this has all been a lot for you, not being used to this life and all. What would you be doing to relax if I wasn't here?" I lean my head more to the left so he has better access. He doesn't even need to do anything else. Just the feel of his beard tickling my skin makes my lower belly flutter.

Some might think having a man with two very different sides is weird. This isn't me considering him mine. I'm not fully there yet, but I love having a prickly, broody man to the outside world. I love that I'm the only one that gets his soft and sweet.

"Evan?" Cain asks after I haven't responded.

"What?" I whisper.

He chuckles lightly against my neck, giving my hips a light squeeze. "What would you be doing to relax if I wasn't here?"

"Um... probably taking a bath," I finally answer.

"Then that's what you'll do. Anything special about it?" he asks while stepping back, making me pout from the lost contact.

"You'll get your cuddles, hellcat. I wouldn't want to wake the demon." He winks before taking off upstairs, not giving me the chance to respond. I finished up in the kitchen before following behind him.

I stop dead when I see what Cain is holding in his hand, just staring at it like he didn't even know such a thing existed. I don't even know what to say. I can feel my face growing warmer with every passing second.

"I was looking for some bubble bath for you when I found

this," Cain snickers as he turns to face me. I can tell he's trying not to laugh. The fucker.

"You mean a bath bomb?" I ask innocently.

"It's a dick, Evan. You have a bath bomb shaped like a dick."

"They're organic and made with essential oils. My skin feels amazing afterward." Don't say it. Please don't say it.

"I got the real thing that will get the job done." He said it.

"Jobs?"

"Job one is making you come so hard around my cock that you can't walk for a week. Job two is coming all over those fucking tits and massaging it in, making your skin softer than this purple glitter dick will."

Oh my fucking god.

Is he jealous of a bath bomb? My mind is telling me that's a fucking weird thing to be jealous of, but my inner walls just let out a little spasm at the thought. If you had told me this was in my future, I would have told you that you were high.

"Jealous of your competition?" I taunt.

"Absolutely fucking not. Clothes off, babe." Bossy Cain is back as he tosses the dick in the water.

"So bossy." I smirk while pulling my shirt over my head. I don't miss the way Cain's eyes flare as they immediately go to my tits. "See something you like?"

He growls while eating up the space between us. His hand reaches around my back and unhooks my black bra. "I see a lot of something that I like." His thumb swipes over one of my nipples, making it harden under his touch. "But this, right now, isn't about that. Now, don't make me ask again, hellcat. Take off your clothes and get in the fucking tub."

"Are you joining me?"

"Do you want me to?"

I duck my head, trying to hide the flush in my cheeks from the intimacy. "Yeah."

"Don't do that," Cain says, coming up behind me where I'm standing at the foot of the tub.

"Don't do what?" My brow furrows.

"Hide from me. If we're doing this, then we're fucking doing it, Evangeline. I want all of it. The good, the bad, and the ugly. Everything you're willing to give and everything you're not."

"I want that too," I whisper, trying to contain yet another set of tears trying to stream free. If you had asked me a month ago if I was a crier, I would have laughed in your face. But Cain is making me do something that no one has done in a long time —something that I thought I had tucked away, sealed in a box, and put a padlock on.

He's making me *feel*.

"Then get in the tub, baby," Cain says just as softly before he steps in and settles his back against the end of the tub.

I lift my leg up, sticking a toe in first to test the water; the fizzy, soft bubbles feel so calm against my skin. I can't have it scalding, but I also can't have it lukewarm. It just ends up feeling cold. He made it the perfect temperature for someone who has never drawn a bath.

Climbing the rest of the way in, I lower myself into Cain's lap. His arms instantly go around me, pulling my back flush against his chest. I lean my head back, resting it on his broad shoulder. I let out a long, soft sigh. "This is nice. Thank you."

"No need to thank me, babe. If you're relaxed, then I'm relaxed," he says as he starts to massage my neck, working his way over my shoulders.

I let out a soft moan as I roll my neck around, trying to give him better access. This is all so new for me—bathing with a man and sex not being the end goal. Now that I think about it, I've never bathed with a man, especially not with a penis-shaped bath bomb. This is all about the connection. The emotional intimacy. The feeling of each other.

"Feeling better?"

"Yeah, I am." I run my hands down his hard, muscular thighs, massaging as I go.

"Good." He rumbles as his thighs flex under my hands. "I want to know about you and Scotch."

I try not to tense at the question but fail miserably. "What do you want to know? Or, I guess, how much do you know?" I knew this was coming. He deserves to know my past. I guess in this moment, I just feel so raw and exposed. Like he can see right into my soul.

"I know you and him met in a foster home, but beyond that, he hasn't really said much. I don't want to dig if you're not willing, so if you're not ready to share that with me, then we'll wait to cross that bridge."

"I'm ready to share." I'm feeling very mellow right now. If he asked for anything at this moment, I would probably do it.

He gives me a reassuring squeeze on the back of my neck before I continue. "I never knew my parents. Well, I never knew my dad. My mom was an addict who didn't want to give it up, so she gave me up instead. I was so young when it happened. It seems like a lifetime ago. I honestly barely remember her."

"I'm sorry you had to go through that, baby," Cain says as he lightly kisses the top of my head. "How old were you?"

"I was almost 7, and please don't be sorry. Some people just don't want to be parents, and that's okay. That part doesn't really bother me anymore. I mean, do I wish I had a mom? Yeah. But as fucked up as this is to say, I think my life would have been way worse if she would have kept me. And I wouldn't have met Zeke."

"I'm glad you found him, babe." Cain pauses. "I hate to admit this, but at first, I was jealous of the relationship the two of you had. That's why I barged into his room that night at the clubhouse. I thought something was going on."

Of course, that's what he thought. I can't tell you how many times this has happened with the girls Zeke dated. They always thought I was fucking him on the side. "No." I let out a light laugh. "It's cute that you were jealous, though."

"I wasn't that jealous," he grumbles, as if he's annoyed he even was in the first place.

I smirk to myself. "Alright, Mr. No Strings Attached. You weren't jealous." I give his thigh a squeeze. "Zeke is the closest thing I have to a brother. I never have or will ever think of him in a sexual way. The thought makes me want to vomit. I saw his bare ass once when I walked in on him and a girl in the living room. Every time I closed my eyes, all I saw was his zitty ass. It scarred me for life." I shudder at the thought.

Cain lets out a laugh before he places a kiss on my neck, letting me know that he heard me.

"We met when I was in my fifth foster home." I pause as Cain tenses beneath me. "It's okay, babe. Some kids just don't ever get adopted, and I was one of them. We just have to ride out the storm."

"I hate that you had to ride that out by yourself."

"I wasn't by myself, though. Well, for a few years, I wasn't. As I said, I met Zeke in my fifth and last foster home when I was 12 and he was 16. There were four other kids in the same home besides us. Richard and Mary were your stereotypical 'I'm doing this for the paycheck and not to better a kid's life' type. We didn't exactly starve, but we went to bed hungry many nights. They did the bare minimum for us." I let out a light laugh as I reminisce, bringing up old memories. "I remember Zeke had just gotten his first job at this little deli down the street from us. I think the owner must have known what was happening in the house because after every shift Zeke worked, he let him take home a sandwich for free. Zeke always hid it under his shirt so Richard didn't find out, and he would split it with me."

"Why do I get the feeling Richard was a massive dick?"

God. Only this man would be able to make me laugh while I'm trying to tell him about my fucked-up childhood. "Because he was. Richard was heavy-handed with the bottle, and when he got closer to the bottom of said bottle, he became a little... handsy."

Cain's whole body is clenched tight as he grits out through clenched teeth, "You better not say what the fuck I think you're about to say."

"He didn't rape me."

"Then what the fuck, Evan?"

"It started out as small sexual comments here and there. He told me he liked how my shorts made my legs look long or how he could tell my boobs were growing," I say with a wince. "Zeke was always there to tell him what a sick fuck he was being." I've tried to tell myself over the years that it wasn't that bad, but therapy really opened my eyes. Because it was that bad. I was just trying to downplay it in my head to cope. I honestly don't think that I would have made it through without him.

I can feel Cain opening his mouth against my neck, ready to say something, but I cut him off. "Things didn't get really bad until I was almost 15."

"What happened?" It sounded like it pained Cain to get those words out.

"It was the first night that Zeke was gone. He had moved out that day. I think that's what gave Richard the courage. There was no one there who would stop him. At this point, it was only me and another younger girl left in the house. They made us leave when we turned 18. It didn't matter if you were still in school or not. Isn't that fucked up?" I turn to look at him.

His face is set in hard lines as if he's bracing for the worst. "Yeah. That's fucked, babe."

"Anyway, that night, he had been drinking. When I came home from seeing Zeke's new apartment in Ravenna Heights, he was trashed. I remember running past him when he tried to get up from his chair to follow me, but he was so fucked up he couldn't stand. Him saying, " My time is coming' is engraved in my brain."

"Where was Mary during all of this?"

"She worked the night shift at the hospital. We honestly barely saw her. If she wasn't working, she was sleeping the day away."

"Gotta keep the lights on."

"Something like that," I say, my tone sounding dead even to my own ears.

"Hey." He rubs my arm. "We don't need to continue. You can tell me whenever you feel ready."

"No. I need to tell you now. I want to tell you now."

Cain places another comforting kiss on my neck, making me relax against his chest.

"Anyway, I made it to my room and locked the door. It was just one of those flimsy locks on the door handle. Anyone could kick it in. I made the mistake of thinking he was down for the count. Whenever he got that drunk, he would be passed out for the rest of the night. Well, that night, I was wrong. So, so wrong." I pause to take his arm and wrap it around me. The bathwater is still warm, but a chill has settled over me. "I was woken up from my sleep by him trying to kick my door in. I froze Cain. I fucking froze. And all I could do was watch it get kicked in. It was like my whole flight response just blanked."

"It's not your fault, Evan. That's a natural response," Cain reassured me.

"I know. Looking back, I don't even know what I would have done. I've replayed this scene over and over in my head about what I would have done differently, and I come up blank. Sorry, I keep getting sidetracked." I shake my head, trying to recenter myself. "By the time I unfroze, Richard had already had me pinned to my bed with my arms above my head. I tried to get my arms out of his hold, but he was so much stronger than me..."

Cain gives me another reassuring squeeze that I needed to continue. "I remember kicking him as hard as I could repeatedly, but it didn't even seem to faze him. It wasn't until his hands were trying to pull down my pajama bottoms to... you know."

"Yeah. I fucking know," Cain clenched out. If I thought his body was wound tight before, it's even worse now.

"It never happened, though," I say softly as I squeeze his thigh in what I hope is a reassuring gesture. Zeke came charging in and pulled him off me before beating the shit out of him. He was in the hospital for a week because of what Zeke did. That was the last time I saw him."

"Good. He deserves to be six feet under," Cain growls. "Why did Zeke come back? I mean, I'm so glad he did, hellcat. He saved you, and I owe him for that, but it doesn't make sense because you said he had just moved out."

"Remember how I said it was just me and one other younger girl in the house? She heard Richard kicking my door in and called him." He didn't even hesitate to come that night. This is part of why I agreed to help Zeke and the club. Even this isn't enough to repay him for what he stopped.

"Thank you for telling me all of this, hellcat. I know it wasn't easy." Cain gently grabs the edge of my jaw before turning my face toward him, placing the most intimate kiss I have ever experienced on my lips. There was no sexual yearning behind it. It was all about the connection we had just shared. Maybe it's because I'm feeling so raw. So exposed. I've never told that story to anyone except my therapist and Zeke. And he was there for half of it.

"Wait," Cain started while pulling away. "You said that was your last foster home, but you were only what? 15? Please tell me you didn't stay after that."

"I didn't stay." The tension immediately left his body upon me saying that. It never occurred to me that he thought my story was about to get worse. "Zeke packed my stuff and took me to his place that night. And that's where I stayed."

"So he adopted you?"

"Not in the legal sense. It was kind of an unspoken agreement between us and Richard and Mary that if no one talked about what happened that night, they wouldn't let the state know that I wasn't living with them. Plus, they were still getting their checks, so it didn't matter. We used that as leverage."

I can feel him nodding against my head. "What about the other girl? Did she stay?"

"No. Her mom ended up winning custody back, so I like to think that her life turned around."

"How did you stay at Scotch's place when he was away in the Army?"

I let out a nervous laugh. I know he's an outlaw biker, but I still don't want to be judged. "He, uh... he still kept the place and paid the rent and all the bills. He even put money into my account for food and whatever random stuff I needed. I just stayed there on my own. I mean, I was already in high school at this point."

"So you raised yourself?" His voice has that edge again.

"Calm down, babe," I say as I rub his thigh for some comfort. "It wasn't like that. Zeke didn't even need to take me in like he did. I told him to go. I didn't want to be the reason he put his life on hold. We both had it rough growing up. I wanted him to go find his happiness."

"I have a newfound respect for Scotch, and I feel like I owe him my life," Cain says before pausing. "So, you two really are just like brother and sister."

It wasn't a question. It was like mine and Zeke's relationship finally clicked for him. I feel so relieved that he finally gets it. I don't even think I noticed how much it was bothering me that it was in the back of his mind that Zeke and I had something going on the side. Cain taps my thigh, breaking me from my thoughts. "Let's get out of this. The water is cold now, and I'm fucking tired."

The funny thing is I didn't even notice the water was cold because, for once in my life, I finally felt warm.

**34**

**Cain**

I don't know what I expected her to tell me, but it wasn't that. I never want to hear my girl tell me she was assaulted ever again. I thought the rage I felt when I found out someone had broken into her place was bad, but that doesn't even come close to what I feel right now. She doesn't need to know this, but Scotch will be giving me that sick fuck's address. There's only one place in this world for child molesters, and that's six feet under.

I watch as Evan climbs out of the bath before I wrap one of her big fluffy black towels around her—the kind I'm sure are in all the fancy hotels.

I love that she's creating her own little slice of paradise. She might be a little slower to finish the house, but no corners will be cut. The more I'm around her, the more I want a spot in that little slice of paradise. I think that's why I jumped on Hash wanting to fix the drywall. I want a part in creating that.

It's just a bonus that she's been living next door to me this entire time. Hell, I should have come over and asked for a cup of sugar months ago. I could have had this sweet piece in my life already. Dick bombs and all.

"What are you over there smirking about?" Evan asks while looking at me like I'm a little crazy as she dries herself off before slipping on an oversized tee that hits mid-thigh. She would look sexy as fuck in my tee. I need to remember to bring some over.

"Nothing, hellcat." I smile softly at her. "Do you need to do anything else, or are you ready for bed?"

"I'm ready for bed," she says before pulling the fluffy teal duvet back. If the guys could see me sleeping in this bed, they would be laughing their asses off. I'd never hear the end of it. "You ready for the meeting tomorrow?"

I knew this was bothering her. "Yeah." I tuck my arm around her and pull her flush against my side, tucking her in. "I texted Hash to tell the guys we're having church first thing in the morning. I want to go over the game plan with them. Figure out where I want everyone to be."

"That will be good." She lets out the cutest fucking yawn before nestling into my chest. "I just hope Storm doesn't do anything stupid."

"Me either, babe. But we'll be ready if he does. I promise you that." Her breathing has evened out, and I can tell she didn't hear a word I said.

There's nothing else I can do for the night, so I hug my girl a little tighter and pass out along with her.

## 35

Cain

"Someone looks like they had a fun night." Cyrus smirks. "I don't think I've ever seen a smile on your ugly mug."

"Fuck off, " I say with no real meaning behind it.

Because he's right. Everyone's on edge with the shit that's been going on, but there's just something about being woken up with a warm mouth around your cock, which then turned into me eating her pussy for breakfast before I had to head out. A guy could get used to being woken up that way.

"Is everyone here? We need to go over the plan in case shit goes south."

Cyrus' face instantly turns serious. "Yeah, they're filing in now."

I nod before heading in. Time to get this show on the road.

I don't even have to get the guys to quiet down. They know what today is. Every one of them wants a piece of this guy. They may not have liked Evan at first, but that changed after last night. She has every single one of them wrapped around her finger.

"Alright," I command the attention that's already on me. "We all know today is the day we finally meet Storm." Every single brother has that glint in their eye — the glint that tells me they're ready to fuck some shit up.

"What's the plan?" Hash asks eagerly.

"My plan is to let him get settled with Evan long enough so that he doesn't think anything's going on. With him already paranoid about Scotch, I don't want to add to it and spook him." The guys all nod in agreement to what I'm saying.

I lean back in my chair, making eye contact with each one. "With that being said, I want someone to always have eyes on her." Pointing to Evan, I wait for another nod of confirmation before continuing. "I want Trick and Ink hiding in the barn in case he makes her go inside. I'm going to make sure she has his shit outside waiting for him, but you never know. The rest of us will be in the woods. I want my eyes on her and Scotch's eyes on him. He's the only one of us who's met him, and I want him to pick up on any weird body language."

"Sounds good, Prez. No one's staying back at the club-house?" Trick asks. We never leave our place unattended. There are too many power-hungry, greedy bastards around here wanting a slice of what we've built from the ground up.

"I'm going to have the prospects stay back."

"What time is he coming?" Scotch asks, tone out for blood.

"Noon. Our bikes can stay on the trail. He won't see them unless he goes behind the barn, and well, if he feels the need to do that, we're just going to have to show him what happens when you snoop around somewhere that you don't fucking belong."

Cyrus cracks his knuckles. "Let's fucking go!"

All the guys cheer as they file out, and I can't help but laugh. Such a bunch of blood-thirsty bastards.

I wouldn't have it any other way, though.

## 36

Evan

I have the nervous shits.

You know, the ones you get when you haven't even eaten anything that day, but the anticipation is too much for your body to take?

Yeah, that's where I'm at.

No amount of Imodium is going to help me this time.

The guys are all in their positions, waiting for Storm to arrive. My head shoots up as I hear a car with a loud muffler turning into my driveway. He's here, and I have a feeling shit is about to get real. "Right on time," I mumble, looking down at my watch.

Cain assured me that if he so much as lays a finger on me, they'll be on him before I can even blink. And I believe him. I've seen Zeke in action, and that was still when he was a scrawny teenager. I couldn't even imagine what it would be like to have all of them on someone now. It honestly would be hot as fuck to see all of that muscle pounding someone you now hate into the ground. God, what is wrong with me? It can't be normal to think that's hot.

"Hey," Storm calls as he opens his creaky car door but doesn't get out. He isn't meeting my eyes. He's too busy scanning the yard, just like he did the day I was at his house. But what is scanning for? I know he can't see the guys.

"Hey," I reply in what I hope sounds like my normal voice, not moving from my spot. "Are you okay?"

"Of course I'm okay. Why do you keep asking me that?" He finally climbs out of his car, his head searching in every direction. Maybe I keep asking because you're acting sketchy as fuck and paranoid as hell. Not a good combination to have. I can't even say hey without him trying to jump out of his skin.

"I don't know. You just seem off and haven't gotten out of the car." I shrug, trying to keep the tension out of my voice.

"Your man isn't here, right?" he asks while walking toward me.

My body is already wound so tight that he doesn't even see me tense. I didn't realize he thought Zeke was my man. "No. It's just you and me. This is the stuff I have for you." I motion toward the product at my feet.

He looks down at it before looking back up at me, meeting my eyes for the first time since he arrived. "Cut the shit, Evan. I know you've been holding out on me. I know there's more shit in there, and I want my fucking cut," he demands.

Um... what?

"Excuse me? You don't know what you're talking about. There isn't anything more in there. I give you what I have." I cross my arms across my chest, matching his glare.

"Look, bitch. I've been playing nice with this whole arrangement for years. I'm not about to be your errand bitch anymore. This business isn't a place for a little fucking girl. Don't make me force my way in. I'm trying to do this civilly." His face is inches from mine, and I'm trying not to freak out, but the freak out is starting to win.

"Civilly? Be fucking for real right now. Your tone and body language are sure as hell not *civil*. You need to back up Storm," I demand as I step back, trying to put space between us.

It doesn't work, and he just takes another step forward. His hand jumps out, grabs my upper arm, and squeezes. Hard. So hard that I wince. "You're going to take me inside and show me what is fucking mine," he spits out. I try not to gag as I feel a few drops hit my face. Ugh, I want to bathe in bleach.

"You're hurting me. Let go," I grind out as I try to pull my arm out of his grasp with no luck. I'm really trying not to let the pain show, but I can feel the tears pooling in the corner of my eyes.

"Take your fucking hand off her now," a voice that I would recognize from anywhere growls out from behind me.

Storm pales slightly at his tone but doesn't release his hand. "I knew you were fucking lying. Just had to fuck your way to the top, didn't you? I just wasn't good enough."

"You're done, you piece of fucking shit." Cain steps forward as I catch something or someone out of the corner of my eye. I look over Storm's shoulder to see Zeke step out from the side of the barn, eyes zeroed in on where Storm is still tightly gripping my arm. Storm looks behind him. I can see him trying to calculate his next move. He thinks it's only two against one. He's an idiot for thinking that.

"I'm going to give you two seconds to take your fucking hand off her before I blow it the fuck off," Cain demands in a tone that commands authority, making both of us jump.

I've never seen this side of Cain before. His presence commands attention, and his face looks like he's about to do a lot more than shoot his hand off. My pussy clenches at the thought of him murdering Storm. I don't know what that says about me. Cain doesn't give Storm the two seconds he said before firing off a round at Storm's feet, purposely missing him.

It does the job, though.

Storm jumps back, forgetting that Zeke is right behind him. Zeke pounces on him and pins him to the ground in seconds.

"Let me the fuck up!" Storm screams as he flails around on the ground, trying to escape Zeke's hold.

"Not a chance," Zeke growls before punching him in the jaw.

"You okay, hellcat?" Cain is at my side, frantically looking me over while he gently rubs where Storm had a hold on me.

"Yeah, I'm okay," I say shakily, looking up at Cain's face, trying to see where his head is, but his eyes aren't on me. They're glued to the bruise that is already starting to form on my arm.

"He's going to pay for that," he grinds out before storming off to where Zeke has Storm pinned.

"This is for thinking you can breathe my woman's air." Cain kicks his steel-toed boot out, nailing Storm right in the ribs. "And this for putting your fucking hands on what's mine." Cain smashes his boot down on the hand Storm grabbed me with. I grin as I hear the crunch of bones. The sound is oddly satisfying.

"Hash! Cyrus!" Cain yells, and the guys come out of the woods looking just as blood-thirsty as Zeke did. "Take him to the clubhouse. You know where I want him."

Hash ties Storm's wrists together while Cyrus ties his ankles before they both grab their respective ends, lifting him up and carrying him back into the woods without a word. Well, without a word from them. Storm, on the other hand, is crying like the little bitch he is.

Cain isn't done giving orders because the next thing I know, he's calling for Ink and Trick. "Take care of this piece of shit and meet me back at the clubhouse." He motions to Storm's car. "He won't be needing it any time soon."

Sensing Cain needs some sort of confirmation that I'm okay, I wrap my arms around him. "I'm okay, babe. He didn't hurt me."

"Evangeline, he fucking marked you," he hisses out, pointing at the bruise on my arm. "That is not okay."

I know he's upset when he uses my full first name. "I bruise easily, Cain. You, of all people, know how pale I am. It's what fair skin does." I try my best to reassure him, but I don't think it's working.

"He's going to pay for that," Cain growls before calling to Zeke. "Let's head back. Get a head start on this while Ink and Trick deal with the car."

My worried gaze meets Zeke's as he walks by. I'm looking for reassurance that shit isn't going to be crazy with this, but I find the opposite of what I'm looking for. "He had it coming, Evan. You don't need to worry about it anymore."

"I want you back at the clubhouse, where I can have eyes on you at all times," Cain cuts in.

"Is that really necessary?" I roll my eyes. "I'll be fine here. He can't do anything to me when he's at the clubhouse."

"Until I know exactly what the fuck is going on and what we're dealing with, you'll have eyes on you. I'm done arguing about this," Cain says before walking off in the same direction as Zeke without looking back.

He clearly needs a minute to calm down, and if I'm being honest, I need the same. So, I take extra time packing an overnight bag, making sure to pack a few nights' worth of clothes because I have no idea how long this will take. Once I have all of my toiletries and clothes in a bag, I grab another bag out of the closet to pack Hades' stuff.

Yes, my baby needs his fuzzy blanket and toys, too. Not to mention food.

With a sigh, I load up my car, get Hades into the back, and head to the clubhouse.

## 37

## Cain

I've always been one to stand by the rule of never hurting a woman. I always thought the guys that did deserve every fucked-up thing they had coming to them. And I would be first one in line to do it. But seeing a guy put his hands on my woman? It's a whole different level of 'I'm going to fucking kill you.' All I want to do right now is take my knife, slowly shove it into each eyeball, and feed them to Hades.

But first, he has a lot of questions to answer. "Is he in the basement?" I ask Hash as I enter the clubhouse.

"Yeah. Cyrus and Scotch are uh... watching him." I don't hear any screaming, so he must still be alive.

"As long as he can still talk, Cyrus can watch him all he wants."

Cyrus, like Scotch, can become a little unhinged. That's why I made them enforcers. They've never met a man that they couldn't make talk, and because of that, they have gained a... reputation that must be maintained.

"Last I was down there, all fingers were still intact," Hash calls to my back.

I let out a laugh before I swing open the basement door and head down the steps. "That's a first," I call back.

"You're just in time for the party, Prez." Cyrus smirks from his chair as I slam my boot down on the last step. He's leaned back in the corner across from Storm, who is now tied down to a chair. Ropes strap down both of his wrists to each arm of the chair, ankles secured to the legs, and there's tape over his mouth. "Had to tape his mouth shut. Hadn't even touched him, and he wouldn't stop screaming like a little bitch. Can't wait to hear what a real scream will sound like out of him."

I slowly cross the distance between the end of the stairs and where Storm is before I rip the tape off his mouth. He didn't even see it coming, letting out a loud grunt in the process.

"Look. I don't know what this is about bu—" Storm starts to say while catching his breath before I cut him off.

"You don't know what this is about?" My tone sounds scary even to me. I heard Cyrus slide to the edge of his seat, no longer relaxed. He's more anxious to let out the release he's been looking for. "You thought it was okay to put your hands on a woman. My woman. That's what this is about, you piece of shit."

"It wasn't what it looked like man."

Scotch snorts from behind me.

"Really? Because what it looked like to me was that you were trying to steal what is Evan's. Then, when she didn't roll over and give you what you wanted, you were going to force her," I grit out. I don't think I've ever clenched my jaw so hard in my life.

The fact that this piece of shit is trying to tell me it wasn't what it looked like is only pissing me off more. Does he think we're fucking stupid? My philosophy is that if you're going to do something and get caught, you own up to it like a fucking man.

"I'm sick of that bitch making all the money. I've been doing the dealing for years! Fucking years! And you know how much she gives me? 10 percent. 10 fucking percent. Fucking bitch," Storm spits out, shaking his head as he rants.

Cyrus moves up behind me next to Scotch, ready to be of assistance for the way he's talking about Evan, but I hold up my hand to stop him. If there's one thing I've learned in this line of work, it's that guys like this who are desperate to be on top will spill their guts out when they're upset. They feel entitled to everything they come across, so money and power-hungry. Their emotions from that entitlement shines bright on their sleeves, all too eager to claim what they think is owed to them. And let's be honest, that will get you dead real quick in this game.

"Other than distribute to the low-life people you associate with, what exactly did you do that you feel so strongly that you're entitled to more?"

"I don't feel! I know I fucking deserve that. It's mine. This business is no place for a woman anyway. Doesn't she realize anyone can grow a fucking plant?"

I share a look with Cyrus, who is now by my side. I called that bullshit. That's another thing you need in this life that Storm obviously fucking hasn't yet. You need to be able to read people. Without it, you better watch your fucking back.

I crouch down so I'm at eye level with Storm in the chair. Direct eye contact makes them squirm, just like he is right now. "Did you break into Evan's house and issue that warning?"

"No." He answers way too quickly, not meeting my eyes. "No man. It wasn't me. I know nothing about that."

I wave Cyrus over as I stand up and step back, tilting my head toward Storm. The poor bastard didn't even have time to register what was happening before Cyrus had one of his fingers bent all the way back until that soothing crunch hit my ears.

"Fuck!" Storm screamed, trying to pull away, which is impossible when you're still tied to a chair.

"Do you want to change your answer?"

"No. It wasn—" His answer was cut off by another scream caused by Scotch, who quickly stepped forward and snapped another finger back.

Cyrus goes in for one more, but Storm has him pausing. "Okay! Okay! It was me, alright? It was me," he rushes out before he pleads. "Just no more, please."

Satisfied for now, Cyrus and Scotch step back so they're standing next to me.

"Care to share why?" I cock my head at him.

"No," Storm says lowly as he sags his head.

"No?" I echo. Well, that won't do. I pick up the crowbar to my right and swing it at his knee. This time I didn't get to hear that satisfying crunch I like because Storm was screaming like a bitch again. I'm really starting to hate this fucker. "If you're going to have the balls to fuck with my girl, the least you can do is take your beating like a fucking man."

I lift the crowbar into position like you do when you're about to swing a baseball bat, ready to go after the other kneecap before he starts speaking, a mixture of tears and sweat pouring down his face. "I can't tell you, man! He'll kill me!"

"And you think we won't?" Cyrus laughs.

"You better start talking, or you're going to leave here with all ten fingers broken, and both kneecaps shattered," I demand, pointing the crowbar at him.

"Okay, okay. Just no more. Please," he begs. And to that, I just cock my eyebrow.

I've never been a patient man when it comes to stuff like this. I have a short fuse and even shorter triggers, and this piece of shit is really testing me.

"I was dealing the last of what Evan had given me. I always meet this dude once a month on the other side of Ravenna

Heights at the abandoned warehouses," he rushes out, breathing labored from the pain.

It makes sense he would meet out there, especially if he's moving a few pounds. It's secluded, and no one likes wandering eyes during a deal.

"He had just left, and I was about to pull out too before this black town car came speeding into the parking lot, stopping right in front of me so I couldn't leave. I always back into a spot that butts up against the building."

"Then what?" I demand, not liking where this is going.

"Two guys got out of the front and then two more from the back. All of them in fancy ass suits. The guys in the front and one of them from the back kind of flanked around the other last dude that got out of the back. Like they were his body-guards or somethin'. I thought it was weird as fuck in this area, but who am I to judge? They looked fucking intimidating. I kind of liked it the more I stared at them." And there's that glint in his eye again. Jealousy. That look that screams he's so desperate for some sort of power.

"Hey," I snap, cutting off his rant. "Fucking focus. I don't want to hear about how you were about to get on your knees and suck their dicks. I want to know what happened."

"They knew what I was doing, and I don't know how. I have never seen these suits in my life. They wanted to know where I was getting my product."

"And you just told some random ass fucks everything?" I ask, growing angrier by the second. Jesus. What the hell is wrong with him? Is there no loyalty anymore?

"He had cash on hand, man! I can't turn away 50k like that. I'd be a fucking fool to," he explains as if that justifies every-thing. As if I'm just going to side with him.

"This is why Evan never gave you a larger cut. She saw what a piece of shit you are. No loyalty whatsoever."

"I'm loyal to who's feeding me."

"That's the thing. You don't get it and probably never will. Loyalty can't be bought. The ones that claim it can will always stray to the next highest bidder," I say, shaking my head. I really can't believe this fucking guy. "What did you do with the money?"

He's back to not meeting my eyes as he says what I already knew he was going to say. "I owed some people some money, so I paid off my debts to get them off my back."

God. What a fucking piece of shit. "How do we tie into this?"

"I think I've said enough." Storm smirks like he somehow still has the upper hand here. Scotch laughs before snapping two more fingers back at once.

"Fuck! Stop doing that! He wants this territory, okay! He knows you're involved with Evan." This bitch is full-on crying now. Fucking disgusting.

"Who is he, and how does he fucking know that?"

"I don't know how he knows. I didn't ask, man. I swear I didn't ask." His voice has a tremor now. "I didn't even ask for a name. I just took the money that they gave me for the info. I heard one of the guys who climbed out of the front call one of the guys Mikhail, but I don't know which one it was. Fuck I don't even know a Mikhail!"

I share another look with Cyrus. This isn't looking good at all. The Russians being at the trailer that day definitely wasn't a fucking coincidence.

"Thanks for the info, man. So much loyalty. I love to see it." I smirk before I swing and bash the other kneecap in, laughing as he cries out. "That's for touching what's mine."

I smile to myself as I hear his cries and head back upstairs.

**38**

Evan

When we get to the clubhouse, Hash is the first one to greet Hades and me, and of course, Hades runs to him like he's his best friend—the traitor.

"I hope it's okay that I brought him," I say to Hash, whose attention is completely occupied by the boy demanding belly rubs. "This all happened so fast, and Cain didn't give me any direction. I wasn't sure what to do with him." I also wouldn't have accepted the answer of pawning him off on someone else or leaving him at home—even if there was someone else to pawn him off on, which there isn't.

"Babe." Hash stands back up, earning a whine from Hades, letting us know he doesn't want the pets to stop. "You're the Prez's girl. Whatever the fuck you want is welcome here."

"Well, we're just seeing where this goes…" I start to tell him before I whip around at the sound of boots coming up from… a basement? I didn't even know this place would have one of those, but here's Cain coming through the door. My belly does a little flutter at seeing him looking almost relieved that I made it one piece. When was the last time someone cared if I made it somewhere?

Hades bounds over to him, tail wagging faster than it had for Hash.

"Were you a good boy for Mom?" Cain asks in a voice I didn't think could come out of a man like him as he crouches down. "You excited to sleep in Dad's bed tonight? It doesn't have Mom's fluffy covers that you're used to, but I'll get you your own blanket."

My heart stopped at hearing him refer to himself as Dad. For someone who wasn't sure where this was going, he seems pretty sure of himself. What girl doesn't want a man to treat her dog like they're an actual child? We haven't even had that conversation, but here he is, being all daddy-like. And damn if that isn't the sexiest thing. But I like this. I like it a lot. A lot, in the sense that I can see myself loving this forever.

Wait, *love*?

No, no, no. I don't love him. Do I?

"Your bags still in the car?" Cain asks, breaking me out of my thoughts. But I can't stop staring at him long enough to answer. I'm not sure I even fully processed what he asked. It was a question, right? I can't get the fantasy out of my head. The fantasy of my future that includes him. And maybe some actual kids. I never saw myself as the maternal type unless it was toward an animal, but now I can't stop picturing a kid with his gorgeous green eyes. Or one green and one blue, like mine.

"Evan?"

"Yeah?" I meet his concerned gaze.

"Are your bags still in the car?" he asks again, this time slower, a concerned look taking over his features.

"Oh. Yeah. Let me go get them." I spin on my heel, ready to head back out the door I just came through when a strong hand grabs my upper arm.

"Hash will get them, hellcat." He spins me back around

until I'm facing him. "You okay?" His eyes dart across my face, looking for what I'm assuming is any sign of me cracking.

"I'm okay."

He must see what he's looking for because he nods before tugging me along behind him until we reach his room, whistling for Hades to follow along the way.

"Have you questioned Storm?" I ask once we're inside his room. "Where did you take him, anyway?"

He lets out a long sigh. "Right. Look, I know this involves you, but we keep women out of our business. If shit goes down, I don't want you involved in any capacity."

Uh, no. "Yeah, that isn't going to fly with me, dude. It's my life. You really think I'll be okay with not knowing what's happening with it?" I ask, genuinely shocked.

"Yup." He smacks his lips, popping the p. "As I was saying, we don't involve women. It's not that I don't want to tell you. It's just that I don't want anything coming back on you. I will tell you something that needs to stay between us, as it concerns keeping you safe."

I nod my head in agreement because I guess that makes sense. It's just like in the mafia movies with the mob wives. If their husband gets caught for something, the wife isn't an accessory.

"Storm is in the basement. So that means you don't go near the basement. I want you to act like you don't even know the basement exists."

Well, I didn't until five minutes ago. "Alright. I can do that. Do I get to know how this at least involves me?"

"When I talk to the guys, and we figure a little more out, I'll fill you in with what I think will still keep you safe. Okay?"

"Okay." My shoulders sag. The events of the day are finally catching up to me. I just feel so drained. I didn't even notice how much I needed a hug until I felt Cain wrap his thick, strong arms around me, pulling me in close.

"I know this day has been a lot for you, baby. I'm going to fix everything, and you don't have to worry about anything."

"I don't want you to have to fix it. It's not your mess that started this," I mumble into his chest.

"We're both tied into this, hellcat. And I'm your man. I'm never going to let you shoulder any stress or pain again. I'm your rock now."

I start to shake my head because that isn't fair, but he stops me. "Don't argue. Not right now. I know you haven't had an easy life. You've had Scotch for a little bit, but you don't know what it's like to have someone you can fully lean on. I'm that for you. I want your laughs, your tears, your smiles, and your rage. I want it all, Evan."

I let out a choked laugh as the tears just burst out of nowhere. "You can't say things like that. I'm already falling, and once I'm at the bottom, you won't be able to get rid of me."

"That's the plan, baby," he says softly while gently rubbing a hand up and down my spine. "I need to go talk to the guys for a little bit, but I want you to stay up here and relax. Take a bath. I don't have any bath dicks, but I bought some bubble bath for you. It's under the sink."

"You bought bubble bath?" I laugh, pulling away from him slightly so I can lean up and place a kiss on his lips. "Thank you for everything. I don't think I realized how much I needed someone like you until your grumpy butt plowed into my life."

"I had a prospect do it." His smile is soft, and his eyes relaxed as I fully pull away and head towards the bathroom. Knowing that's a look that only I get to see makes a wall around my heart crumble.

I think I'm already more than halfway in love with this man, and that scares the absolute shit out of me.

"Try not to take too long. I want to cuddle with my man tonight," I call over my shoulder, throwing him a wink before disappearing into the bathroom for a bath that my man had planned out for me. I don't miss the shocked look on his face when I finally acknowledge it.

I went in there thinking things would settle down and we could all finally have some peace. If only I knew how short-lived it was about to be.

**39**

**Cain**

It takes me a second to pick my jaw up off of the fucking floor. I know I've been pushing her in this direction every chance I get but hearing her call me her man shocked the shit out of me. And fuck me because I can't do any of the things that I want to do to her. All the filthy fucking things. The thought of Evan in my bathroom, soaking in my tub, naked, with her skin all wet and glistening, begging for me to touch and lick every inch of her.

"Down, boy," I say to my dick as I finally make my way downstairs to talk to the guys. Ink and Trick should be back by now, and I can't have a serious conversation like this with my dick hard. But that's what Evan does to me. I'm constantly sporting a semi when it comes to her.

"How'd it go?" I ask, looking right at Ink and Trick, who are now sitting around the bar with the rest of the guys. "Prospects." I nod to Brock and Levi. Rules are rules, and until they're officially patched in, all the information they get is on a need-to-know basis. "Stay outside and let me know if you see anything unusual. We aren't trusting anyone but our own right now."

"Car is taken care of," Trick says after they both head outside. "You get anything useful out of him?"

"Yup. Turns out it wasn't just a coincidence that the Russians were at Storm's place that day," I say while pouring myself a glass of Jameson. "They caught wind of him dealing, cornered him in a parking lot, and paid him for info on where he was getting his product. Sold Evan out for 50k."

"Fuck."

"What a piece of shit," Trick and Hash say at the same time, both looking equally disgusted.

I look over at Scotch, who is using his pocketknife to scrape blood out from under his nails. "I got bad vibes from the guy, but it never crossed my mind that he would sell her out like that." Scotch grumbles while shaking his head. "Fuck. And to the Russians at that."

I can hear the guilt slipping into his tone. Guilt, I imagine, is from all of this getting as far as it has. "Don't take the blame for this brother." He meets my gaze and holds it for a long moment, saying nothing. Finally, he nods in confirmation that he heard me, but it doesn't reach his eyes.

"My guess is that Storm looked into who paid him and got spooked more than he's letting on." I get a chorus of grunts of agreement. "I think they were there the day Evan went over there by herself. Or he thought she found out he leaked shit." Anything is possible at this point.

"He the one that broke into her house?" Hash asks.

"Yup. Claimed he deserved a bigger cut than what Evan was giving him. My theory continues with the Russians finding him after he tried to flee and got him to do this shit. It screams amateur."

"But how do they know we're tied in?"

I shake my head. "That's the thing. I have no idea, and

neither does he. That was the only thing I believed out of his mouth on the first try."

"He could have recognized Scotch's cut and not let on," Ink offers.

Our club is still small. Yeah, we can all hold our own pretty well, but we're still only a club of six, not including the two prospects we have left. It sucks we lost two during the shipment getting jacked, but that's the life.

"I think we need to feel out the Reapers. I know Spider came busting in here ready to bust some balls, but I'm not fully trusting that he doesn't know what's going on." I say, pausing to take a sip of my drink. "I'm going to call Matteo to see if he knows anything." Matteo is the head of the Italian Mafia in Ravenna Heights. I wouldn't say we're friends, but we have become acquaintances over the years. Civil enough that there's a silent agreement we'll back one another.

"What's our next move if he doesn't know anything?" Scotch asks in a hardened tone.

"Well, we have Storm, and I think we need to use that to our advantage."

"You think he'll draw them out?" Trick asks.

Nodding my head, I say, "I do. The fucking idiots think he's valuable for some reason. They've paid him and kept him around this far."

"You think he's working his way up the ranks?"

"Fuck no." A laugh bursts out of me. Seeing Storm in the Mafia? No way. I'd pay money to see that. "I think they see a desperate man and are taking advantage of that. Once they get what they want, Storm will either be taken care of or just used as an errand bitch."

"It could work," Ink says. "They now know he has a huge connection with Evan, who, let's be honest, probably sells just as much, if not more, than some of the other players in town."

"I think that's our best bet. We can figure out how they

know we have anything to do with Evan." I look back over at Scotch. "Go downstairs. I want you and Cyrus to get him to set up a meeting with them or whatever the hell he does to contact them face-to-face. I want us there when that happens."

"My pleasure, Prez," Scotch says as a wicked smirk takes over his face. He chugs the last of his beer before slamming it down and heading toward the basement.

I finish the last gulp of my drink, too. "I need to go check on Evan. You fucks try not to get too crazy." I grin, knowing none of that is even in their vocabulary.

"Why not? You want us to hear the sweet soundtrack of your latest porno that will be coming from your room?" Trick says as the rest of the guys whoop and cheer.

"Yeah, yeah, yeah." I flip them off as I head back upstairs to my room, grabbing Evan's bags set at the bottom of the stairs on the way. I open my door, and the view I have is like a sucker punch to the gut.

Evan is out of the bath, just lounging on the bed in one of my old tees. The shirt hits about mid-thigh. Showing off her long, silky legs but leaving just enough covered that it makes you wonder what's waiting for you underneath. Makes you want to push the shirt up a couple inches to see that pretty pussy you know is already warm and wet for you. Just waiting for you to come inside.

"Hey." Evan smiles warmly at me, and damn if it doesn't feel like another punch to the gut. One more, and I'd be down on my knees for this girl. "How did it go?"

"I think I'm supposed to be the one asking you that," I say as I kick off my boots.

"Ask me how what went?" Her brows furrowed in that cute way I like.

"Your bath, hellcat. Did you get to relax?"

"Oh. Yeah, I mean as much as I could. Your bathroom is nicer than I expected."

A laugh bursts out of me. I've never laughed so much in my goddamn life until she came into it. "What did you expect it to look like?"

She looks sheepish now as she shrugs a shoulder. "I don't know... dirty? Like your typical biker bar bathroom, but in your personal room."

I can tell she isn't trying to offend me, and I'm not. I get it. Bikers are known for living life in the moment and partying our asses off. Plus, I've seen Trick's bathroom, and it's exactly what she pictured mine to look like. "I like my space clean, babe. Guys who want to be one of us and girls who want to get with one of us are constantly coming and going. This is the one space that's mine, so I try to take care of it. Can't promise you it will always look like that." Now, it's my turn to look a little sheepish as I climb onto the bed next to her. "I may have had a prospect quickly clean it before you came."

"Trying to impress me?" She quirks an eyebrow up, tone teasing.

"Maybe."

"Don't make poor Levi clean it. I'll do it."

"That's part of the job, hellcat. He knows the score."

She lets out a long sigh as if she's accepting defeat. "The aromatherapy bubble bath that you, I mean a prospect," she pauses to smirk, "got me really helped. It's my favorite. The scent just makes your head feel so clear. Thank you again," Evan says softly before resting her head on my shoulder. I just got my arm around her when she asks her next question.

"Why are you avoiding my question?"

I should have known that she wasn't going to let this lie.

Sighing, I rub my hand up and down her arm. "You know I can't tell you much, babe. But I will tell you that he was the one who broke into your place."

"That motherfucker," she hisses, shooting up straight. "Can I have a minute alone with him?"

"Absolutely fucking not."

"But—"

"No," I cut her off. "I know you want your time with him to rip him a new asshole, and I promise that you'll get it. Just not right now. There's still some shit that we're trying to piece together, and I don't want his hands on you again." I don't even want him breathing her air.

"I don't have to like what you're saying, but I get it," Evan says reluctantly. She makes the perfect old lady. She has a spine of her own and doesn't shovel anyone's shit, mine included, but at the end of the day still lets me lead.

I tuck her head under my chin, coaxing her to relax before continuing. "Storm was greedy, hellcat. Fuck, still is greedy."

"What do you mean?" she asks, tensing up.

"He felt like he was owed more of your business than just the cut you were giving him. And he didn't tell me this, but it was just a vibe I picked up on, but I think he wanted to take over completely and be the boss of the whole operation."

Evan has fallen silent to the point where the only noise in the room that can be heard is the true crime documentary she has playing on the TV. Fuck. Just when I get her to relax, I stress her out all over again. I wonder if you can buy those bath dicks in bulk. If the brothers found those, though, I'd be done. I don't know how I would recover from having a bunch of dicks in my bathroom.

"Ugh. I guess that doesn't really surprise me," Evan says, breaking the silence.

"Why do you say that?"

"I don't know. The last few times, he kept asking for more and more product each time. I didn't think anything of it because it had always been the same amount since we started, and I assumed stuff was picking up. And I mean, who doesn't want more money?"

Can't fault her for that logic. I haven't met a single person outside of the club who's actually content with their cash flow. No matter how rich you are, there will always be something you can't afford that makes you strive to get it.

"But since everything has happened, it does seem... greedy." She facepalms her head. "God. I feel like such a fucking idiot for not seeing the signs sooner."

"No," I say, pulling her hand away. "None of this is your fault, so don't blame yourself. What did I tell you earlier?"

"That you're going to take care of it."

"Good girl," I rumble. "Daddy's going to take care of it."

Evan's cheeks turn a light shade of pink. "You can't just say things like that."

"Uh-huh." I grin while shaking my head. "I sucked those pretty toes and that pretty pussy. That makes them mine now." I wink as her cheeks turn an even darker shade of pink at the mention of that.

"That was a onetime thing." Evan sniffs.

"The fuck it is. You were dripping. Try denying it. I dare you."

"We were in the shower. It was hard to tell because everything's wet anyway!"

A deep laugh escapes me. It feels good to finally be with someone who can make you laugh during chaos. It feels good to finally have something that feels like home.

**40**

Evan

He just had to bring it up.

Cain has this whole silver fox thing going on. Mix that with the tattoos and energy that commands your attention when he enters a room? Yeah. This man knows the effect he has on the opposite sex. I want this man to worship me until I can't walk for a week.

The way I'm laying on him puts me at the perfect angle to see that his dick is semi-hard, just resting down the leg of his jeans, begging me to take it out to play. Why should I deny my new favorite thing what it wants?

I drag my hand that is resting on his leg up his thigh, lightly swirling the head of his cock with my thumb on my way up to his belt. Cain sharply inhales, making his stomach tense underneath me. I pluck open his belt like I've been doing this every day of my life, making quick work of undoing his jeans. He helps me out by lifting his hips up so I can slide his jeans down over his hips, making his cock spring out because, once again, this man isn't wearing underwear.

"You going to suck my cock, little hellcat?" Cain rumbles out the question as I blow lightly on the head. "Don't tease."

"Sorry, daddy," I whisper before darting my tongue out and sweeping along the head, using the same motion that I did with my thumb just seconds before. His control snaps as soon as I wrap my lips around the tip, hollowing my cheeks and sucking hard.

"Fuck," he hisses as his hand grips my hair, tugging. "That mouth is almost as lethal as my pussy."

The ache between my thighs grows as I continue to blow him. Every little tug of my hair, every groan, grunt, and moan makes me that much more wet. My body is already taking over before my mind can even catch up. I rub my thighs together, trying to create any sort of friction to ease the ache that keeps building. I can tell he's getting close by the sound of his grunts as I take him deeper.

"Let up, hellcat." He groans as I hollow my cheeks again, only this time with most of his cock down my throat. Knowing he's so close to the edge makes me suck that much faster and harder. "Babe, slow up," he says with no real force behind it. Tears are pooling in my eyes, and saliva is dripping down my chin and onto his balls.

"Fuck, Evan, stop." He tugs hard on my hair, making his cock pop out of my mouth. "As much as I like to see your greedy mouth sucking my cock, I want to come inside you. Come up here." He pats his chest.

I kiss my way up his chest until I reach his mouth. A moan slips out of me as he takes control of the kiss, alternating between nipping my bottom lip and sucking on my tongue. The action has me squirming in his lap. The only barrier between me and his cock is the thin fabric of my g-string.

Cain rips his mouth from mine, breathing just as hard. "Fuck, little hellcat. Your soaked panties are getting my dick all wet." I let out a whimper as I grind down on him, making his cock brush my ass, leaving the stud at the base to tease me through my panties. Cain picks up on the movement almost instantly, creating the friction I desperately crave. "Cain..." I moan out as he growls and snaps off my thong. I'm too gone to care that he's destroyed another pair of panties.

"Fuuuuck," Cain groans as his hands grip my hips hard enough to leave bruises. "You're so hot and wet, baby. You need more?" he asks on my whimper. "You need my thick cock in there to ease the ache?"

"Yes," I barely get out. That light tingling sensation is starting at the base of my spine. "Please."

"Please, what?" he asks, tone letting me know I better give him what he wants.

"Please, daddy."

Cain rumbles his approval as he reaches into his nightstand for a condom. "Only because you asked like such a good girl. Good girls get rewarded."

He makes quick work of protecting us before he slides his cock through my wet slit, coating himself before positioning at my entrance.

My pussy sucks in the head, clamping down on it. "Shit. Take me in, hellcat." Cain curses as I sink all the way down until he's seated to the hilt, walls tightening around him. "My greedy fucking pussy is gripping me so good. Ride daddy." Cain slaps my ass, and that's all I need before finding my rhythm, chasing after that release. Cain is meeting me thrust for thrust.

Every moan from me is matched with a grunt or curse from him. It isn't long before I can feel that familiar tingle from a minute ago reappear, this time stronger. My inner walls grip Cain's cock even harder as he pushes me back slightly so I'm resting against his thighs. He creates the perfect angle, hitting that sweet spot every time he thrusts his hips. The stud at the base of his cock brushes my clit every time.

"Cain," I moan out in a slightly higher-pitched voice than normal, my breath caught in my throat.

"Let go, hellcat. I got you." He growls as he pounds into me.

That's all it took, him commanding me to come. My pussy clenches him so hard that I almost black out. Cain slams home one last time before exploding. I barely register his long stream of curses as he comes right along with me.

I collapse against his chest, both of us trying to catch our breath.

"Just when I thought it couldn't get any better, you surpass it with flying colors," Cain says softly, running a hand lightly up and down my spine.

"I think it's just different when it's with someone you care about," I admit, shocking myself. A few months ago, I would have thrown up at the mushiness.

"Yeah," Cain says softly, wrapping both arms around me and squeezing me tight. "I want to ask you something..." He starts before there's a fist pounding at his door.

"I know you two are busy playing Where's Waldo, but we got a meeting," Hash calls through the door, not waiting for a response as I hear his boots already walking away.

We both laugh before Cain lets out a long sigh. "I'm sorry, this moment just got ruined. I need to go deal with that. We'll finish this later, yeah?" He gives me another squeeze.

"Yeah." I smile. "Go. I'm just going to veg and watch TV."

I can't help but feel a sense of dread in the pit of my stomach as I watch Cain put his clothes back on and head out.

## 41

Cain

"What time?" I ask the room. The guys are already waiting around the table for me.

"They want to meet with Storm tonight at midnight," Hash answers.

"Where are we meeting?"

"Out at the abandoned warehouses where Storm first met them."

"Do they own them?" I ask. It's weird that they knew Storm was even there in the first place. Makes me think that they just want everyone else to believe they're abandoned. "When I called Matteo the other day, he didn't know anything about this. Last he knew, Mikhail wanted nothing to do with our area."

"Not that I know of," Hash replies.

Well, we're going to fucking find out who does. "Where's Brock?" I ask as Trick nods towards outside. "Go get him."

"What are you thinking?" Hash asks. I can tell by the look on his face that he already knows where this is going.

"I think it's about time Brock proves himself to be patched in." I scan the room for hesitation or disapproval but don't find one.

"The way he's stepped up with installing all the cameras at Evan's house made me want to put that bug in your ear, but then more shit hit the fan, and I forgot." Scotch shrugs from his seat. "I think he'll be a nice edition. Especially with his nerd shit."

That, right there, is how Brock is going to prove himself. Scotch is right, though. Brock has stepped up. He brings valuable assets that none of us have to the table. When he first approached us at DD's wanting to prospect, I wasn't too sure. I remember laughing in his face. You can't blame me. He looked like an adult who lived in his mom's basement.

Brock doesn't exactly strike you as the type that wants to get down and dirty. Hell, the kid didn't even get his first tattoo until Ink basically told him you can't have virgin skin in the club. He was joking, but the kid took him seriously and got some code of some shit on his arm. Looks kind of badass, even though I don't know anything about that stuff.

"Yeah, Prez?" Brock asks as he makes his way inside.

"Have a seat." I nod to the empty seat next to Repo.

The tension in Brock's body is coming off in waves as he clenches his fists at his side and walks to the seat, probably expecting the worst. I don't think the kid has any family. At least he hasn't mentioned anyone. But then again, neither had Scotch, and look what fucking happened with that. "You're good with computers, right?"

"Yeah." He nods tightly.

Perfect. "I want you to try to find out who owns the abandoned warehouse on the other side of the city. Hash did a basic search, but it came back as bank-owned."

"You think it's a cover?"

"I do. Can I trust you to get me that info?" Do you have the balls to hack a government database and get me the shit I want?

"Absolutely," Brock agrees all too eagerly. The tension is gone now that he knows he isn't getting kicked out. "When do you need it by?"

"As soon as you can get it. Preferably within the next couple of hours."

"I'm on it, Prez." Brock moves to stand. "I'll let you know when I have something." I nod my head, dismissing him.

Waiting until the door shuts behind him before I continue. "Let's hope gets the info we need. Something in my gut tells me that the Russians own that."

"But why would they cover it up like that?" Ink asks.

"I'd cover something up like that if I was storing something that I didn't want anyone to know about," Hash answers.

"Exactly," I agree. "And it doesn't sit right with me that they just happened upon Storm doing a deal that day. It makes me think they've had eyes on him a lot longer than he even realizes."

"Evan did say that she felt like she was being watched that day when she went over to Storm's alone," Scotch adds.

"You ever get that feeling when you did drops with her?"

"No, but I was also too busy trying to figure out why Storm rubbed me the wrong fucking way. Dropped the ball on that one. Sorry."

"Don't beat yourself up. None of this is your fault. We're going to figure out what the fuck is going on." I look around the room at all the brothers, who share the same hard expression on their faces and are nodding in agreement. "Tonight," I growl.

"What's the game plan for this?" Hash asks.

"I want all of us going. I don't want a repeat of what happened at Storm's place. I want us all suited up."

"What about Evan?" Scotch asks. "You know she isn't going to be okay with all of us going and her staying back."

Yeah. I knew that was going to be a problem. "I think it's best if she knows as little as possible right now. I finally got her to relax—"

Cyrus cuts me off by snorting, "Yeah, I bet daddy did."

The guys all burst out laughing while Scotch slaps Cyrus on the back of the head. "Hey!" Cyrus exclaims while ducking his head and rubbing it.

"I don't want to hear that shit. It's fucking gross. That's my sister you're talking about," Scotch grumbles, looking like he might actually throw up.

I can't help but grin because, yeah, I love it when my girl calls me daddy. "Alright, alright. Calm down. Scotch is right. Show Evan some respect. She's mine."

The room instantly becomes dead silent at that comment.

"You officially claiming her?" Scotch asks. He looks almost pissed off at the idea.

Am I claiming her? I haven't been able to get the woman out of my head since I saw her standing in the clubhouse, looking so out of place. Those mismatched eyes snatched my soul without me even realizing it. They locked me in and threw away the key. Not to mention, no one has ever sucked my cock like she does. And I've had a lot of blow jobs. And that cunt. Fuck. It's always so tight and warm. Just waiting for me to come inside. She's the first person to make me feel like I'm home. So yeah, I guess I am. "I'm claiming her. Evan's mine."

"It's about goddamn time!" Cyrus cheers as all the guys whoop and holler.

"Congrats, Prez," Hash smiles.

"Yeah, congrats, Prez. Who knew your old ass would be the first to settle down." Trick smirks. "Wait. She does know how old you are, right?"

And now it's my turn to smack someone on the back of the head. "Yes, she knows how old I am fucker." I can't help but laugh.

A knock sounds at the door. "Prez?"

Brock. That was faster than I expected. "Come in." Oh, yeah. He found something. Unless that excited look in his eye is because he just rubbed one out. "You find something?"

"Oh, yeah," Brock says, and if the look in his eyes didn't already confirm it, the excitement in his voice does. "I did some digging around, and well, you were right to be suspicious," he explains as he takes the seat next to Repo again.

"The bank doesn't own it?"

"Nope. Well, I mean, I guess they did. They gained owner-ship of it due to foreclosure eight years ago when the economy took a nosedive. They found a buyer three years ago, though."

"Who was it?" I growl, making Brock look up from his laptop.

"Someone that goes by the name Mikhail Petrov."

Motherfucker. "I knew it." I slam my fist down. "So you're telling me they've been in our area for three years, and we're just now finding out about it?" My voice sounds lethal, even to me.

"Uh, yeah. I think so," Brock hesitates before he answers. "I'm not sure if that's when they came here, but it's when they bought the warehouse. Based on the pictures I saw, it doesn't look like they've done much with it."

No. No, they haven't. An unsettling feeling has settled in the pit of my stomach. "What are they hiding?" I ask out loud, more to myself than the brothers, but Hash answers.

"Drugs." He simply shrugs.

"What makes you say that?" Trick asks, brow raising.

"Think about it. Our shipment got stolen, and the Reapers don't know anything about it. They've clearly been watching the fuck face that's in our basement deal for years without him even knowing. And if they've been watching him for that long, I'm willing to bet all the cash I have buried out back in my titty piggy bank that they've seen Scotch with Evan when she meets up with Storm. It wouldn't take much to piece it all together and figure out what club Scotch is with."

Fuck. "And they would just assume Evan is in on everything based on that association," I finish.

"Yup." Hash looks grim.

"Alright," I start. "Everyone is coming, including you, Brock. Levi will stay back with Evan. Someone needs to take a cage to bring Storm." I snort as the other guys snicker. "If questions get asked, just have Storm explain that he had a little accident and needed a driver."

"I'll do it." Cyrus looks all too pleased with himself. "Wouldn't mind cutting a finger off this time if he gets out of line."

"Leave some for the rest of us," Ink tells Cyrus, looking a little put out that he didn't get to participate earlier.

I let out a laugh while shaking my head. "Glad that's settled. Load up the back with some extra guns, just in case. I don't know how many men we're about to bust in on." I turn to Brock before continuing, "If there are cameras when we get there, can you hack them so we can see what we're working with or cut them?"

Brock rears his head back as if I've offended him. "Can I hack them? Does a biker eat pussy?"

"There he is!" Cyrus booms. "I knew there was some swagger underneath all that virgin skin. Just had to hack it out."

"Not virgin skin anymore." Brock smirks while showing off his half-sleeve, making all the guys crack up. It's like watching a bitch turn 18 getting her first rose.

"Alright, alright." I laugh while trying to get their attention again. "Let's get our shit together. I'm going to deal with Evan. We're heading out in two hours. I want to scope some shit out before Cyrus comes with Storm."

I leave the guys to it as I head back upstairs to my woman,

knowing the conversation we're about to have isn't going to be easy.

So much for daddy getting her to relax.

**42**

Evan

Usually, I have no problem lying around like a potato with Hades. Staying in bed all day and watching TV is our favorite pastime. However, it's hard as fuck to do when you know the man that was probably going to hurt you and tried to steal your business from you is just two floors down.

And then there are all the what-ifs.

What if I'd have been home that night he broke in? What if the guys wouldn't have been there earlier? Would he have killed me? I'm so zoned out with my spiraling thoughts that I don't even hear Cain come back into the room. It isn't until I feel Hades doing his violent, happy booty wiggle on the bed that I'm pulled from my thoughts.

"True crime still?" Cain smiles while petting Hades and looking at the TV. "You don't think you've experienced enough crime lately?"

"True crime documentaries are comforting. The narrator's

voice is so soothing that it can put me to sleep," I explain. And I'm not lying. There's something so comforting about the deep level of his voice that it just kind of lures you in. Then, the next thing you know, you wake up, and it's 5 a.m., and the show is still playing. "How did it go with the guys?"

Cain lets out a long sigh before sitting on the bed next to me. That feeling of dread that was in my stomach earlier sinks deeper. "It went as expected. We have some stuff to do tonight. I want you to stay here. Levi will be with you."

"Where are you going?" I don't like that he's not telling me the full story. I understand that I'm not allowed to know every-thing that goes on with the club. Club business and all that shit. I get it. I really do. What I have a problem with is being left in the dark about something that directly involves me.

"Can't tell you that, hellcat," Cain says softly.

"It's unfair that this involves me, and I'm being left in the dark," I say honestly as I cross my arms over my chest.

"I know, but you just have to trust me, okay? I'll be back tonight after we get all of this shit taken care of. We can finally move the fuck on with our lives and not be so on edge for a moment."

"For a moment?" My brow furrows because I feel like he's insinuating this won't be over.

"I'm the president of a one-percenter club, hellcat. Some fucker always thinks he's grown a pair big enough to try us. This means that there's bound to be a problem every now and then." He shrugs. Just shrugs as if it's not a big deal.

Just another thing I need to learn to deal with. I sigh. "I guess I can live with that. But I want to be filled in as soon as you get back. Just be careful, all right? I'm too young to pick out funeral cactuses."

"Cactuses?"

"Because you're prickly." I snicker.

Cain's eyes go soft at that. "Never had anyone care if I live or die before." He places a light kiss on my lips. "Feels damn good that it's you. I'll be careful. Maybe tomorrow I'll take you on a date."

"A date?" I laugh because I can't picture Cain on a date. Or dating in general.

"Yeah, a date. Since you're my first relationship, I don't know much about romance, but I'll figure it out along the way."

"And you think I'm okay with being your trial run?" I have to give him a little shit for that line because, honestly.

"Yeah. Want to know why?"

"Why?"

"Because you'll be my first for everything in between."

And there goes my heart. Who is this man, and what has he done with Cain? Part of me thinks my heart took control of my body by what I do next because my brain was not up to speed. "I love you," I whisper.

I watch as Cain's eyes widen, almost as if he can't believe what he's hearing, like no one has ever told him that they love him. That look breaks my heart almost as much as it makes it feel whole. The emotion swirling in his eyes takes over. "You can't take that back," he rasps out.

I frame his face with both of my hands. "I'm not taking it back. I love you. I've never met a man quite like you. You'll stop at nothing to make sure I'm safe and cared for. I'll never stop thanking Scotch for getting me to help you guys even after you were an epic fucking asshole." It's my turn to place a light kiss on his lips. "I don't need to hear the words back. I just wanted you to know how I feel before you leave tonight."

Cain swallows. "Evan—"

"We're ready when you are, Prez!" Hash yells through the door, cutting Cain off.

"Fuck." He runs a hand roughly through his hair. "I feel like we're always getting interrupted here. We'll finish this when I get back, okay?"

"Okay." I blink back the tears threatening to fall at how he's leaving this.

"Hey." His features soften again. "It won't be bad. Nothing about the conversation will be bad. I just don't want to start it when I have to leave."

I can accept that for now. I did just drop a bomb on him.

"Be a good girl for Levi, and daddy might reward you." He smirks before planting a rough kiss on my mouth, his tongue dominating mine before he pulls away and leaves the room without another word.

ITS BEEN about an hour since Cain and the guys left. I feel bad that I haven't gone down to say hi to Levi yet, but dammit, I'm sad. You know that feeling you get when you wish the other person would say what you want to hear, but they don't? It just leaves you feeling... empty. Even though I know I told him he didn't have to say anything back, it doesn't mean I didn't want him to. And I am feeling hungry. Maybe I can talk Levi into eating with me.

"Come on, Hades. Let's go see what Levi's doing," I tell him as I head to the door to go downstairs.

I find Levi lounging on the couch.

"I'm sorry you're stuck with me." I grimace. It can't be fun always being on babysitting duty.

"Nah, come on. It isn't like that," he says while sitting up. "Plus, you're my favorite girl." His eyes widen at the realization of what he just said. "I, uh, didn't mean it like that. I swear. I know you're Prez's girl."

I can't help but laugh because he literally looks scared for his life right now. "Relax, Levi. I know what you mean." The relief on his face is instant as he slumps back into the couch. "Are you hungry?"

"I could eat."

Perfect. A fellow foodie. "Let me look around the kitchen and see if there is anything I can whip up." It didn't even take me a full 30 seconds to realize there was nothing but booze and some crackers in it. How are all of these guys so fucking big if there's no food?

"I think we're out of luck," I say when I return. "There's literally no food here. What do you guys live on?"

"Uh... we usually just eat at DD's."

I sigh. "Of course you do." This place is literally a giant bachelor pad. No wonder why they were all so excited for a home-cooked meal the other night. "Want to order a pizza?"

Levi looks uncomfortable again. "Yeah, I don't know about that. Prez said to stay in."

"We can get it delivered," I add, seeing that he's still hesitating. "I'll even stay in here while you go out to meet him. And honestly, I doubt a delivery driver is going to want to kill us." I roll my eyes. I've never met so many overprotected men in my life.

Levi thinks over what I just said for a moment before reluctantly agreeing. "Make sure mine has pepperoni."

"Deal." I smile, cheering inside my head for winning this one. Sometimes it's the small things in life.

After the pizza is ordered, I lounge on the opposite end of the couch. He's watching some show with a guy redoing a classic car. It's not my cup of tea, but I find this more relaxing than being up in Cain's room stressing over what's going on. It sucks not being involved when it's your mess.

I must have drifted off because my eyes are opening at the feeling of Levi getting off the couch.

"Pizza is here," he says before going out to get it.

"Finally. I'm fucking starving," I say while snuggling back

into the couch. I plan on eating my food right here and never leaving this spot.

It isn't until the next episode of the show starts that I realize Levi didn't come right back. It's been what? Ten minutes? It doesn't take that long to pay the driver.

Another five minutes go by before I start to get really worried.

"Ugh, Levi. Don't you know not to mess with a girl when she's hungry?" I grumble to myself as I get up and head to the door.

Hmm.

No sign of Levi or a delivery driver. I don't even see a car. What the fuck is going on?

Just as I'm about to go back inside and call Cain, I hear a quiet moan coming from the other side of the clubhouse.

"Levi?" I call.

No answer.

My heart is pounding so hard I can feel it in my ears as I wait to see if I hear anything again. I'm getting flashbacks from the night I saw someone in my backyard, making that funky, dreadful feeling come back times a thousand this time. You know that one you get when you're watching a thriller and the girl is being chased, but you know she's probably going to die? That feeling of absolute terror.

Yeah. That's how this feels.

"Levi?" I try again. My heart feels like it's going to explode out of my chest as I rub a hand over it, trying to get myself to calm down. It can't hurt to just peek around the corner, right?

I quickly dash to the edge to peek my head around, and that's when I freeze. Levi is on the ground with the pizza splattered all around him, and the box is discarded off to the side.

I rush to his side. "Oh my god. Oh my god. I'm going to get you help! Just hold on!" I frantically tell him, unsure if he can even hear me. It looks like he's been hit in the head. There's so much blood dripping down his face that I can't even tell where it's coming from. I hate that he's hurt because of me. I caused this.

I reach into my back pocket for my phone. My heart stops when a deep voice comes from behind me. "I knew you would come out eventually."

That's the last thing I hear before everything goes black.

**43**

**Cain**

All of us, minus Cyrus and Storm, park just down the road from the warehouse two hours before the scheduled meeting. Could we have gotten closer? Yeah. But I'd rather walk the rest on foot. Our bikes don't exactly allow us to have the element of surprise on our side. I don't know what kind of cameras or sensors these guys might be operating with. And if there's one thing I know about organized crime, it is that there's a fuck ton of money there. Which is why we didn't know for three fucking years that they even bought the place. Hell, if all of this shit hadn't gone down, I probably would have never known.

"Find anything?" I ask as Brock and Hash make their way back.

"Cameras all around like we thought. Didn't pick up on any sensors, though," Brock replies.

"They probably think they're flying under the radar," Hash grunts.

"You think there're cameras inside?"

"I'm going to say yes. Once I hack into their system, I'll know more. I highly doubt they have different servers for something way out here."

"How long do you need?"

"Maybe a half hour. Just depends on what type of security they have."

"Good work, Wiz." I pat his back as I step away to let him work. I didn't miss the small smile he gave at the nickname.

"What's up?" Hash asks in a low voice as he comes to stand by me.

"I don't know, man. Everything seems to be going well here, but I can't seem to shake the feeling that some shit is about to go down," I admit as I look around. "I feel like we're missing something. It just seems too easy."

"I was thinking that too. When we were looking for cameras, I didn't see any cars. It doesn't look like anyone is even here."

"Unless they opened one of those bay doors and parked inside."

"Maybe." Hash didn't sound convinced, and honestly, I'm not either.

"Cyrus just said he's 5 minutes out," Ink says at the same time Brock says, "I'm in."

Hash and I share a look because, again, this shit is just too easy. "What's it looking like, Wiz?"

"There's a camera in each corner of the exterior and one in each room of the warehouse." He waves us over to look at the screen as he points. "So far, I've only seen these two guys throughout the whole place."

"Only two guys?" Hash asked, wariness clearly present in his voice.

I lean in to get a better look. "Neither of those guys looks like Mikhail." I point to the corner of the screen. "Can you zoom in over there?"

Wiz hits a few buttons on the computer, and a couple of seconds later, I'm looking at a shit ton of heroin.

"Oh fuck. Is that what I think it is?" Hash asks.

"What is it?" Trick asks, coming up behind us. "Are you fucking kidding me?"

"We don't want that shit here," Ink growls.

No, we definitely fucking do not. "Explains all the overdoses lately." The guys grunt in agreement. "Wait. Go back." Wiz clicks a few more times, and the cameras change angles. "These motherfuckers. How much do you want to bet that's also our missing shipment in there?" How did two guys that we didn't even know fucking existed pull this off?

"They're dead," Ink grumbles. "Fucking dead."

They absolutely fucking are.

Soon enough, Cyrus is pulling into the parking lot with Storm in the passenger seat, looking like he's about to pass out. "Showtime." I motion to the guys to spread out. We all watch from a distance as Storm rolls down the passenger side window, and the same two men Brock saw exit the building. "Why aren't you driving?" I can hear one of them ask.

"Had a small accident," Storm answers, looking like he wishes he was anywhere else but right here. "He's cool." He nods towards Cyrus. I wait until they approach the side of the truck before I head towards them.

"Who the fuck are you?" The guy in a black turtleneck shouts, both of them drawing their guns.

I snicker. "Just wanted to have a friendly chat, gentlemen." I raise both of my hands as I approach them. "No need for all of that."

"I don't think you're in a position to make demands," the other one said. No accents. Interesting. I doubt these guys are high up. This brings me to my next question: why are only two guys like this guarding this much heroin? From what I saw on camera, there's at least a million dollars worth of product in there. And if you have that much in heroin, why do you need a bunch of weed?

"You sure about that?" I smirk as I sense the guys coming up behind me. Judging by the looks on the two dipshits' faces, they know they're fucked if something goes down, and by doing that, they have no clue that they just confirmed it's only them here.

"What is this?" the turtleneck asks. "Are you double-crossing the Pakhan?" His tone has taken a dark edge as he looks at Storm.

"They fucking know it all, man," Storm cries before spilling his guts. "I tried to take over shit at Evan's like he wanted, and they were there waiting for me. I didn't stand a chance. Tell him I didn't stand a chance," Storm is full-on trembling now as he pleads with Cyrus to bail him out.

What a little bitch.

I knew he would crack under the slightest amount of pressure.

The turtleneck lets out a deep laugh. "Begging won't help you here. You're a means to an end."

"What does that mean?" I growl. That bad feeling I felt when we arrived has permanently settled in my throat.

"It means that we're handling what Storm couldn't."

I'm on him before he can even register what's happening. My brothers behind me come up quickly, guns drawn, yelling at the other guy to drop his weapon that's currently pointed right at my head.

Turtleneck drops his gun as soon as my hand wraps around his throat, slowly cutting off his air supply. "If he so much as touches a hair on Evan's head, he's going to wish I put a bullet between his fucking eyes." I hiss out as he gasps for air.

"You have five seconds to take your fucking hand off him." The guy beside him yells, gun aimed right at me.

"I don't think you're in a position to make demands," Hash mocks, earning a chorus of snorts. I don't need to take my eyes off of turtleneck to know that every single one of my brothers has a gun aimed at both of them.

"You have five seconds to start telling me what the fuck is going on," I taunt as I squeeze a little harder in that sweet spot that's just below the jawline and right by the ear. I've completely cut off his air supply, and his buddy knows it.

He holds one hand up while lowering the other to the ground after realizing he's outnumbered. "Mikhail wants it all for himself. He's just taking out whoever is in his way." He nods his head to the guy whose throat is seconds away from being crushed with my hand. "Now let him go."

"Wants what?"

"The territory. He's had his eye on Evan for a while. Knew Storm would be an easy in. Once he realized you all knew each other, he decided to take out two birds with one stone."

"Why did he kill two of our men and take our shit? You obviously don't fucking need it."

"He just wanted to send you a message. Just like the one he's sending now."

I swear my heart just stopped fucking beating. "Call Levi." I don't even care who does it. Seconds have gone by since I gave that order, but it feels like ten years. My stomach is in my throat at the thought of anything happening to her.

"He's not answering."

"Keep trying," I growl. It's taking everything in me not to crush this guy's throat right now. Information first. Fuck this bitch up afterwards.

"Where is she?" I yell while shaking the guy by his throat, making him make a few gurgling noises as he tries to take the smallest breath.

"He's taking her to Storm's!" his buddy yells just as his partner's face turns blue.

"You're coming with us," I grit out through clenched teeth as I shove turtleneck's body toward Hash, his gasps for air coming in short and fast. "Tie them up and throw them in the back. Tie that fuck face up too." I nod my head toward Storm.

"You better fucking hope she's untouched when I find her, or you're going to beg me to put you out of your misery.

Don't worry, little hellcat, I'm coming. I'll burn the world down if I have to.

**44**

**Evan**

I slowly open my eyes, trying to blink away the brain fog. My head is pounding as I try to get my bearings. "Where in the hell am I?" I whisper to myself as I look around the dark, furniture-less room, trying to focus. I'm really hoping that's dirt on the walls and not blood. The sliding closet doors have been taken off their tracks, letting me see more blood splatter in the empty space. The bars on the window make it feel like a jail cell. It isn't until I notice the thick metal lock on my ankle with a chain attached that's anchored to the wall that everything comes flooding back to me.

"Levi!" I gasp, jerking up. The quick movement makes me wince as a wave of nausea hits me.

Oh, my god. Oh, my god. Oh, my god.

Okay.

This is really happening, isn't it? I've been kidnapped. All the true crime documentaries I've watched over the years didn't prepare me for this. I feel like all they talk about is what the victim was doing before and then how they died or escaped. Nothing really in between.

"God, I hope he's okay," I whisper to myself. *All of that blood.* That's all I remember before I was hit over the head. I run my hand over the bump that's throbbing on the back of it. The lightest touch feels as if I'm being hit all over again. I squeeze my eyes shut as they begin to burn. I try to hold back the tears. Now isn't the time to break down. I need to be strong, or I'll never get out of here alive.

I get a huge whiff of something foul and wrinkle my nose. It's disgusting enough to make you gag but familiar at the same time. A smell this bad shouldn't be familiar to me.

"Wait." I rush out and frantically look around, only this time really noticing the room—specifically, the blood/dirt/matter in question covering the old wall panels.

Wall panels that match Storm's living room.

"This motherfucker," I hiss just as the door flies open. My eyes squint as I try to adjust to the light until I see a shadowy figure standing in the doorway.

"You're awake. It's about time. If you weren't up, I was going to find a real sweet way to wake you up." He smirks before walking away and leaving me alone again. I couldn't see his eyes, but I felt them crawling over my skin.

"I'm really sorry it had to come to this, Evangeline," a new voice says from the doorway as they enter the room.

"Come to what?"

"Your life ending at my hands," he answers as if I just asked the stupidest question in the world.

The light from the moon coming in through the window lets me see an outline of a tailored suit. I know I should be scared. I know I should shut up. I definitely shouldn't be running my mouth to this man who is probably about to shoot my brains out, but here I am. Instead of fear, I just feel rage.

Lots and lots of rage. "Would you like to educate the class on why you think my life is ending?"

"Because I warned you." His tone is sharp now. As if I've pushed a nerve. "I warned you to stay away from that club. And if you had given what I wanted to Storm, we wouldn't be in this mess." He lets out an exasperated sigh. "But here we are because, of course, you're too fucking stupid to listen."

"I don't listen to men that think it's a power move to flex their tiny dick around."

"Shut the fuck up!" he roars before backhanding me across the face. My head snaps to the left from the surprise blow. I bring my hand up to my face, pressing my palm against where he just hit me, trying to ease the sting. Tears are falling from my eyes before I can stop them. The ringing in my ears only makes my headache more intense.

"If you had just given me what I wanted, you wouldn't be here, Evangeline." He says in a soft tone that's borderline creepy. All the anger from before is nowhere to be found. He closes the distance between us before kneeling down in front of me. "But you just won't give it up. And then you had to go and fuck the biker." His tone is just above a menacing whisper now as he sneers while reaching his hand up to twirl a section of my hair around his finger.

I stop breathing at the contact, and my skin starts to crawl. I don't know what I did in a past life to deserve this.

"You're ruined now, Evangeline. And it's such a shame. I would have proposed an arrangement. You could feel like you still had a little piece of what you started. A woman like you needs authority and to run under a firm hand." He clucks his tongue. The disappointment he's feeling from I don't even fucking know what is suffocating the room.

My head flew back as if he slapped me again, proud of myself for not showing how much it hurt on my face. "Proposed an arrangement? Like a marriage proposal?"

"Yes," he grits out. "You would have married me."

"You don't look high." I study his face now that I can see it up close. His eyebrows are almost more manicured than mine. Other than that, his facial features are hard. My butt crack is probably as deep as his forehead lines. It's clear this guy is off his fucking rocker. I've never seen him a day in my life.

"Enough!" He yells quickly, standing up. On instinct, I duck my head, covering it with my arms, expecting another blow to the face. Instead, he gives me a swift kick to my abdomen, which sends me flying into the wall.

You know when you were a little kid and swinging really high on the swings before you jumped off? And sometimes you didn't stick the landing and would end up flat on your back with the wind knocked out of you? Making you fear for your life for the longest five seconds ever? That's what that kick just did to me.

I press my palm against my ribs, inhaling short, quick bursts of air. I feel a sharp pain with each one, which is only making me freak out more.

"I'm done listening to you run your mouth. A girl like you needs to learn her place," he bites out as he raises the butt of his gun and brings it down on my temple. "And you're going to learn today."

And once again, the world goes black.

**45**

**Cain**

I'm driving like I did when I first got my bike.

Going 90 down the freeway while weaving in and out of cars like I have nine lives. The amount of fear I currently feel would do that to any man. I've always been told it would be different when you found the one. I never imagined it would be like this. The thought that I might lose her before I really even have her is fucking terrifying. Before I could even tell her that I love her.

I can hear my brothers hot on my heels behind me. They know how I am. I'll go in guns blazing, ready to burn the world down without a second thought.

It takes us about forty-five minutes to get from where we were outside of Ravenna Heights to Storm's trailer. We were about five minutes out when I started to smell smoke.

I turn onto Storm's road when I see a car, matching Storm's description from the day he was approached, leaving the driveway.

The driveway where all the smoke is coming from.

"Motherfucker," I hiss, reaching back and grabbing my gun.

I don't hesitate before I start shooting out their tires before they see me. A shot rings out from behind, nailing the windshield, making the car swerve off the road and fly into a huge oak tree.

"Go!" Hash shouts over the bikes, motioning with his hand. "We got this! They'll be here for you to deal with!"

I must have blacked out from adrenaline because the next thing I know, I'm body slamming the front door of the trailer that's on fire, with one end completely up in flames.

"Evan!" I yell over the roar of the flames. "Evan!" "Evan!" I get out once more before the smoke chokes me. Lifting my shirt up to cover my mouth and nose, I move further into the house.

"Help!" I hear from the opposite end of the trailer. The end where the flames haven't reached yet. My heart feels like it's about to beat out of my fucking chest as I move toward the screams.

"Evan!" I yelled again before slamming my shoulder against another locked door. "I'm coming, hellcat!"

Two more slams, and I'm in. The splintered door slams against the wall as I try to make out Evan through the smoke. I find her slumped over in a corner.

"Fuck, baby." I cradle her head in my hands, quickly assessing the situation. I have to swallow down my rage at seeing her face beaten to shit. He'll pay for every one of those marks. "We have to get out of here."

"Can't," she wheezes, making my heart ache. "Ankle."

Fuck. How did I miss that her fucking ankle is chained to the goddamn wall? I frantically shoot off a text to Cyrus, hoping the cutters are still in the cage.

"Just go." Her eyes slowly start to close, and I can tell I'm losing her. "Take care of Hades..."

"Evan. You need to stay with me for just a little bit longer, baby." I gently shake her. I'm full-on freaking out now. I can't fucking lose her.

"Tired.." she rasps. Her breathing is coming in short pants now.

"Eva—" I start to say again just as I hear the sound of a drill undoing the bars on the bedroom window just enough to smash it in.

"Prez!" Cyrus shouts, holding the cutters through it. "Hurry the fuck up. I couldn't even get inside the front door."

I make quick work of cutting the chain off a now passed-out Evan before I gently pick her up and pass her through the window to Cyrus. I follow through and make it out just before the flames barrel into the room.

"I'm going to kill this motherfucker," I grit out as I take Evan from Cyrus. I'm trying to be as gentle as possible, but it's a little fucking hard to do while running. "It's okay. I got you."

"Cain?" Comes the faintest whisper.

Jesus fucking christ. "Yeah, hellcat. It's me."

"Put her in the cage. You can drive back with her; I'll take your bike," Cyrus says as he opens the door for me.

"Where's Storm and the two dipshits?" There's no way in hell he had time to run back to the clubhouse.

"Look in the back." Something in his smirk tells me he thinks he just came up with the greatest fucking idea.

I peek in the back, and sure enough, there is Storm and the two dipshits. All three are tied up and weighed down. Mouths covered in tape.

"Nice work. We need to get the fuck out of here. He still alive?"

"Yup. Hash has him. Let's go."

I pull out of the drive and stop about half a mile down where Mikhail had crashed.

"Call Doc and drive Evan back," I tell Cyrus when he catches up. "I want her taken care of while I deal with this." I can tell he's about to argue, but I cut him off. "I need to deal with this."

He gets in the cage with his phone to his ear, calling Doc, and I walk around to the passenger side.

"I'll be with you soon, Evan." I gently kiss her forehead, getting a small twitch in return. Not enough to make me feel even the slightest bit better about this whole fucked-up situation. I slam the door shut and pound twice on the bed, watching them drive off before I make my way over to the guys.

"You," Mikhail hisses as I take him in. Blood is running down from a massive cut on his head, and his arm is bent in a different direction.

"I'm feeling a little put out that I wasn't the one to break that." I nod to his wrist.

"Do you know who I am?" he rages.

"Nope. Just know your name and the three guys you have working with you. And I've got you all." I smirk. I don't give him a chance to respond before I fire off a shot into each of their feet, talking over their cries. "Did you think it was okay to touch what's mine?"

"I didn't know she was yours."

"Liar." I shoot another round into their kneecaps.

The guy with him flops over on the ground, screaming in pain and grabbing at his leg with his bound hands. "Just end it! Just fucking end it!"

I arch an eyebrow at Mikhail.

"Stop crying like a bitch! You're embarrassing me," Mikhail hisses at him.

I let out a sinister chuckle. "Here's what I think, Mikhail. I think that you are associated with the Bratva. But I don't think you're as high up as you want to be. I think you're trying to prove yourself, saw what you thought was an easy opening, and took it without a second thought." I see his eyes flare as I hit the nail on the head. "The way I see it, you're a dead man either way. Which one of you hit her head so hard that you made her bleed?"

This time, they all remain silent, looking around everywhere but at me.

"Which one?" I roar.

Mikhail doesn't answer verbally, but his eyes track to his partner. I don't ask for confirmation before I shoot him right in the dick. I might have one more good shot before he bleeds out.

"Oh fuck. That's got to hurt." Trick winces behind me.

"You can finish him. But Mikhail is mine," I say to Scotch behind me. I know he needs this almost as much as I do. I know if I had a sister, and some shit happened to her, I would want my hands in on the sentencing.

I barely get to finish my sentence before Scotch puts a bullet in his head. "Damn. I wanted to draw that out." He pouts, making all the guys laugh.

"Give me the cutters."

"Prez, don't make too much of a mess. We still need to clean this shit up," Trick says with a smirk as he hands me the cutters.

"What are you do—" Mikhail starts to ask before I start cutting off his fingers one by one, making sure to draw it out as his screams get louder.

"Anyone in your organization will think twice before touching what's mine again," I grunt. I hand a finger to Hash, who takes it with a look of disgust on his face. "I want to find out who the Pakhan actually is and send him a little message."

"Now I need to get back to my woman," I say before I put one last bullet between his eyes, ending it.

46

Evan

My eyes slowly open as I hear someone moving around beside me. Blinking away the fogginess, I look around at what looks like a makeshift hospital room.

"You're awake," a man I have never seen before says from the left corner of the room. He is wearing a white lab coat, but I can still see the tattoos on his neck peeking out from it. He looks pretty clean-cut, minus the tattoos and ruffled hair. His glasses make him look a lot younger than he probably is, almost giving him an innocence. "I'm Doc."

"Where am I?" My voice comes out hoarse. I wince at the sound. My throat feels like I swallowed a bunch of sand.

"Oh shit. My bad. I probably should have started with that, huh?" He cringes before grabbing me a cup of water and bringing it over. "You're at the clubhouse. Prez should be here soon. He was just tying up some loose ends. Drink that slowly. Baby sips."

Loose ends, as in the guys that kidnapped me and hurt Levi.

"Is Levi okay?" I ask after taking a sip.

"He's good. His head will be sore for a while. They knocked him out from behind. His ego is a little bruised, but what are you going to do?" Doc shrugs before looking back at my chart as if dealing with something like this is a normal occurrence for him.

"Are you a member of the club?" I have never seen this man in my life, and I am pretty sure I have met everyone over the last few months.

"You can say that. I'm their resident doctor, and I like to ride in my free time. That's about as far as that goes."

Huh. I guess that makes sense. You can't have shit reported if you're also doing something illegal. Cain has never mentioned him.

"What's the damage?" I ask while holding up my arm, which currently has an IV in it.

"You have a mild concussion, which I'm assuming is from when they knocked you out as well. Your ribs, luckily, aren't broken, just severely bruised. They're going to be really sore for a while. Smoke inhalation did your throat in, but keep pushing the fluids, and you'll be good as new. Take some ibuprofen. If you feel that you need something stronger or have any questions or concerns, I'll leave my card." He had just finished explaining before Cain burst in through the door.

"Fuck, hellcat," Cain breathes as he rushes over to me.

"I'm okay." I wince again at the sound of my voice. Apparently, water isn't going to be my cure-all for that. "Thank you for coming for me."

"I'll always come for you," Cain says while lightly caressing my cheek as he sits on the side of the bed. "They paid for touching you." His tone turns deadly as he looks me over. "How is she?"

"She's fine. Nothing's broken. I do want you to keep an eye on her for the next 24 hours. Her concussion is mild, but if you notice her getting very disoriented and vomiting, bring her in because I'll want to do some tests. Otherwise, just a little R&R." Doc winks.

"You want to take a bath with one of your bath dicks?"

I never thought I would laugh after the recent events, but here I am. The fact that he knows exactly what I need without me having to tell him is more than I could ever ask for. Some people search their whole lives for the type of connection we have.

"Yeah." I smile at him. "I'd like to take a dick bath with you."

**47**

**Epilogue**

**Evan**

It's been a month since everything happened with the Russian mob and Storm. Cain has officially moved into my house. We're almost completely done with the renovations. Who knew that the process would go a lot faster if you asked people for help? It might seem like a big house for two people, but it's never just us. Someone from the club is always staying with us. Cain says they just like to have a little break from the club girls, but I think they just want to eat our food.

I'd be lying if I said it's been a walk in the park. Everyone was so tense, waiting for someone higher up to come and finish the job, but it never came. Cain wouldn't give me all the specifics, claiming it was 'better that I didn't know everything,' but apparently, they had been wanting to take out Mikhail for a while now. He had been putting on a front for a long time. The guys he had been working with thought he was more of a big shot than he actually was, and it pissed off the guys that are actually high up in the Russian Mob. The club just did them a favor by taking them out, which in turn allowed them to form some sort of loose alliance. The cartel got their product, and the Dirty Devils were able to semi-smooth things out with the Reapers. Everything finally seems well in our world.

I still have random nightmares from that night. Each one is always the same. I wake up with the trailer on fire, except instead of Cain saving me, I burn alive. Luckily, I've found the best man in the entire world to help me through those.

To celebrate things calming down, Cain wanted to have a cookout. Family and friends only. Nothing huge. And honestly, as introverted as I am, I'm actually looking forward to it. The guys have welcomed me into the fold with open arms. They were constantly checking on me when I was recovering. It's nice to feel like you're a part of something. I'll never be able to thank Cain enough for giving me a family.

"Those ready for the grill?" Trick asks as he comes into the kitchen, nodding at the burger patties on the tray.

"They're ready. I'll follow you out," I say as I grab the two sides I put in large bowls and follow him outside. Hash requested mac and cheese, and well, who am I to deny that request? IBS be damned.

Cain clears his throat just as I set everything down on one of the tables outside. "Can I have everyone's attention?"

A speech? This ought to be good.

Cain grabs my hand before continuing, "Hellcat, you came into my life when I least expected it." He lets out a rough laugh. "Fuck, I didn't even know I needed someone like you until you barreled in. You remember those three words you told me before I left you here with Levi that night?"

I swallow before answering, "I do." I'd never tell him this, but it's been weighing on me that he never said them back. He hasn't even brought it up, and honestly, it hurt.

"I spent the last month trying to rack my brain around how I should respond," Cain says before he gets down on one knee.

Oh my god.

Oh my fucking god.

"Evangeline, I love you. You're the first woman ever to get those words from me, and I want you to be the last. Will you marry me?" he asks while pulling out a little black coffin-shaped ring box. He lifts the lid, revealing the most gorgeous teardrop black diamond ring surrounded by little sparkling chips. It's absolutely perfect.

"Yes!" I cry as all the guys cheer in the background.

"Scotch!" Cain snaps as he stands up and spins me around, grinning from ear to ear.

I look over his shoulder and see Zeke carrying a large box to the table.

"Congratulations, Ev. I can't say I'll ever be happy seeing Prez hanging off of you like a bitch, but it's nice to know we're all family." He hugs me before stepping back.

"What's this?"

"This is for you. I should have given it to you a month ago, but I wanted it to be perfect," Cain says almost shyly, as if he's embarrassed I'm not going to like his surprise.

I give him a smile before lifting off the lid and moving the tissue paper aside, pulling out a brand-new leather jacket. "Holy shit."

"Turn it around."

I give him a raised eyebrow because, of course, he had "Property of Cain" engraved on the back.

"Does this mean I'm finally your old lady now?" I smirk as I put it on, the smell of new leather hitting my nose.

"Fuck yeah. No going back now, hellcat." Cain lands a hard kiss on my lips while slipping my dream ring onto my finger.

"You're crazy," I mumble against his lips.

"You wouldn't have it any other way," Cain mumbles back.

He's right. I wouldn't have it any other way.

# ALSO BY D. VESSA

If you liked this book, please check out these other titles in the
Ravenna Heights Universe:

<u>Dirty Devils MC:</u>

Cain

Ink

Hash

<u>The Adduci Crime Family:</u>

<u>Cavaliere</u>

<u>Dangerous Games</u>

<u>Standalone:</u>

<u>Wrapped Up in You</u>

# ACKNOWLEDGMENTS

Mike and Odin, thank you for always supporting and never doubting me. This has been a dream of mine for as long as I can remember, and I'm so grateful for you two being at my side.

Meg, thank you for always listening to me bitch about anything and everything. You're a real one. I love you no matter how much you talk about, and make me listen to, Taylor Swift.

Ashe and Blake, thank you for always listening to my crazy ideas and answering every little question that pops into my head with no judgment. Your support means the world to me.

Taylor at Deliciously Dark Editing, thank you for taking on my very first book baby and making it shine.

# ABOUT THE AUTHOR

D. Vessa is a romantic suspense author who loves a morally gray alpha, the color black, and a good Aperol Spritz. She lives on the East Coast with her family. When she is not writing, she spends her time running from her problems and wondering what color to dye her hair next.

authordvessa.com

**<u>Facebook Reader Group:</u>**

D. Vessa's Twisted Little Ravens